I0545140

THE GATHERING

AFTER THE FALL

BOOK TWO

JOHN PHILLIP BACKUS

JONDHI MEDIA GROUP U.S.A.

This novel is a work of fiction—of future events, yet to happen. The characters, incidents, and story are drawn from the author's imagination and should not be construed as real. Any resemblance to actual events or persons, living or dead, is purely coincidental.

THE GATHERING—AFTER THE FALL. Copyright © 2012 by John Phillip Backus. All rights reserved. Produced in the United States of America. No part of this book may be used or reproduced in any manner whatsoever without written permission, except in the case of brief quotations embodied in critical articles and reviews. For information contact legal@jondhi.com. Published by Jondhi Media Group, a division of Jondhi Holdings, LLC., 677 Spartanburg Highway, Suite #172, Hendersonville, NC 28792.

Covert Art by Duncan Long
Layout by JPB
Illustrations by Jesse Duke and Chad Schoenauer

Book Two in the AFTER THE FALL ™ series.
AFTER THE FALL ™ is a trademark of John Phillip Backus

FIRST EDITION - May 2012
Library of Congress Control Number: 2012954705
ISBN 978-1-935812-05-0

ACKNOWLEDGEMENTS

With the release of The Gathering-After The Fall, Book Two, I wish to extend my gratitude to the many persons who have been instrumental in helping to make this project a success. As it is a truism that "no man is an island," artistic endeavors rarely result from isolated efforts, and this example of my own creative imagination is no exception. The following individuals have graciously contributed their valuable time, talents, and observations directly to this project. Each is owed a tremendous debt of gratitude for their help in bringing this novel to fruition:

My tireless reading crew: Chris Backus, Mareka Backus, Ryan Backus, Troy Backus, Wayne Beardwood, Nancy Guarino, Lucy James, Dr. Diana Claire Jones, Jeremiah Miller, and Koya Pimenta, each of whom read the draft manuscript and offered insightful comments and invaluable advice and encouragement.

Troy Backus, webmaster and electronic frontier wiz, www. troybackus.com, for coding and maintaining the Jondhi Media Group fiction series' websites, Facebook and Twitter fan sites, and the www.johnphillipbackus.com blog site. Troy works wonders in the realm of all things web.

Frances Augusta Hogg, FAHOGG.wordpress.com, multi-talented author and editor, who painstakingly sifted through the manuscript, offering brilliant recommendations and insights which helped me to improve my craft, resulting in higher quality prose for my readers to enjoy.

Tommy Smith, social media guru, for pioneering my plunge into Twitter.

Duncan Long, renowned author and illustrator, for his world-class cover art and general technical expertise. www.duncanlong.com

Last but not least, gifted illustrators Jesse Duke, www.Facebook.com/jessedukeart and Chad Schoenauer, AshevilleIlluminator@gmail.com who captured the images from my imagination and brought them beautifully to life through their captivating drawings.

DEDICATION

To my granddaughter,
Isabelle Marguerite Brousseau,
Her tireless curiosity and self-determinism are inspiring.

To my mother,
Mary Aideena Lee,
Who occasionally pretended to believe my feigned claim of
illness so I could play hooky from school to spend the day
in bed reading adventure fiction.

And to fiction lovers everywhere,
Who enjoy nothing more than curling up with a good book
and becoming immersed in a stirring tale of high adventure.

THIS STORY WAS WRITTEN FOR YOU.

ILLUSTRATIONS

YEAR 19 – AFTER THE FALL...

CHAPTER ONE

THE CALLING

Everyone has a path that is uniquely their own, as individual as a snowflake, each person unlike any other. To find one's unique way in the world, that is the secret, that is the key: to discover one's calling and to know beyond the shadow of a doubt exactly why you have come into this world...

WHEN THE FIRST West Coast caravan arrived in New Eden after spring thaw, Anna Planchet was ready. She'd been feeling strange—slightly agitated or off balance and dissatisfied with her life somehow—her perfect life, in this perfect place, in this wide, imperfect world. Her restlessness had been brewing all winter. No matter what she did, it was not enough. Whatever this longing was, this *angst,* she had no clue, but something inside was stirring, impatiently trying to emerge from within her soul and she just had to let it out. It didn't matter to Anna what it was, as long as she could be delivered of it and return again to her peace.

The instant she saw him she knew. He was beautiful. His thick black hair, plaited in twin braids down to his midchest, was adorned with feathers and wrapped in ermine skins. His clothing was tailored and fringed—deerskin leggings, moose-hide moccasins and a long deerskin over-shirt belted at the waist by a finely-woven sash.

He was of Native blood from the Pacific Northwest, a bit older than she, perhaps twenty-five. Strong, lean and muscular, with straight white teeth and an easy smile that revealed slight dimples in his beardless cheeks. His skin was the color of copper with a sheen as smooth as silk and he had the most remarkable eyes she had ever seen—eyes as blue as the ocean, or the deepest blue sky, with little specks of gold in them reflecting the sun and flashing like tiny sparklers in the dark embrace of his long, black eyelashes.

She hung about his wagon pretending to shop. He was a woodcarver by trade and crafted the most incredible masks and totems, flutes and pipes—all from western red cedar—with a fragrance she inhaled like perfume when she picked up his offerings to examine them more closely. She ended up choosing an ingeniously carved box with mother-of-pearl inlaid lid, copper hinges, and colorful designs carved into the top and around the edges.

When she asked his price, he only looked at her, smiling—those amazing eyes gazing deeply into hers—and she felt a tremble within and was transfixed there in his presence, waiting, unable to move from that spot. Finally, he spoke and placed the box gently back into her hands, "It is yours, sister of the sun." He smiled assuredly, bewitched by her strawberry-blond locks and hazel eyes, "I made it for *you*."

Anna never questioned it—and from that moment forward never wanted to leave his side. Now, one month later, the couple was headed northwest, angling toward the coast and then north up into Old British Columbia, Canada to join his people there. Anna was learning him, understanding him more clearly each day. Their nights were filled with loving and he gave her ecstasy and release beyond her wildest imaginings. Her yearning within was gone and her peace had returned in full measure. Within her womb a tiny life now grew, multiplying its cells moment-by-moment. She felt anointed and blessed, and wondered what a child created from their pairing would be like.

Skye Ravencloud was a man of many talents, many gifts. Life was his opportunity and his challenge, and he lived it with purpose, reverence, and dignity. Back home with his People, he was recognized as a shaman—a spirit-talker—and the magic flowed from his fingertips as he fashioned his art, invoking his spirit guides. Where the power came from, he never questioned, knowing as far back as he could remember that all things came from the Great Spirit.

He was a man of peace, not of strife, though was not known to back down from a just fight. He'd rather give than receive and didn't ask *why* he was in the world. He understood that he was simply a conduit channeling something greater than himself and he accepted that for what it was.

For Skye Ravencloud there was much work to be done, much wisdom to gain, and *the calling* provided insight into that which was and that which was to come. He had traveled to old Colorado because his spirit guide, the Raven, had landed on a tree branch outside his shop one day, speaking plainly to him that it was time to take a wife—and so he went forth and found her.

She was the one for him, for sure, his spirit bearing witness when she chose the cedar box, the one with the special markings foretelling of his mate. Now they were heading back to his village on the coast, to his People, and the road was before them—each day an adventure, each night like heaven in the arms of his golden-haired goddess, Anna, his sun-sister, who carried their offspring in her fertile womb.

She had talked him into a detour on the way back—to pass by the Wind River Range up in Old Wyoming to visit her sister, Elise, and Elise's partner, Hunter, whom Anna hadn't seen since their visit to New Eden two summers before. Skye's friends from the caravan had agreed to escort his mules and wagon back along the Overland Road to the Pacific Coast Highway—now known as the *Old Coast Road*—where he would pick them up in three month's time. Anna provided their mounts and pack animals from the community herd, and with her family's blessing, she and Skye headed north toward South Pass.

She recounted her previous journey along this way, and Skye was surprised and encouraged to learn that his Anna was such a fearless and able woman. He discovered her history a little at a time and was impressed when she shared the battle of New Eden and the heroics of Elise's man, Hunter. He looked forward to meeting such a mighty warrior who would do whatever he decided was necessary in order to honor an oath once given.

The weather was mild this time of year and the days passed pleasantly with temperatures in the seventies— dropping into the fifties at night under wide open skies alive with brilliant stars and planets. Occasional rain showers were rare here with most of the precipitation taking the form of snowfall during the long, cold winter months.

The landscape was breathtakingly beautiful in its vastness, rich and varied in red and yellow sandstone canyons with towering granite mesas and stone monoliths refusing to succumb easily to the weathering of time. Big skies stretched the limits of one's eyesight and there was always something interesting to see among the myriad native plant and animal species.

They would sit together around the campfire in the evenings, sharing stories of their lives and speaking about how they felt and what they believed. He told her the ancient tales of his People, and how they first came to be *The People* in the mists before the reckoning of time. She spoke of her family and community, of their struggles and triumphs, of the End War and the Siege. In this way, they came to know one another's histories, hopes and dreams, and made plans for their own new chapter in this unfolding human saga of generation-following-generation, from time immemorial into whatever distant future lay in store for their descendants.

After South Pass, they skirted the foothills of the Wind and rode north toward the Tetons and Yellowstone Valley—and beyond that, Skye's Old Canada. The snow-covered peaks of the Continental Divide towered to the east as they drew ever closer to their interim destination, with Mt. Gannet, the tallest of them, rising 13,800 feet into the blue. At the Green River they turned to follow it up to its headwaters, finally crossing over the ridge into Hunter's valley.

From the crest, Anna looked down and spotted the two-story stone-and-timber cabin that Elise had told her they were building. She was excited to see what the couple had managed to accomplish in their five years together here. It looked like a respectable ranch—with a barn, sheds, corrals, a garden and orchard, and goats and sheep wearing tinkling bells wandering about the hillsides.

Someone exited the house and Anna immediately raised her face to the heavens, calling out a long coyote greeting. Skye looked on surprised, and even more so when, far off, Elise returned the spirited howl, beckoning the travelers, who nudged their curious horses forward down the faint trail toward the bottom.

CHAPTER TWO

THE OFFERING

HUNTER CROUCHED IN the shade of a massive rock overhang, senses poised, crossbow ready, waiting for a clear shot. The wounded cougar was out there hiding in the scrub, camouflaged in the jumbled rocks and sagebrush of the rugged mountain pass. It was lying very still, very close, watching. Wound up tight as a spring and ready to explode in a bursting flash of fury; it was as dangerous and unpredictable a threat as only an eight foot, two-hundred pound wounded mountain lion could be, armed with three-inch fangs and two-and-a-half-inch retractable claws.

Hunter knew it was badly injured; he saw his bolt pass right through its body before it jumped sideways off the kill and vanished into the bush. He'd checked over Elise's badly-mauled foal for any sign of life, but the three-month-old filly was already gone, its spine crushed by the big feline's vise-like jaws. Hunter immediately gave chase, tracking its blood sign into the rocks. He glanced at the height of the sun in the stark azure sky, droplets of perspiration beading up on his tanned, wind-blown brow.

In a blur of motion, the enraged lion sprang across the rocks and Hunter shot it straight through its heart as it flew

7

through the air above him. Rolling left, the beast fell dead where he'd been kneeling a moment before. Removing its hide, he opened the skull and removed the brain, wrapping it in the pelt to be used in the tanning process to make the skin feel baby soft. Heading home, he pondered the best way to present Elise with the bad news about her precious filly and decided that there was no easy way to go about it. She so loved that little thing—but that was just her way.

* * *

AN EXCITED ELISE cantered out to meet Anna and Skye on her newly saddle-broke Mustang mare. On the way back she walked the pretty paint alongside her sister's chestnut gelding, the two siblings chattering a mile a minute. When introduced to Skye, Elise could tell at once that he was the perfect match for young Anna, who had blossomed into the fullness of womanhood in the years since seeing her last.

When she heard the news about the baby, Elise was thrilled for her sister, but inwardly wounded by the reminder of her own disappointment at still being childless after five years with Hunter. She'd always wanted to have children, but not way out here alone, away from community—so perhaps it was a blessing in disguise. Children needed others their age to grow up and play with, and to come of age with in this world, but her longing for tribe was a pain she bore quietly alone.

When Hunter arrived home a few hours later, he was surprised and happy to see Anna and glad to meet her man. They were welcome to stay as long as they liked, and he could see the joy it brought Elise, who he knew suffered greatly, though stoically, from the lack of female companionship. It was a touchy subject between them and was avoided most of the time, but there was nothing to be done about it. He had never been comfortable around a lot of people, especially since the End War. Not much of a herd animal, Hunter was more the solitary predator type, preferring the quiet solace of the wilderness to the constant busy comings and goings associated with towns.

Well aware of his self-imposed social isolation and its effect on Elise, Hunter had tried to accommodate her in other ways. Like moving from cave to house, for example, or in his embrace of a more agrarian lifestyle than he would have personally preferred. When he received the happy news about the baby, he smiled and nodded his head, remaining silent. He and Elise had hoped to have children, but there was something not working right—he wasn't sure what. Perhaps they couldn't. It was a fairly common scenario since the End War, and even before, that some couples weren't blessed in that way.

After supper, they sat around the table and Anna and Skye shared their vision of the future out on the Pacific Northwest Coast. Elise listened enraptured, while Hunter read between the lines. He was curious to know what was happening out there, and was rather surprised by much of what Skye related.

Civilization, it seemed, had returned. Towns and villages were vibrant and all manner of arts and crafts had experienced a tremendous renaissance. There were blacksmiths and brewers, carpenters and masons, jewelers and potters, glassblowers, basket makers, weavers and tailors.

Shepherds tended flocks and herds, and wineries and orchards prospered in the mild micro climates of the Willamette and Yakima valleys. Northern Old California still grew plenty of pot and a powerful cannabis guild coordinated with its northern sister guild in Old British Columbia to set prices and keep the quality of the bud at a premium level—to the enjoyment of all who partook.

Amidst this period of cultural renewal and human industry, there was, of course, the usual chaos. Bandits plagued the Coast Road, hijacking wayfarers and kidnapping women and girls to sell or keep for themselves. Slavers were an even worse scourge of the new world, indiscriminately taking the young and strong of either gender to sell to work farms and plantations.

Walled towns and communes were well armed with organized defenses against depredation. From their base on Vancouver Island, brash pirates plied the seas in swift vessels, raiding up and down the coast by night, plundering and pillaging whoever and wherever they could.

Notwithstanding the challenges, the Pacific Northwest Coast was reasonably hospitable and navigable as long as you kept your wits about you and knew how to take care of yourself. Traveling alone was not recommended, so folks on protracted journeys banded together in caravans. A common defense force of sorts had evolved along the road, with stockades and guardhouses strategically positioned on the highway where travelers could stay the night, safe from the ubiquitous creepers and leeches who sniffed out an existence on the fringe—conscienceless predators, stalking the edges of the safe zones for unwitting prey.

Elise served the pumpkin pie that she and Anna had baked in a dutch oven as Skye answered questions about his life out on the coast.

"Is it true what they say about the Sisterhood Alliance?" Elise asked, curious to learn about the controversial cavalry of warrior-women that was sworn to avenge crimes against the weak and helpless—women and children in particular.

Skye related that while many admired their courage and supported their cause, others felt threatened by their methods and maligned them unjustly. Men without malice toward those less physically powerful than themselves need not fear them. It was Skye's understanding that misogynists alone had reason to dread the knock on the door in the black of night when the Sisterhood warriors would suddenly appear, hundreds strong, and there was no hiding from their vengeance. Their symbol was a red winged triangle within a circle, with an all-seeing eye in the center above an inverted cross.

Proficient in the martial arts, these women were silent weapons experts, specializing in the short bow and throwing knife, and they especially abhorred slavers, pirates, and pimps. They had been known to coordinate ferocious large-scale attacks on enemy strongholds and brothels to free their sisters from bondage. Their numbers grew larger, and their army more powerful each season, as rescued women and children found love and acceptance within their ranks. Some towns and communes refused to allow them inside their walls for fear they might lose wives and daughters to what the less enlightened inaccurately referred to as *that man-hating cult.*

New forms of self-government had evolved across the region, decentralized and responsive to those whom they immediately served. Ruthless warlords, too—as in the Middle Ages—ruled certain districts with an iron fist, coveting the resources of others and subjugating entire populations by use of force. Their brutal private armies were another scourge upon the land, and as they squeezed their people for some sort of tax or tribute, woe unto those who refused to meet their demands.

Without a national anything, or a mass communications capability, news traveled slowly and conversations took place face-to-face. Books were treasured, even revered. Libraries had become irreplaceable repositories of knowledge, cherished by all those with a view toward a brighter future.

Within the various enclaves, tremendous ongoing creativity and invention took place, with the ingenuity born of necessity resulting in the unusual—and unexpected—use and reuse of components from the old world. Certain locales had even restored some form of electrical power, either through the repair of a dam or by salvaging bits and pieces of wind and solar systems.

The most well known of the new cultural creations in the region was the *Gathering,* something unique in the world. The sprawling walled city—declared neutral territory by its

Keeper—had become the vortex for a constant stream of bustling humanity, and generally anything needed or wanted could be found there. A town had grown up around it—the place where deals were made and news passed along. It had evolved into a commerce and communications hub where merchants brought their wares and received credits, which they could trade for desired goods offered by other vendors. Twenty years after the End War, the Gathering was a vast living entity, inhaling goods and services and exhaling the dreams and desires of the neoculture.

* * *

ANNA AND SKYE stayed three days and Elise was overjoyed to have someone with whom to share her secret thoughts. On their final evening together, they all sat at dinner enjoying some tender lamb, and salad fresh from their abundant garden. In the midst of the meal, Skye stood up and walked over to stand behind Elise's chair.

Hunter half stood, unsure of what was happening but Elise gestured to him that it was okay. Skye closed his eyes and spread out opened palms toward her lower back, speaking words unknown to the others in a sing-song voice. After a minute or so, he ended and returned to his seat.

Afterwards, Elise experienced a warm tingling within her belly and a realization that some kind of quickening had occurred inside her body. Inexplicably, she felt that her barrier to conceiving a child had somehow been removed. She turned to tell Anna and they embraced while Hunter sat back observing, curious, but skeptical, not knowing exactly what had happened.

Later that evening when they were alone, Elise shared what she believed had occurred within her and he was intrigued, though not yet convinced, trying to work out with logic how Skye could have made a difference in her long-standing barrenness. Hunter was familiar with how babies were made and his understanding of the process included neither faith healing nor magic. It wasn't until a month later, when Elise was late and the morning sickness began, that her illogical theory about Skye's mystical influence on her reproductive capabilities began to impinge upon Hunter's metaphysically-conservative mind.

* * *

WITH THE COMING of their child, Elise understood that her life with Hunter was about to undergo a significant transformation. He, too, began to experience a growing restlessness, a stirring desire to go someplace new. Not that he wanted to suddenly embrace community, but he had been living in the wilderness for nearly two decades in this same territory, and the familiarity—though comforting in many ways—limited his innate sense of curiosity and yearning for discovery.

Their intriguing conversations during Skye and Anna's visit had altered his perception of the world beyond his mountains. The biowarfare viruses seemed to have played themselves out, with those having lived through them apparently developing an immunity. The social landscape, as well, appeared to be evolving rapidly and transforming itself in many positive directions and ways. The *Great Purging* had done a remarkable job in selective adaptation, bringing out the best in the human DNA and psyche. There was a brand-new world out there to be discovered and Hunter had a growing realization that perhaps he had been in exile long enough.

When he informed Elise that he was ready to travel to the coast to see this new land of milder winters, abundant water, and game-filled forests for himself, she almost fell out of her rocking chair. She had wrestled with the thought of joining Anna, Skye, and his People up in Old Canada and had even considered going there alone, just until the baby was born and old enough to return. She was completely taken by surprise at Hunter's decision to move on and was pleased beyond words.

What to do with their livestock and belongings that would remain behind was another challenge that resolved itself rather nicely when Hunter suggested that they offer the animals they wouldn't be taking with them to a young couple that had arrived in the territory about three years earlier, and who had a modest spread two valleys west. When Hunter and Elise traveled the twenty miles to talk to them, they were overwhelmed by the generous offer, and returned to see what they would be inheriting. Two weeks later, Hunter and Elise said their goodbyes to home and valley, and with a string of mounts and pack animals, headed northwest to rendezvous with Anna and Skye.

CHAPTER THREE

WINDSONG

THE SLENDER WOODEN vessel skimmed buoyantly across Beggar's Bay under full sail, heeled slightly to starboard, slicing the whitecaps with her sharp, gracefully curved dragon prow, like a Norse warship of memory past. Her mainmast was spruce, tall and solid, her ivory sails stretched, lines taut as she chased the wind down the coastal waters south of Vancouver Island. Lars was her captain, strong and steady, with curly, red-blond hair and beard, and eyes like the sea that he loved. Sometimes bluer than the deep water, at other times gray like the storms that pounded the rugged coastline in winter, but mostly they were a misty sea-green like the foaming breakers churning up the kelp beds where harbor seals chased fish near the shore.

He stood at the helm, hair blowing wildly in the brisk onshore breeze of morning, eyes concentrating, counting the rock formations jutting from the water on both sides of his ship. He steered her through the passage with precision as he had done a hundred times before, each voyage risky, each journey flirting with disaster. His course was strewn with shoals, shallows, and half-submerged rocks and shipwrecks, all just waiting to rip the keel out of his darling—his mistress. She had taken two painstaking years to build. Piece by piece, board by board, a labor of love for a man who was only at peace on the ocean riding the swells, surrounded by endless horizons.

He'd discovered his prize while scavenging wrecks amidst a dilapidated marina north on the Coast Road. She was hidden beneath a rotting tarp in the back of a custom shipyard, in a large warehouse near the wharf where someone had commissioned a wooden sailboat fitted with the up-swept dragon prow of a Viking ship. With her frame already in place atop a rolling gurney that would facilitate moving her to the water when complete, her owner had left behind a detailed set of plans and all lumber and hardware neces-sary to finish her. So there Lars lived and there he worked, the inherited genes and skilled hands of his master-carpenter father helping the vessel take shape, day-by-day, beneath the skylights of the lofty warehouse ceiling with the huge bay doors rolled open, inviting in the mist-soaked world.

When his beauty was finally complete, he moved her from the workshop to the water on the gurney, rolling her out to the end of the wharf. Using a series of cables and winches, he eased her onto the launching ramp, where she slid down, crashing into the cold waters of the Pacific, bobbing sweetly on the gentle swells.

He had done it alone, without any help. Lars didn't need help—didn't need people, couldn't trust them. Besides, he was alone here. Stepping the mast on his own was a bit of a challenge, but the shipyard was filled with all manner of use-ful tools, supplies, and equipment, and he used his wits and the laws of physics to his advantage and got the job done.

When the End War arrived without warning nearly two decades earlier, everyone who didn't die right away moved down south, fleeing the brutal two-year nuclear winter, but eight-year-old Lars had followed his father north. Sven Mor-gan led his wife, Jenna, and their boys in the opposite direc-tion of the migration, striving to get as far away as possible from the hordes of desperate survivors. Here they lived much better than most on the old world's leftovers. When the thaw finally came, they turned to the sea for food and lived off her bounty. With rod, net, or speargun, the father taught his sons to fish for cod, flounder and salmon, or to don a wet suit and scour the seabed to harvest crabs and mussels—but that was then...

* * *

SUNRISE PAINTED THE dawn sky crimson and the onshore wind blew a steady ten knots, smelling of rain. It was mid-April and still cold enough to wear layers. Lars was very excited, for today was *the* day for which everything had been made ready. He looked his graceful ship over and was pleased. His final task was to painstakingly paint her name across the stern in dark green oil—*Windsong*—and was she ever a beauty.

Thirty-three feet long at the waterline with an eleven foot beam and four-foot draft made her nimble in the wind and agile in the water—immediately responsive to his slightest touch. She was well-provisioned and well-appointed, having spare sails and lines, spare hardware, and two extra anchors with chain, all in waterproof lockers on deck. Belowdecks was a forward cabin, an amidships galley and bath, with an aft captain's cabin hosting a king-sized bed. She was set up for a single man to sail her, which Lars found challenging at first, even harrowing at times.

After mentally going over his seaworthiness checklist a dozen times, he decided to make a practice run over to an island about twelve miles off the coast. On a clear day, perched atop the old lighthouse ruins on the cliff, he could barely make out its profile on the horizon with his telescope. From a set of laminated charts scavenged from a former harbor-patrol office, he'd plotted a course and made final preparations to get under way.

Lashing the helm to starboard with a bit of line using a quick-release knot, he cast off the dock lines and ran back to tighten the slack jib sail. As Windsong came around, the wind blew the luff out of her sails and she jumped ahead, cutting nicely through the swells on a WNW heading away from the dock. Minding the rocks and shoals, he headed her out into the straits, referring constantly to chart and compass, tacking toward the distant island, wind off his port bow, full mainsail and jib taut and lines humming.

Two hours later, on the western side of the rock-guarded isle, he cut back some sail with his windlass and slowed, discovering a perfect little inlet protected by a curved rock jetty, built sometime in the distant past by men and machines long-since forgotten. Inside the half-mile-long cove was a rocky shoreline with a sturdy dock at the far end next to a narrow darkened opening that appeared to be a cave.

Back and forth, plastered to the cliff face, a steep stairway zigzagged eight-hundred feet or so to the only house in sight, perched precariously on the extreme edge of the precipice and underpinned by what appeared to be the massive beams and footings of the type used in bridge building. Putting out the fenders, he coasted in next to the cedar and redwood structure and jumped to the dock, tying *Windsong* off to the tarnished brass cleats that, surprisingly, still held firmly to the wood.

With adrenaline kicking in, Lars swept the rocky beach for signs of life or recent activity, but came up negative. Just in case, he strapped his sidearm to his waist and grabbed an oil lantern, heading toward the narrow cave. Inside it was dark, so he held the lantern aloft as he climbed the aluminum steps that ran along the beach side into the grotto. Beyond the tiny entrance, the cavern opened up into a roundish, playing field-sized chamber with a high, arched ceiling. He was surprised to see another small dock hidden safely within, perfect for tying up *Windsong* out of the weather.

From inside the grotto, a second set of stairs led up and out a rusting metal door near the roof. Scouting these stairs he emerged from the cavern into the sunlight to join the stairway he had seen from the water, that scaled the cliff and led to the house perched on the edge of the world. He decided to go on up and take a look and was pleased to discover that the stairway infrastructure was also fabricated from aluminum and, thus, practically corrosion-proof. Still, Lars took no chances, and made his way carefully to the top, checking for loose fittings or storm and weather damage as he went along.

Cautiously ascending the last few steps to the top, he came to a large balcony decked with composite flooring— apparently some sort of acrylic or epoxy planks designed to look like wood. The house itself was amazingly intact with huge floor-to-ceiling windows looking out over the water below. Standing at the railing, he looked down to see *Windsong* resting peacefully next to the dock.

Trying the door knob, he was a bit surprised when it turned freely and he stepped inside where the stale smell of dust and disuse assailed him and he instinctively covered his mouth with his shirt. Relighting his lantern, he scouted the place, which was larger than it appeared to be from below. Upstairs was a bedroom loft with a second covered balcony boasting an expensive high-powered telescope on a tripod. Looking through its lens out to sea, he felt as if he had just returned home from a long, trying voyage. Dubbing this newfound estate his *Crow's Nest,* he claimed the house, cave, and docks all for himself.

Over the next few weeks, Lars investigated the small island and found it deserted, but for a few skeletal remains and a mummified corpse or two, impelling him to christen it *Skeleton Island.* It was approximately two miles wide and five miles long with high cliffs and small rocky beaches here and there peppered with jumbled piles of driftwood. He also found several freshwater springs that could supply him drinking water and there was even a small waterfall pouring into a perfect swimming hole.

The fourteen luxury vacation homes occupying the rocky paradise were more or less intact—some faring better than others. It seemed that none of the former inhabitants had been back here since the End, and he found it amazing how well provisioned some of the houses remained—replete with stockpiles of basic necessities and many luxuries. Lars determined that before the End War, all food supplies must have been ferried in by boat or flown in by helicopter; on the far side of the island he found a small helipad. It was surprising to discover that certain survival-type items such as dried goods and spices, and some canned foods like tomato-based sauces and fruit preserves, were still edible—even decades beyond their expiration dates, depending, of course on how they had been prepared and stored.

The fishing here was excellent and Lars was content with plenty of everything he might need. He enjoyed nothing more than taking *Windsong* out every day he could, weather permitting. Sailing was an incredibly *in the moment* experience for him—a time when he felt in total concert with the natural world surrounding him—guiding his ship through the water with the wind on his face and salt spray in his hair.

* * *

AS SUMMER PROGRESSED, he further familiarized himself with his island paradise and fixed up the Crow's Nest to better suit his needs. One bright day, with a ten-knot breeze out of the west, Lars was a couple of miles offshore, hauling in an overnight net he'd set the day before, when he saw something moving out of the corner of his eye. Reaching for his binoculars, he scanned the horizon and spotted some type of low-riding vessel passing by—a large canoe with outriggers—about a mile away and heading toward the mainland, but coming from where? He watched it until it disappeared over the horizon.

He was puzzled and went to his maps and charts to consider the possibilities. Whoever they were, he wasn't sure whether or not they'd spotted him since *Windsong's* sails were down and her varnished hull reflected the colors of the sea and sky. *Who could they be?* he wondered, not happy about the prospect of having other seafarers in his territory.

If they navigated the ocean currents, they could find him. If they found him, they could make trouble—perhaps even ransack his home while he was out fishing, or worse. He wondered about the crew as there must have been several men aboard to paddle the forty-foot sea-going canoe. He had seen such a vessel in a book once; the oceanic islanders had used them long ago on long-distance voyages from Polynesia.

23

Lars spent the next ten days fortifying the Crow's Nest and beefing up his defenses. He devised several alternate battle plans, customized according to how many attackers might be in the raiding party and their specific assault approach. Finally, he felt very well-prepared.

When the End War had arrived almost two decades earlier, residents of his island had either fled, never to return, or died here. One of those who had chosen to stay on was apparently a gun aficionado, who died, literally with his finger on the trigger. Lars added two battle rifles to his personal arsenal from the corpse's collection, selecting an M-25 sniper rifle in .308 Win. with a Leupold Mark 8 scope, and a heavily upgraded Adams Arms AR-15 in .223 caliber/5.56 millimeter with a Trijicon ACOG ECOS scope plus Doctor RMR red dot. There were ten cases of vacuum-sealed ammunition for each rifle, plus a case of .45 ACP's for his pistol and a thousand 12 gauge shells in various configurations—slugs, double-ought buckshot, and birdshot—depending on the specific application they were to be used for. With the mummy's remaining stash worth a fortune in barter value, Lars removed all of the remaining weapons and ammo to a hidden location in the center of the island. He made sure the weapons he took for his own use were clean, well-oiled and functional, and had full bandoliers with loaded magazines ready to go.

Down below in the cave, he prepared some oil bombs—Molotov cocktails made from wine bottles filled with spirits pilfered from a house that hosted a full bar. He capped each with a piece of cloth stuffed into the top that he could readily light with one of the disposable lighters he always carried with him.

Two uneventful weeks passed and Lars had begun to relax when a three-day storm moved in, bringing torrential rainfall with lots of thunder and lightning. The morning of the fourth day dawned clear and sunny with a mild breeze and sparkling waters. Deciding it was time to get back to a normal routine, Lars prepared to take *Windsong* out for a little fishing when he heard something unusual in the distance.

Looking out to sea, a dark ship belching smoke suddenly appeared from around the jetty guarding the little inlet's entrance, powered by some type of motor. It was a 45-foot pilothouse motor-fisher and Lars could make out several people moving about on deck. As it headed into his inlet, he turned and started to sprint back up the steps, heading for the Crow's Nest where he could watch her through the telescope. He made the top, breathing heavy with his heart jumping out of his chest, and peered down through the scope.

The ship was halfway across the inlet, heading straight toward his dock. He could make out a crew of about eight men and it appeared as if they had two or three women on deck with them. His mind raced through twenty different scenarios. *They might try to assault the house—no, if they did that they would be exposed the entire way on the stairs.* He watched the noisy boat approach, and as she got closer, he counted a total of ten heavily armed men and three scantily dressed women, probably slaves.

The unfamiliar smell of exhaust fumes from the internal-combustion engine eventually reached him and he wondered where the hell they had come from. He was amazed

25

that people were still able to maintain that old mechanical technology—but why not? Internal-combustion engines were invented back in the late 1800s. Fuel was still easy to distill. There were tons of spare parts and tools lying around if someone only had sufficient knowledge and skills as a mechanic to use them. It made sense, but seemed bizarre to Lars, as if he'd suddenly been transported back to civilization *before* the Fall.

He heard gruff voices over the sound of the motor as she tied up alongside his dock and several of the crew jumped off, heading toward his cave. He'd forgotten about *Windsong!* What if they tried to take her? The cave entrance was too narrow for them to drive their wide-beamed boat into, but he watched with dismay as the men disappeared into the opening, reappearing a few minutes later carrying armloads of his precious supplies.

Lars turned and picked up his long-range sniper rifle, resting the bipod on the deck railing. The crack of his warning shot echoed off the cliff walls and rang out across the calm inlet. Down below, the crew dropped their pilfered goods and raced back aboard their boat. He could hear the captain in the pilothouse yelling at his men to hurry as he pulled the exhaust-belching, steel-hulled workhorse away from the dock, heading back toward the entrance to the cove.

Suddenly, one of the women broke free from the others and leapt off the side of the boat into the sea. He watched the crew run to the rail, yelling and gesticulating wildly. The girl swam hard for shore as the captain began turning his boat around to go back for her.

Instinctively, Lars took careful aim at the roof of the pilothouse and slowly squeezed the trigger. *Boom.* He blew a large hole in the cabin roof, top dead center, and the boat swerved back toward the mouth of the inlet. The captain increased her speed and drove in a zigzag pattern to avoid being picked off. Lars watched the crew hustle the remaining females belowdecks as the boat made fast tracks toward the open sea. Down in the 64 degree Fahrenheit water, the young swimmer was nearly at the dock. Grabbing a towel and an extra sweater off a peg, Lars dashed out of the house and raced down the stairway to the beach.

CHAPTER FOUR

JESSI

ARRIVING AT THE bottom of the stairs, Lars discovered that the swimmer had vanished. He could make out her telltale water trail where she had climbed the ladder to the dock, leaving wet footprints on the decking, headed toward the cave. Skirting the water, he approached the dark opening cautiously, not wanting to further frighten her. More than likely she was already scared, having just executed a daring escape from God-knows-what kind of treatment at the hands of the trawler's crew.

Slipping through the cave mouth, Lars lit the lantern hanging just inside the entrance. He called out to let the swimmer know that he intended her no harm, but his voice sounded gravelly from disuse and not very soothing. As his eyes became accustomed to the flickering shadows, he followed her wet footprints to *Windsong's* deck, again attempting to reassure her by announcing that it was he who had fired upon the ship, allowing her time to escape.

As his vocal chords relaxed, he continued speaking in a warm, even voice, offering his help and inviting his hidden visitor to follow him up to the house where she could warm herself at his fire and enjoy a hot meal and a cup of tea. Passing the wooden canopy covering the helm station, he heard

28

her moving above him and turned just as she jumped down from the roof with his fillet knife clenched tightly in her fist.

"You stay away from me, mister, you hear me?" Jessi threatened.

Lars was shocked to discover that she was only a girl—thirteen or fourteen at most.

"Stay away or I'll cut your heart out!" she warned.

She glared at him with her meanest face, teeth clenched and lips drawn back in a snarl. Poised before him in a classic fighting stance with legs shoulder-distance apart, knees slightly bent with one foot forward, her bare, goose-bumped limbs trembled from the cold. Dripping blond curls lay plastered to her cheeks as she shivered in her skimpy cotton top and skirt, lips blue, feet bare and scraped raw from the barnacled steps.

Lars looked on her with pity, yet was duly impressed by her courage. Her physical condition was atrocious—arms and legs covered in bruises where she'd been grabbed and manhandled, and with numerous hickeys and bite marks adorning both sides of her neck beneath the jawline. Holding his hands high, palms out, he attempted to reassure her.

"It's okay, no one will hurt you here. I have brought a dry towel and a warm sweater for you." He placed the articles on the ship's deck, took a few steps back and sat down. "You'll need to warm up quickly or you might catch cold and get sick." He smiled warmly, willing her to trust him as he covertly studied her skin tone for evidence of the early stages of hypothermia.

The girl looked beaten and bedraggled, yet she still had some fight left in her, and while the expression in her eyes

29

was one of back-against-the-wall desperation, he sensed her unwavering resolve to secure her freedom, whatever the cost.

Lars sat back on his heels, arms wrapped around his knees, and waited, hoping that seated thus he might appear less threatening. Shaking from the cold, the girl eyed him suspiciously, daring a quick glance down at his offerings. After a tense standoff, during which she rapidly weighed her limited options, the desperate youngster finally inched forward with her knife outstretched and reached down with her free hand to quickly snatch up the offered items. Retreating to a safe distance, the trembling girl continued threatening Lars with her blade as she fought to bring her thoughts and breathing under control, finding it quite an effort to think logically about what to do next.

Sitting perfectly still and intentionally avoiding eye contact, Lars started first humming, and then softly singing a silly tune—something he remembered from his childhood.

"Merrily, merrily, merrily, merrily, life is but a dream. Row, row, row your boat gently down the stream..."

He kept this up for a minute or so, finally pausing to look up at her again and smile, and this time she relaxed her guard long enough to place the knife between her teeth and wrap the lovely, thick bath towel about her head and shoulders like a hooded cape.

Seeing that the stranger took no threatening action, Jessi placed the knife atop the canopy and rewrapped the towel around her waist, pulling the heavy lambswool sweater down over her arms and head. As the natural fibers began trapping her body heat, she experienced welcome relief. Looking down at her trembling legs, she wished for a pair of trousers; the pirates had allowed her only a skimpy top and skirt with nothing underneath, or on her legs and feet, which were presently turning purple in the sunless chill of the cave.

Welcoming the girl's response to his overtures, Lars calmly introduced himself, briefly explaining that he was alone on the island, and again offering to lead her up to the house where she could sit by the fire and enjoy some hot tea. After further inner deliberation (and more shivering), the young escapee nodded her head and he stood as she backed up, allowing him to lead the way up the stairs. Carefully zig-zagging their way across the cliff wall to the house, he glanced back from time-to-time to see how she was faring and noticed the handle of his razor-sharp fillet knife peeking from the waistband of her skirt beneath the towel.

At the top of the stairs, Lars held the door for her and Jessi slipped quickly through, heading straight for the red-enameled, *avant guard* fireplace suspended from the ceiling in the midst of the room where a bed of hot coals still smoldered in its rounded basin, throwing off a wondrous, intoxicating warmth. With hands outstretched, she stood as close as she dared, barely moving aside to allow her host to add a couple of seasoned hardwood chunks which soon burst into flames, heightening her pleasure and relief. With a smile threatening to soften her furrowed brow, she momentarily let down her guard and relaxed for the first time in weeks as she gratefully offered her frigid person to the life-giving radiance of the blaze.

Disappearing down a hallway to rummage through bedroom drawers and closets for appropriate clothing for his shivering young guest, Lars returned with jeans, socks, knit cap, long-sleeved shirt, fall jacket, and even a pair of sheepskin-lined boots that looked as if they might fit her, dropping them off in a pile before continuing on into the kitchen. While Jessi tried on clothing in the other room, Lars stoked the fire in the antique stove, filling the teapot with fresh spring water from the gravity-fed spigot and placing it on the stovetop to boil. Retrieving two mugs from the cupboard and a pair of English Breakfast teabags from their tin on the shelf, the seafaring recluse-turned-rescuer mulled over the morning's bizarre encounters, pondering their far reaching implications with a growing degree of concern.

Mentally sifting through the recent events, he prepared steamed wild rice and sauteed salmon fillets in a Dutch oven and served them piping hot. Eating in silence, seated on supple leather beanbag chairs in front of the fireplace, it was obvious to Lars that the girl was famished. Therefore, in spite of the many burning questions begging to be asked, he patiently held his tongue, affording Jessi an opportunity to enjoy her meal in peace.

He felt it important to grant her the personal space to process the realization that she was no longer in danger. Although having escaped from her immediate life-threatening situation, he knew that she had most certainly been traumatized, more than likely assaulted, and obviously abused and humiliated by the retreating crew. And though he had not known her before her trauma, Lars understood intuitively that she could never be the same—and had probably been forever altered by her harrowing experience.

Seated cross-legged on the supportive cushion, Jessi devoured the delicious fish and rice from the wooden bowl in silence, washing it down with hot, sweetened tea while doing her best to block out the memory of her brutal two-week ordeal at the hands of the merciless slavers. She shuddered at the thought of them—degraded beings who reveled in practicing cruelty toward women. Treating them badly was apparently one of their favorite pastimes, but she figured that she was probably the lucky one, since the captain had taken her all for himself—in private. She closed her eyes, trying to shut out the taunting voices and sadistic laughter of the crew as they had their way with the others.

Rising to fetch the teapot to freshen their mugs, Lars brushed past Jessi, inadvertently startling the girl who instinctively grabbed for her blade, withdrawing it too quickly and slicing a deep, nasty gash in her side.

"Owww!" she cried out as Lars stepped in, calmly, but firmly, retrieving the knife from her hand and applying direct pressure to her wound with a folded kitchen towel. After a few seconds he checked it, knowing already that she would need stitches.

"Press down firmly with the cloth," he told her. "It will control the bleeding." He went for his first aid kit.

Returning with hot water and sutures, he cleansed her injury, warning her and apologizing in advance for the coming pain. Working quietly with confidence, he deftly sewed her up, taking fifteen tight stitches to close the wound. Afterwards, he cleansed and rinsed the area again and applied antibiotic ointment and a sterile gauze dressing. While he was stitching her, Jessi hadn't made a peep, though he knew she must be experiencing a good bit of pain.

Sitting perfectly still with her face a stoic mask of indifference, Jessi revealed zero discomfort, but inside she cringed, loathing the proximity of his presence. *Another strange man with his hands on her body.* But Lars was different, his manner poised and professional, his concern for her wellbeing genuine. His was a healing touch, not groping like the Captain's, yet still, she felt uncomfortable being handled by him, all the while fully acknowledging its necessity. During her captivity she had become very clear about one thing—no one would ever again touch her against her will the way that Captain had. She would resist such an affront by any means necessary, preferring to kill her attacker or die defending her right to live as a free human being on this earth.

As he finished bandaging her wound, Lars sensed Jessi's turmoil and was empathic. It was likely a tragic probability that for the rest of her life she would feel threatened and, through subconscious mechanisms, be compelled to withdraw whenever anyone got too close—no matter how kind or well-intentioned that person's approach might be. This was simply her basic survival instinct at work and Lars understood from personal experience that even given the passing of time, some wounds might never fully heal.

C H A P T E R   F I V E

THE OLD COAST ROAD

THE STURDY WOODEN cargo wagon with its cramped living quarters perched on top rolled north on cracked rubber truck tires over the disintegrating remains of the Pacific Coast Highway—U.S. Highway 101— the Old Coast Road. Its team of four patient mules leaned into their traces, trudging up the long, gentle grade toward the crest at Promontory Point. More than fifty wagons followed single-file in a long line down the narrow thoroughfare.

As the wagon drivers arrived at the wide plateau on top, Ephraim Smith, the caravan's headman, allowed them each a short break from the lively pace he'd set all morning— but only long enough for them to water their livestock and stretch their legs. Ephraim was more determined than ever to make it to the final stockade at Widow's Creek before nightfall. The burly caravan master hopped down from his wagon seat to look south, down the winding, dusty track, at the wagon train strung out along the debris-littered roadway.

To the west, the rocky ground—hidden beneath a tangled forest of delicate ferns and sprawling dark evergreens— dropped steeply to the sea. At just after midday, the thick coastal fog had finally burned off, allowing the warm sun-

35

shine through, to tap dance upon the vast blue panorama of the Pacific. The sun's reflection rippled across the tops of long arcing waves breaking against numerous massive off-shore rock columns topped with vegetation. Towering hundreds of feet into the sky, these monoliths stood guard like silent stone sentries, having sworn—in some unremembered past age of the world—to protect the jagged coastline from the relentless assault of the sea.

Above in the brilliant, cloudless blue, countless seabirds wheeled and swooped, diving into the ocean for fish and then soaring up on the freshening breeze, lighting and taking off from thousands of nests hidden away in tiny niches scattered among the black-and-tan cliff walls. Ephraim watched as a squadron of brown pelicans passed by far below, skimming the water's surface in a tight V formation, like a low-flying jet squadron of a previous age. Ephraim had always marveled at the large, gangly birds that managed to look so graceful in flight and when bobbing on the surface of the water, but who appeared so completely awkward when hobbling about on land. They seemed barely able to waddle, much less take to the air as if they were swallows. Struck by the improbability they represented, Ephraim turned back to the business at hand, reflecting on his caravan's four-month round trip journey that was rapidly coming to an end.

Overall, it had been a successful trading run, with nothing particularly unusual to report. They'd started out from the Gathering with fifty-three wagons, all of which were accounted for, and now they were on the last leg of their return trip home from far-flung settlements out in Old Colorado, Utah, and Nevada. Hearing the chirping call of a passing bald eagle, he lifted his squinting face toward the bright sun, hanging midway in the cobalt sky. For once, even the weather had cooperated for the most part, being milder this spring than in recent years, with moderate rainfall encouraging the blossoms in the fruit and nut orchards lining the vast agricultural valleys to the south.

Looking again at the long line of ponderous wagons, Ephraim counted back to the fourteenth outfit and stopped. *Interesting story about that one*, he reflected. It belonged to a Native woodcarver who had dropped out back in the Old Colorado community of New Eden. He had apparently found himself a woman there and stayed behind. Normally it was the other way around—especially with younger females from isolated communities far removed from social interaction with the outside world.

Such stagnant backwater settlements offered limited choices and opportunities, and after experiencing a caravan or two—with the accompanying exposure to news and goods from the greater world-at-large—some folks would invariably become infected with the idea of going someplace new. Especially after hearing romantically whispered tales of far-off places and the wondrous happenings elsewhere, some had opted to join the caravan, finding passage with a willing driver with room in his wagon and a desire for companionship. Some just wanted a change, others, to escape a bad relationship or some other problematic situation. Though he generally frowned upon casual interaction between caravan personnel and settlers, Ephraim mostly strove to remain neutral and out of other people's private affairs, unless, of course, it adversely affected his business.

He could think of several instances when he had been forced to turn over a runaway or an otherwise previously obligated person—perhaps an unhappy wife or other such stowaway who had become involved with one of his drivers. When the upset father, brother, husband, partner or other interested party finally chased down Ephraim's caravan demanding their return, he was obliged to hand the culprits over, regardless of the circumstances. After all, his was an officially sanctioned caravan, commissioned to sell and trade all types of useful goods—and not a social justice movement.

In the absent woodcarver's case, the man's friends had agreed to look after his team and wagon on the return trip to the Gathering. Ephraim didn't much give a damn what their arrangement was, as long as the Keeper got his customary share of the profits and the drama remained at a minimum. Behind him in his own wagon, Ephraim's personal treasure was carefully stashed away, safe from prying eyes. He smiled to himself, pleased with his own cleverness, and looked forward to the generous profits he would soon enjoy.

Hearing the sound of rapid hoofbeats ahead, he glanced up to see a heavily armed rider approaching from the north on a dusty black stallion. Riding in at a full gallop, the man waited until the last second to rein in his horse, wheel about and fall into step next to Ephraim's wagon.

"Mornin Ephraim," Coleman Black greeted the head-man with an easy smile, his spirited horse breathing heavily through its bellowing nostrils and shaking his head against the reins.

"Coleman," Ephraim nodded, noting the other's custom-ary all-black garb and military-like bearing. Much to the wag-on master's relief, the congenial gunslinger had arrived three days earlier with a thirty-man detachment of armed outriders to personally assume responsibility for the caravan's secu-rity on the final leg of its journey. The Road Defense Force, or RDF, founded by Black, had been established some years back to generally keep the road open and free from bandits, and to escort caravans at critical points along the road to help ensure their safe arrival at the Gathering.

Black had been riding shotgun for the official caravans for as long as Ephraim could remember, earning a handsome living by escorting any outfit with the wherewithal to afford his fee. It was comforting to know that the rough-and-tum-ble enforcer was close at hand and keeping an eye out for trouble. As the official Old Coast Road security boss, it was rumored that Black had been personally appointed by the Keeper himself.

Commanding a private security force of some 300 outrid-ers posted up and down the sparsely populated Coast Road was not a simple task. The RDF operated under a lucrative, longstanding contract with the Guilds to protect officially sanctioned caravans and ensure their safe passage. Private parties were free to hire Black also, and he did quite well for himself, mostly due to his spotless record and reputation, and the fact that if one chose to attack travelers who had hired him to protect them, there was no hiding from his vengeance.

It was common knowledge that in the early days before the RDF was commissioned, Black had single-handedly fought off a dozen bandits who had foolishly attacked a wagon train under his protection—a mistake none of them survived. Throughout his tenure on The Road, he'd introduced countless highwaymen and outlaws to justice, Coleman Black-style, either at the end of a short rope, or via a red-hot chunk of lead, shot from the bore of his .44 Winchester.

It was also true that, over the years, various thugs and criminal organizations had placed a generous bounty on Black's head; forcing him to keep his personal schedule a secret—so that one never knew when or where along the road he might show up. One thing was certain, Ephraim Smith always felt more at ease when Coleman Black was around.

Truth be known, the caravan master was relieved that the trip was nearly over. Another day and a wake-up and, barring unseen complications, he would be home free. Ephraim stretched his stiff muscles and yawned. Three months on the road was a long time to be away from home, but the credits were good and he could get ahead by not spending much during the crossing—not to mention the bit of lucrative smuggling he occasionally engaged in when the deal was right.

Ephraim customarily piloted two major trading runs per year as well as a couple of shorter regional circuits before the harsh winter weather rolled in and shut things down until spring. By the end of the season, he was looking forward to taking some well-deserved time off to engage in less stressful domestic pursuits: primarily the wooing of an occasional romantic interest, or otherwise simply enjoying the pleasure of waking up in the same geographic location more than twice. High on his list of things to do were fishing, hunting, and generally kicking back at his snug homestead nestled on the shores of a pretty little lake where he dabbled in brewing what the locals claimed was some of the best ale in the territory.

It was a lifestyle that he would have chosen regardless of the state of the world. He'd always been a bit of a Gypsy—hell, as a young man he used to drive a big rig himself up and down this road back in the day—before the lights went out. A journey that used to take three days now took three months, weather permitting. With occasional bad storms or mudslides, detours might double or triple the travel time in affected sections, as overworked repair crews figured a way around objects such as boulders the size of houses, or huge fallen coastal redwoods blocking the thoroughfare's one twisted lane.

With a tip of his hat, Black gently nudged his horse with his knees and the magnificent charger leapt forward, extremely agile and light on its feet for so large and muscular an animal. Of the twenty or so mounts he'd received this year from Jedediah Cobb, the big stallion, Spartacus, had become Black's immediate favorite. The renowned Cobb was a highly respected horse breeder and trainer with a reputation for producing the finest animals in the region.

As a man of particular discernment when it came to horses, no one appreciated the experience of riding a finely bred and trained animal more than Black. In the case of Spartacus, the bond of mutual respect between horse and rider had been instant and irrevocable, and their daily excursions were a mutually rewarding experience that each looked forward to with pleasure.

Ephraim watched as Black was joined by a pair of subordinates, and the trio huddled a short distance from the passing wagons to converse in private. Afterwards, the two rode back toward the tail end of the strung-out caravan while Black urged his mount ahead with a single word. Without hesitation, Spartacus broke into a full gallop—taking long, powerful strides, hurtling horse and rider rapidly down the gradual decline. Freshly trimmed and shod hooves pounded out the horse's pleasure upon the dirt-covered roadway—his glistening black mane and tail trailing behind him like ebony streamers in the wind. Leaning forward over his stallion's arched neck, Black became one with his steed's fluid momentum while his sharp eyes roved from side to side, examining the bordering trees and rocks, ever watchful for an ambush or similar form of treachery that might readily befall an unwary traveler along this notoriously violent passage.

From his vantage point atop the wagon, Ephraim Smith watched the horse and rider race away, until they finally disappeared around a bend beyond the tree line, far below. Turning in his seat, Ephraim climbed through the narrow doorway into his cabin where a quartet of carrier pigeons perched and cooed in a bamboo cage suspended from the ceiling. The snow-white birds—property of Royal Chen, Keeper of the Gathering—were provided to all caravan headsmen. This enabled Chen to keep tabs on the progress of widespread, multiple caravans, regardless of their distance from home.

Refilling the birds' water bottle, Smith offered them a handful of sprouted birdseed before returning to his seat. Picking up the reins, he called to his lead mule, Blue, who nonchalantly glanced his way with large, liquid eyes, his tail patiently swishing flies while his harness mates nibbled greenery at the sides of the road. Soon, the good natured beasts were again plodding along, moving forward at a casual downhill pace. Behind Ephraim in the cabin, his pigeons swayed to the rhythm of the steady cadence, awaiting a final opportunity to carry the daily report back to the dovecote on the roof of Royal Chen's cliffside palace.

CHAPTER SIX

THE KEEPER

ROYAL CHEN, KEEPER of the Gathering, languished comfortably in his tea room on a silk-covered futon supported by soft pillows. Opposite him on a slightly raised dais framed in fresh cut flowers from his expansive gardens, a petite Asian beauty sang a melancholy love song in Cantonese while plucking a traditional seven-stringed instrument with delicate, manicured fingernails. Incense smoke wafted lazily toward the ceiling as Chen leaned back, taking a deep pull on the jade mouthpiece of an ornate opium pipe filled with the finest from his private reserve.

His consciousness drifted across the room to the exquisite young lotus blossom seated among the balusters— a recent addition to his already extensive harem. He'd first noticed her six months earlier on a rare visit to New San Francisco while being entertained by his good friend and longtime business associate, Venerable Wu. It was there, while enjoying Wu's superb hospitality, that her beauty had entranced him, and he hadn't been able to get her out of his mind since.

Enchanted, Chen had difficulty taking his eyes off her. Dressed in luxurious silks with long, obsidian hair held in place with jade and ivory hairpins; her flawless skin, inviting lips, and almond eyes mesmerized his soul. Exhaling a blue cloud of aromatic smoke, he smiled—his heavy-lidded eyes mere slits in his rounded cheeks. Having fantasized about her for months, he'd been looking forward to this moment with eager anticipation.

* * *

ACROSS THE ROOM, young May Ling was nervous, but concealed it well. She had arrived at Royal Chen's palatial estate only yesterday, but had been schooled and groomed for this moment since the day she was born. Her esteemed uncle and patriarch of her family clan, Venerable Wu, had planned this life for her and she was obligated to honor his wishes. As head of the powerful Red Dragon triad in New San Francisco's burgeoning Chinatown, Wu had been doing business with Royal Chen for nearly two decades and was, by far, the wealthiest and most influential personage in the Bay Area with expansive connections and multiple business interests throughout the region.

Wu's diverse holdings—in which Royal Chen held a significant stake—included silk and clothing factories, rug and textile mills, as well as craft shops producing everything from bamboo and reed basketry, hardwood furniture and cabinets, to pottery, cookware, jewelry, and weapons. In the outlying districts his interconnected network of farms produced rice, soybeans, tamari, garden vegetables and medicinal herbs. In addition to large-scale vineyards and vast fruit and nut orchards, Wu's widespread livestock and ranching operations produced poultry, sheep, meat and dairy goats, beef and dairy cattle, horses and mules. Related business ventures included a tannery and a footwear factory. Along the coast, fishing collectives provided his markets and restaurants with a constant supply of fresh seafood from the Pacific's plentiful bounty.

May Ling clearly understood that Uncle Wu was a key player in Royal Chen's sprawling matrix, but even more importantly, she was aware of her esteemed uncle's secret, most ambitious plans. Someday, when the time was right, Venerable Wu intended to *replace* Royal Chen as the Keeper, and rule both the Bay Area and the Gathering—and everything in between. In order to bring his plans to fruition, Wu required trusted spies inside Chen's stronghold to learn everything he could about the Keeper's habits, routines, strengths, and weaknesses. Already, he had dozens of informants employed by Chen as cooks, housekeepers, gardeners, laborers, horse trainers, accountants—even a member of his own personal bodyguard—with all of them secretly reporting back to Wu. But none of these would be able to get as close to Royal Chen as May Ling might. Placing her into Chen's bed as his number-one concubine was a key element in his takeover strategy. He was supremely confident that the girl would become Chen's favorite lover as soon as he discovered her expertise in the pillowing arts—erotic skills that no normal man could resist.

May Ling finished her song and flashed her new master a shy smile, gracefully reaching up to remove the pins holding her hair in place. Allowing her waist-length tresses to cascade down her lithe body she moved slowly toward him, unfastening her robes. The obvious desire radiating from her liquid eyes further intoxicated Royal Chen's drug-heightened senses. As she slipped out of her silks, her lustrous black hair lay in stark contrast against her pale, youthful breasts. Overcome with longing, Chen knew that he could wait no more—he *must* have her now!

Hours later, as he rested on his back enjoying the time lessness of perfect bliss, May Ling lay snuggled against his side, her head resting delicately on his chest, an arm and leg wrapped tenderly across his body. He could feel her gentle heartbeat tapping against his ribs and was vaguely conscious of the heat from her smooth pelvic mound pressed up against his thigh, lying in wait to again capture his charging man-hood, should he somehow gain the strength to indulge himself once more in her wondrous pleasures.

Never before had he experienced the erotic intensity that this new lover had managed to extract from his now-spent body. What beauty! What skillful passion! She was worth ten times the price he had negotiated for her. A perfect lov-er—creative, energetic, intuitive—and willing to satisfy his every desire. With a final pull on his pipe, Chen drifted off into a dream, pleased to have acquired such a rare jewel with whom to share his boudoir.

Lying wide awake beside the dozing man nearly three-times her age, May Ling feigned sleep, acutely aware of her new master's slightest movement. His breathing, she noted, was good—deep and steady—occasionally punctuated with momentary snores. His smooth limbs twitched from time-to-time as his body sank deeply into a contented slumber. She wondered how long it would be before she could extricate herself from his presence. She dare not fall asleep in his bed as there was the unpleasant possibility that she might snore, or bump him while he was dreaming and wake him, thus rousing his legendary wrath.

May Ling was not worried as long as she remained alert. She could lie awake all night if need be. Amah, her wise pillowing tutor, had thoroughly trained her in all aspects of the erotic arts, and especially in the much more challenging and oh-so-subtle *pacification and manipulation of the male ego.* Thanks to Amah's tireless instruction—initiated when she was still just a child—May Ling had transported Royal Chen to blissful ecstasy three powerful times—once more than she had dared hope for! She was now certain that she had already begun to gain access to her new master's secret heart, and thus, his trust—an essential step in her strategy to become Chen's most intimate confidant in order to successfully fulfill her honorable duty to Uncle Wu.

* * *

ROYAL CHEN HAD everything a man could ask for and much more. His three story limestone mansion dominated a cliff overlooking the sea and boasted terraced grounds and magnificent gardens surrounded by a tall stone wall with massive iron gates. The imposing chateau was further protected by a moat fed by a thundering waterfall—the driveway entrance incorporated a drawbridge over the raging torrent—and an ornate iron portcullis was embedded in the arched gateway to the inner courtyard. All of this protection was further enhanced by an elite corps of bodyguards sworn to kill or die in Chen's defense, ably assisted by a unique breed of vicious canines.

Situated adjacent to the sprawling Gathering complex, Chen's private fortress-like residence encompassed sixty-thousand square feet of living area. Its grand interior rooms boasted twenty-foot ceilings and intricately inlaid wood and stone floors, and were furnished with the richest tapestries, draperies, rugs, and carpets. The rooms held the most exquisitely crafted furnishings and decor, gleaned and collected from nearly every Age of Man. Surrounded by the best of the old and new worlds, Chen displayed only a small portion of his innumerable possessions throughout the thirty-three rooms—the remainder of his treasured cache were secured in vast underground storerooms, carved deep into the bedrock.

The Keeper's personal sphere of influence radiated out across the entire Pacific Northwest. Up and down the coast, from Old Northern California in the south, to Old B.C. in the north, and east all the way out to the Continental Divide, a network of carefully developed spies and allies watched over Chen's interests, and reported on progress and developments across the region. This well-entrenched organization ensured that he was always the first to receive any timely information that might affect his thriving empire, and thus enabled him to adapt and adjust his business dealings accordingly.

If a large shipment of wine, silks, or cannabis left northern California on the new moon, Chen wanted to know every detail—quantities, qualities, varieties—and the cargo's expected time of arrival. Timely weather and climatic data affecting the sensitive growing conditions of vineyards and orchards in particular, and rice paddies, poppy fields, and soybean farms further south, was critical in predicting crop yields and the future availability of staples such as cooking oil, wheat, tamari, tofu, tea, opium and alcoholic beverages.

Production levels from silk factories south of San Francisco Bay, labor and supply issues affecting the region's numerous sweatshops, pleasure houses, food venders, spice traders—everything to do with anything that might influence the wealth that flowed to him via the Gathering and back to the people in the form of goods and services—Chen was the first to know about it.

The Gathering was his crowning achievement—his golden horn of plenty—supplying him with an unlimited abundance based upon one defining principle: all who wished to trade at the Gathering forfeited a single percentage of their offerings as a participation fee. Anyone in the vast region having a serious going concern eventually came to do business with Royal Chen, and after nearly twenty years of trading and accumulating, he had amassed wealth seemingly beyond measure, (though he prudently employed seven full-time Chinese whose sole purpose in life was to record, tally, and account for each and every item of value that he owned).

Strategically utilizing his vast fortune to further strengthen his influential position in the world, Chen—in concert with partners such as Venerable Wu—was heavily vested in farms, ranches, ships and caravans, and a myriad of diverse business interests. Through his far-flung network of spies and informants he maintained a close watch on his business partners and associates, whose loyalty was guaranteed by the threat of death or worse from Chen's stable of highly trained and experienced assassins.

The Keeper's reach was long and he manipulated every financial opportunity—his thin, yellow fingers firmly on the pulse of the emerging Afterworld economy. Chen's physical wealth, however, was not his greatest asset; his real power resided in the many *secrets* he possessed and favors that he was owed. What he knew about the crimes, abuses, and indulgences of powerful and influential people gave him an inordinate degree of leverage over them. During the course of the past two decades, countless individuals and groups had come to him, asking a favor here, seeking some assistance with their dreams there, to which, of course, he gladly complied, *always* securing an interest in whatever it was they were involved. After these many years, he owned a piece of nearly everyone's pie, an advantage that enabled him to literally control prices and determine the individual value of things and commodities—and control them he did.

Everything in the new world was assigned a value represented in *credits*. When a shepherd brought his sheep to the Gathering, his animals were accepted and evaluated, and he was issued a certain number of credits which he could then use to procure whatever available goods or services he might desire. The same was true in the case of a potter, blacksmith, or woodcarver. Each brought their goods to the Gathering and received credits which they could, in turn, spend on the things they needed or wanted.

Others offered services, and in the same way, they were awarded credits to "spend." Hours of service were assigned a value, and teachers, carpenters, prostitutes, gardeners, laborers, and musicians received credits from clients as they provided their services to Gathering attendees.

The value of a given product or service at any particular time was determined by a number of interrelated factors such as: current inventory levels, present market saturation, the number of potential short-term and long-term buyers, and the quality of the merchandise in question. If an artisan, craftsperson, or farmer was unhappy with the value placed on their goods or items, they were simply escorted back outside the thirty-foot-high gates, and not allowed to trade.

To keep track of his larger, long-term accounts, Chen maintained an accounting department billeted on the second floor of one of the sprawling Gathering structures. Inside its fortified, high-ceilinged room without windows, rows of shelves held hundreds of handwritten ledgers providing a running record of every transaction ever conducted. Volumes bearing red spines denoted accounts receivables records of amounts owed him by the large agricultural or manufacturing enterprises. These were annual credit accounts, usually based upon yearly crop yields or other long-term factors, wherein the client required extended credit throughout the year until their crop or product was harvested and the accounts were settled. Several large wineries, orchards, cannabis and berry farms fit into this category, as well as the usual livestock operations and the only significant shipbuilder on the west coast.

Gathering attendees not requiring a long-term credit account conducted their business using actual physical credits: small kiln-fired ceramic disks of varying colors and patterns representing various denominations from one to one thousand. Anyone possessing physical credits could spend them as they pleased, and even many transactions up and down the coast beyond the Gathering's borders were conducted using Chen's credits as legal tender. Over the years, the physical tiles themselves came to be known and referred to as "chens."

"I'll give you a hundred *chens* for that horse."

"How many *chens* will you take for that firearm?"

Of course, chens were not the only popular currency of the day. Mankind's historical fascination with precious gems and rare metals remained strong. Fine jewelry made from pearls, diamonds, emeralds, sapphires, or rubies; and gold, silver, platinum, and even the rarer palladium, were highly valued as a means by which to consolidate one's wealth. All were universally accepted as legal tender and welcomed at the Gathering, where the Keeper insisted on their exchange for chens to ensure that he always maintained a slight advantage in every transaction. After twenty years of trading, it was whispered that deep within the subterranean catacombs of Chen's palace, lay secret vaults hidden in rooms overflowing with accumulated treasure.

C H A P T E R S E V E N

NORTHWEST PASSAGE

HUNTER CRESTED THE rise and came to a halt above a rushing stream, allowing Sagebrush enough rein to nibble the lush grasses growing along its banks while Elise gathered plant specimens from the nearby creek bottom. Her lifelong interest in herbal medicine compelled her to remain watchful for useful botanicals they might find along the way.

Beginning at age nine, she had been schooled in the craft by an ancient Cheyenne medicine woman named Little Bird who had lived out her final years at New Eden, patiently escorting the young girl into fields and forests to collect beneficial plants. At her mentor's kitchen table, Elise had learned to preserve and prepare them for later use in poultices, salves, teas, and tinctures. Still spry into her nineties, Little Bird was delighted to have the bright, inquisitive child underfoot, sincerely grateful for the opportunity to impart her vast treasure chest of knowledge to such an apt pupil.

Until her passing at the respectable age of 102, Little Bird shared with Elise everything she knew about the art and science of preparing and employing medicinal remedies. Her passion for the craft was the seed of Elise's lifelong interest in the healing arts which she fastidiously applied wherever she found a need. Beyond herbal medicine's obvious *human* health benefits, she found the practice invaluable in maintaining the vitality of livestock—especially her beloved horses.

Decades earlier, research by twentieth-century botanists had confirmed that long before the first Europeans so graciously *blessed* the shores of the New World with their "enlightened" presence, the Aboriginal First Peoples and early Native American tribes throughout North America had already categorized and codified some three-thousand individual medicinal plants. Incorporating their unique healing properties into diverse tribal databases and treatment regimens, these indigenous practitioners carefully passed down their vast storehouse of collective knowledge, generation-to-generation, master-to-apprentice, from their ancestors' earliest memories.

With the recent Fall of modern civilization and the dissolution of the high-tech pharmaceutical industry along with it, this rich cultural heritage was more relevant than ever. Regrettably, Nature's wondrous pharmacopeia remained a mystery to most, largely overlooked and neglected except within certain subcultures, or by rare individuals already proficient in its use and familiar with its benefits.

After Little Bird's passing, Elise continued her education, absorbing everything she could find on the subject and carefully interviewing anyone she met with demonstrable skills in its application. Over the years, she compiled an extensive library, and with two-and-a-half decades of experience now under her belt, Elise was able to identify and employ the healing properties of nearly 700 of the most important broad-spectrum botanicals.

Nearly every day she had discovered yet another beneficial plant or two along their way. Some were identical to those back home, but as their trip to the west coast progressed, variants appeared, divergent from those she'd grown up with in Old Northwestern Colorado, and distinct as well from plants native to Hunter's valley in the northern reaches of Old Wyoming's Wind River Range.

Referring often to a well-worn *Peterson Field Guide*, she collected samples of the more important specimens, tying them with homespun yarn and lashing them in bundles to the pack animals' rigging to dry in the warm sun and fresh air. Some days, depending on her harvest, the mules and horses appeared amusingly adorned, as if intentionally camouflaged to blend in with the surrounding flora. Remounting her spirited buckskin, Elise flashed Hunter a smile, ready to continue tracing the old I-90 roadbed west.

*   *   *

SOME TWENTY YEARS after the cessation of motorized traffic, concrete and asphalt roadways were now buried under two to three feet of topsoil and overgrown with numerous grasses and shrubs. Over the years, colonizing plants had sent down roots, that chiseled their way into tiny fissures in the surface of the underlying tarmac, and allowed moisture to seep deep inside. Freezing in winter and expanding, the ice further widened the cracks to help break up the pavement underground.

Scattered here and there along the way were trees up to thirty feet in height or more, depending on the species, that spread their branches to the heavens above the buried road. Though rapidly reclaimed by nature, the route carved out by 19th and 20th century civil engineers was still fairly well-preserved, albeit certain sections of the roadbed—low bridges across narrow ravines in particular—had suffered washouts by flash floods during years with heavier than usual runoff from record snowfalls and their subsequent snowmelt. Some portions running through especially steep terrain were blocked by rockslides and difficult to navigate due to the sprawl of unstable sediments, boulders, and downed trees.

Freeway overpasses, stained and cracked by the passing of time, still spanned the buried interstates, covered in shrubs and grasses, and overgrown with vines. Protected from the elements, these shaded bridge underpasses formed cave-like refuges often claimed as nesting areas by bats or barn swallows, as dens by bears or wolves, or, if uninhabited, were frequented by random species of wildlife seeking shelter from inclement weather. The once-familiar freeway signs had long since oxidized and were no longer readable, defaced by lichens, with the majority fallen over, their awkwardly leaning support posts wrapped in wild grape and weathered with age.

In spite of the challenge of negotiating tangled undergrowth or having to detour around larger obstacles, the old interstate and state highway roadbeds were generally the most direct routes across country. Local and migrating wildlife preferred their relatively gentle grades when navigating the territory, especially while crossing mountain ranges. Their well-worn game trails, in turn, were easily managed by mounted travelers and their pack animals, although in the more seriously overgrown sections, Hunter and Elise were forced to proceed single-file along narrow, hemmed-in tracks.

Leaving the familiarity of their Wind River valley, the couple and their entourage had headed west, passing south of Yellowstone Lake before picking up the Old I-15 roadbed north. Tracing it for a week, they arrived at the I-90 interchange on the outskirts of the crumbling remains of Butte where they again turned to follow the setting sun. Presently, they were passing south of Flathead Lake in northwestern Montana, and would soon cross a narrow slice of northern Idaho before entering the eastern Washington desert on the outskirts of Spokane.

Just beyond that derelict city's sprawling ruins they would depart the interstate to trace several consecutive state highways angling northwest across the expanse of Washington State, crossing the Columbia River to continue over the Cascades until they bisected the I-5 corridor south of Bellingham. In a final push north, they planned to cross into Old British Columbia, Canada, and to arrive at Skye's village a few days later. Hunter figured the entire trip would take roughly seven to eight weeks, depending on the weather and the number of delay-causing surprises they encountered along the way. All told, their angular trek to the coast would cover more than a thousand miles of rugged wilderness.

* * *

ON THE TRAIL ahead, Hunter suddenly raised his hand, signaling for silence. Elise instantly reined in and went still. Quietly sliding the crossbow from her shoulder, she cocked it, pulling the stock in tight against her body for accuracy while sighting down the freshly loaded bolt in the direction of Hunter's gaze. She waited, poised to fight or flee as the situation demanded, though frankly, she didn't seriously entertain flight as a viable option. Considering the value of their precious livestock and belongings, she was calmly prepared to make a stand to defend what was theirs against anything or anyone who dared challenge their presence in this place.

After half a minute, Hunter relaxed his arm, pointing downhill toward a thick, wooded glade. Standing just inside the trees, a cow elk patiently suckled her energetic twin calves. Jockeying for position on stilt-like legs, they butted her udder to start her milk flowing and hungrily nursed her swollen teats. Lowering her weapon, Elise relaxed, reassured by the familiar backcountry sight so common this time of year.

Throughout the western wilderness, hundreds of species of wildlife thrived, with prolific bands of Rocky Mountain elk and mule deer populating the hills and meadows, joined by their larger moose cousins in the wetlands, feeding knee-deep in ponds along swollen streams blocked by jumbled beaver dams. On the windswept plains, herds of pronghorn antelope and North American bison ruled the open spaces, their frolicking offspring chasing one another recklessly across the landscape, racing the wind and reveling in the simple joy of being alive. In the craggy heights above, bighorn sheep and Rocky Mountain goats scaled the cliffs, defying gravity to nonchalantly walk where other species dare not tread.

Rarely seen, but ever-present in the background, large carnivores shadowed the herds: coyotes and gray wolves, mountain lions, and the great bears—ever watchful and hungry—each doing their bit in the overall scheme of things to maintain a natural balance. By vigorously culling the old, sick, weak, or injured, the predators ensured that only healthy, genetically superior specimens embraced the fullness of their potential, helping to bring out the best in each species in this ever-evolving dynamic momentum humans referred to as *the survival of the fittest.*

For Elise, traveling cross-country with Hunter and their string of spare mounts and pack animals was reminiscent of their first epic adventure together some five years earlier. In that autumn journey south from Hunter's valley they covered more than three hundred miles of wilderness in their desperate attempt to rescue the besieged community of New Eden—her entire world hanging in the balance. Unforeseen and significant life-changing events had transpired along the way: miraculously finding her missing brother William alive and on the mend, and nearly losing her own life when her horse plunged through a weak section of river ice and was swept away by the frigid current.

Rescued at the last possible moment, Hunter had coaxed her back from the brink of death through sheer will power and competent wilderness skills. He had been utterly committed to her survival, refusing to have it any other way. During the precarious days that had followed, Elise drifted in and out of consciousness while her quiet champion remained at her side like a devoted fire carrier of the migrating Paleo-tribes of prehistory, doing whatever he found was necessary to keep the flame of her essence alive.

The subsequent retaking of New Eden and the defeat of their enemies from New Hope was bittersweet—the price of victory far greater than she could ever have imagined. Her beloved father and youngest sister had both been taken from her during the final battle and Hunter himself nearly paid with his life on the old trestle bridge. For Hunter and Elise, their budding love eventually blossomed despite their stubbornness, and now the origins of their relationship seemed like ancient history; to her it was as if they had always been together.

Much personal growth had transpired during their first five years together, both in their understanding and awareness of themselves as individuals, and in their relationship to one another. Their deep interconnection—born of mutual trust and respect—had been tempered in the fires of adversity and had remained strong. In the interim, she and Hunter had fashioned a satisfying life for themselves, working diligently to create a harmonious personal oasis filled with peace and companionship.

It was a hardy, demanding lifestyle, requiring each to embrace a multitude of diverse duties and responsibilities necessary to ensure their daily survival. Beyond the mundane, the pair stretched the limits of what they felt they could accomplish together, committed to working tirelessly to improve the everyday conditions of their lives.

With their long-hoped-for child now forming in her womb, both she and Hunter recognized the wisdom of moving to the coast where the sisters would have the benefit of each other's encouragement and support—a comforting thought for the first time mother-to-be. Placing a hand low on her soon-to-be-expanding belly, Elise smiled contentedly, happy to be on this journey and looking forward to a bright future ripe with possibility and promise.

* * *

TRACING THE SHORELINE of a placid lake, Hunter noted the plentiful bear sign, including several smaller sets of tracks made by grizzly cubs. Determined to avoid a risky confrontation with a mama bear protecting her young, he withdrew a string of sleigh bells from his saddlebags, stored there for just such an occasion. Hanging them over his saddle horn to sound out sufficient warning of their approach, he gave any creatures inhabiting this place plenty of opportunity to temporarily move out of their path, allowing the riders and their pack animals to pass through unharmed.

Moving northwest across the former state of Washington, they had chosen to circumvent a derelict ghost town nestled along State Road 20 to their south. Hunter didn't really know or care which one. He always preferred to give a wide berth to such ruins rather than chance an attack, keenly aware that bandits liked to employ such places as cover from which to ambush unwary travelers who ventured too close.

Not that one couldn't be ambushed in the raw wilderness; there were no rules when it came to such things. Hunter knew that an attack could take place anywhere, but attuned as he was to wild places, he found it easier to detect a human presence in them rather than in the crumbling wastelands of overgrown urban sprawl.

Conversely, permanently inhabited communities presented their own challenges. When Skye Ravencloud had spoken to Hunter and Elise about the cultural renaissance taking place, he had mentioned several successful settlements out on the coast—his own in particular. These were communities raised up from the ruins of the past where people of conscience lived together in relative peace and security, embracing and enforcing a *civilized* code of conduct. It was rumored that many such towns existed, each a unique version of social success—much like New Eden in Old Colorado.

In spite of acknowledging the possibility that his fellow human beings were capable of selfless acts of great kindness and compassion, Hunter still had serious reservations about how truly civilized this new world had actually become. He agreed that those who staked a claim and put down roots in a place were generally more stable and predictable, however, the now-infamous social experiment at New Hope had blown that theory all to hell—a vivid reminder of Man's inherently flawed character. Founded with good intentions, New Hope had soon fallen into the hands of violent men who wreaked havoc on their neighbors for potential personal gain, and ultimately hastened their own demise. As history often repeated itself, Hunter preferred to judge the persons he came into contact with based on their individual merit rather than their affiliation with one community or another. His trust in his fellow man was clearly tempered by his life experience and he preferred to withhold his allegiance from strangers, settler or vagabond, until convinced it was prudent to do otherwise.

While many post End War survivors preferred to fort up together in permanent communities, a vibrant transitory sub-culture had evolved since the Fall as well. Its adherents embraced an essentially nomadic existence, and periodically moved from place-to-place for perfectly logical reasons of their own. Some sought fresh pastures for grazing flocks or herds, while others moved up and down between the latitudes chasing milder weather. Some such Gypsies roamed the continent in caravans of elaborately decorated wagons, entire tribes with livestock and worldly possessions in tow. When they moved, the whole community went with them and their passing was a colorful spectacle not soon forgotten.

Existing in an altogether distinct category, *ghosts*—the colloquial term for sociopathic drifters inhabiting the derelict *ghost towns* commonly found along the overgrown roadways—generally depended on scrounging and scavenging from the ruins and relics of the past. Unwilling to embrace the paradigm shift required in adapting to the ultra-challenging post-civilized world, and unable to assume responsibility as a productive member of the new social reality, such beings became predators of a lower nature, preying upon anyone unlucky enough to fall into their snares. These hellish creatures passed over into the twilight of a macabre netherworld in which murder and cannibalism had become just a normal lifestyle for certain of these fiendish ghouls.

Hunter wasn't particularly interested in meeting up with any cannibals today and had no remaining curiosity about the burned-out ruins of the past. Instead, he remained focused on living purposefully on the Earth during his allotted time upon it, and reveling, as best he could, in the wonder and beauty of the present moment. In his pragmatic worldview, integrity and free will were the ultimate qualities potentially possessed by anyone. Along with the remaining survivors of his race, Hunter was *free to choose* in any given situation, and he chose to follow his *conscience*. This inner compass bore witness that there *was* a moral high ground, a right and wrong, not based on a particular religious dogma, but anchored to a respect for, and a belief in, the sanctity of life and in what he intuitively believed to be the right thing to do in any given situation. All of this was underpinned by his personal live-and-let-live philosophy—in which he allowed others to follow their own prerogatives as long as their actions didn't encroach upon his own or another's inalienable rights.

Not that he was a saint. Hunter killed to eat and felt no remorse, but neither did he despise his prey, believe himself to be superior to it, or harbor animosity toward other living creatures and lifeforms. On the contrary, he recognized his place within the grand scheme of things and fostered a deep appreciation for the plants and animals that sustained his physical existence.

Embracing the survival principle forged into his DNA during eons of natural selection and adaptation from the earliest hominids through to *Homo sapiens* throughout the past couple of million years—Hunter daily experienced and acknowledged his compelling urge to *survive*. If he wished to remain physically fit and healthy, he required nourishment which he was willing to procure from available sources in the natural environment around him. He was a hunter-gatherer in the purest sense of the word, an opportunistic omnivore, willing to appropriate the life-sustaining energies of other species in order to maintain his own.

This was not a moral issue for him and while he was keenly aware that other living organisms gave up their lives to supply what he needed to survive, he also understood the cycle and circle of life within the food chain on this unforgiving planet. Not only was he a predator, but he was hunted as well, and there was no doubt in his mind whatsoever that the bears, mountain lions, wolves—even many of the smaller flesh eaters—would have no qualms about ripping his body to shreds and feasting on his bone marrow to satisfy *their* urge to live—and that was acceptable to him. He had no problem with dying. Everything died, eventually. It was all part of the cycle. In the present moment, however, he had no intention of rushing into that experience unnecessarily ahead of schedule.

* * *

LATER THAT MORNING as the trail dropped into a wide valley carpeted in bunchgrass with scattered groves of mixed hardwoods and conifers dotting the flanks of the bordering hills, the pair made an unsettling discovery—a second roadbed merged with theirs, showing evidence of fresh wagon tracks and a large number of outriders. Kneeling beside the road to study the sign, Hunter picked up as much information as possible about the recent visitors. Scanning the horizon with his field glasses, his furrowed brow revealed his immediate concern. Neither he, nor Elise were pleased to suddenly find themselves in such close proximity to a large party of strangers with unknown intent. The travelers had passed through here within the past forty-eight hours and could be miles away by now, or just around the bend—there was no real way of knowing.

In the sky ahead a bad omen appeared—dozens of red-faced turkey vultures circled in wide, lazy spirals, their two-toned wings outstretched, feathered tips making nearly imperceptible adjustments as they drifted effortlessly on the rising thermals. Drawing closer, he watched them drop, one-by-one, into a grove of trees a half mile north of the trail.

Signaling a halt, Hunter dismounted, passing Elise his reins and indicating his intention to singly scout the glade, curious to know what had attracted such a large group of scavengers to this place. As Elise watched over their livestock and gear, Hunter headed down through the meadow on foot, loaded crossbow resting casually in the crook of his arm. A few minutes later, he caught a glimpse of an old homestead on the far side of the thicket. Entering the shade beneath the trees, he froze.

The pungent odor of death permeated the space and he immediately realized why the meat eaters had gathered here in such numbers. Suspended from the trees were five naked corpses, intestines from their vivisected abdomens dangling nearly to the ground. The decomposing bodies were in the process of being consumed by clouds of insects and a bevy of large, raucous birds lining the branches of the neighboring trees.

Covering his nose and mouth with his bandana, Hunter watched as the jostling vultures took turns jumping onto the swinging bodies long enough to rip off a bit of flesh, before losing their balance and awkwardly plopping to the ground below. Flapping back up into the trees for another try, they challenged one another in a grotesque game of *king of the hill*, vying for the right to perch on the head or shoulders of the dead, to tear off strips of tasty, rotting meat before being buffeted by a rival who was just as determined as they had been to have a turn at the grisly feast. Crowds of crows and ravens also partook of the hearty repast, darting in and out amongst the bodies, determined to take full advantage of the sumptuous fare.

As far as Hunter could ascertain, the victims were all adult males, but due to the warm temperatures and depredation by numerous species of animals and insects, it was difficult to determine much else. It had probably only been a day or two since they'd been strung up by their necks—feet and hands hog-tied behind them with barbed wire. In addition to the five corpses in the trees, two headless bodies lay sprawled out on the ground, their picked-over skeletons nearly stripped clean by hungry, earth-bound scavengers who feasted and fought over their remains. Like macabre Christmas tree ornaments in an imaginary scene from a revised version of *Dante's Inferno*, their heads still dangled from the branches above, strands of rusted barbed wire wrapped tightly around skulls filled with orgies of writhing maggots.

The ground beneath them had been churned up by the hooves of many horses and Hunter followed their tracks back to the homestead, trying to get a sense of what had happened here. The modest spread consisted of a two-story cabin, a large timber-framed barn, and several smaller outbuildings. The cabin showed signs of a fire that had caused a blackened section of its roof to collapse. From the look of the scorched grasses and heat-withered shrubs immediately adjacent to the structure, it had been recently torched.

Alongside the burned-out home were wheel tracks made by more than one heavily-laden wagon pulled by large draft animals judging from the size of their hoof prints. A corral and adjacent shed held more clues as Hunter noted fresh horse manure and uneaten hay. He paused, taking in the scene, pushing his emotions aside to simply observe what was and what had been.

Inside the cabin were blackened bunks, a table and chairs, and a few meager belongings scattered about. In a back room he discovered two pools of dried blood and blood-streaked trails leading out the back door where the bodies had apparently been soaked in lamp oil and lit on fire, their charred remains left there to be ravaged and rot. Noting the recent bullet holes in the doors and shutters, Hunter could easily imagine the intensity of the desperate drama that had recently engulfed this place.

Poking through the smaller outbuildings for clues, he was struck by the violence of the assault and the gruesome manner of the executions. *So much for the return of civilization that Skye Ravencloud spoke of*—but to be fair to the shaman's analysis, this wilderness was hundreds of miles from any positive influence that a West Coast renaissance might have affected.

Hunter was puzzled; it was very unusual to come upon a scene like this way out on the edge of nowhere. With the surrounding territory sparsely populated, those responsible for the slaughter were probably not locals. The timber-framed barn held no further insights into the mystery. There were a few rusting tools and some odds and ends from old farm implements, but nothing here to speak to recent events. Back outside, he noted the well tended garden plot, sufficient to supply a couple's table, now trampled and stripped of its bounty, solid evidence that someone had definitely been living here long before the outriders arrived with the wagons.

Back on the roadway, Elise had allowed the animals to graze as she checked over their tack and rigging, making adjustments where necessary to ensure that saddles and packframes weren't causing blisters, or pinching and digging into their skin. She and Hunter had decided to bring a total of eight of the big, gregarious equines with them on their migration—the twin mules and six favorite horses with whom Elise couldn't bear to part. Rotating pairs of horses as mounts, spare mounts, and secondary pack animals, allowed each of their hard-working stock to bear lighter loads, avoiding fatigue and over exertion.

Watching Hunter return across the field, Elise instantly perceived his somber mood as reflected in the way he carried himself and the deliberateness of his stride. Curious to find out what he had discovered out there, she searched his face as he drew near.

"We must leave quickly, Elise" he said in his most serious voice, obviously upset by what he'd witnessed. "A large cavalry apparently attacked a small homestead on the far side of those trees, killing the inhabitants along with several newly arrived wagoners." He paused as he and Elise mounted their horses and he collected their string of pack animals to continue their journey. With Elise riding beside him, he continued, "After setting fire to the cabin, the killers gathered up the heavily-laden wagons and the remaining livestock, and withdrew."

Predictably, Elise became instantly concerned by his report, scanning the surrounding hills and feeling vulnerable. Hunter, too, searched the immediate environment for sign, looking for anything out of place that might reveal a potential ambush or trap. Still processing what he had seen beneath the trees, Hunter formulated a theory about what had taken place. He was fairly certain that the newly arrived wagoners had attacked the homesteaders, eventually storming the cabin and dragging the murdered occupants outside to be burned.

A short time later, the large group of riders had shown up and, in turn, overwhelmed the wagoners, who were stripped naked and hung up in the trees. Whoever the large cavalry was, they departed this place as suddenly as they'd arrived, hastily torching the cabin, and taking the horses and wagons—including their mysterious cargo—with them. Hunter believed that whatever those wagons contained held the key to the mystery. Whatever it was, men obviously considered it something worth killing for.

Whatever prompted these grisly events, the victors were long gone, and Hunter and Elise were relieved to have avoided serious trouble, if only by a day or so. Resuming their journey, the couple instinctively picked up the pace, crossbows ready and senses alert for any further sign of the marauders. With nightfall rapidly approaching, they pushed steadily northwest, determined to put as many miles as possible between themselves and the disturbing scene of the massacre.

CHAPTER EIGHT

HOUSE OF CHEN

HIGH ATOP THE roof of his cliff-side palace, in the comfortable reception area of his dome-shaped dovecote, Royal Chen sat on a dark leather sofa admiring the hundreds of snow-white pigeons cooing and fluttering in their respective bamboo cubicles. Moving purposefully about from cage-to-cage, a dozen children, aged nine to eleven, made sure the birds remained happy and healthy under the watchful eye of Old Chang, Chen's venerable pigeon wrangler. Behind his back, the children called him Old *Mean* Chang for his strict, no-nonsense disposition and unswerving devotion to duty, but to his face they were reverently respectful for fear of the consequences. It was the children's responsibility to keep the pigeons fed and watered, and their cages immaculate, and Old Chang saw to it that they did so—or went without supper.

Royal Chen came here two-to-three times a day to sit and read his messages, eager to receive news and updates from dozens of stationary and roving outposts scattered throughout the surrounding territory. He was intrigued by these interesting little birds that had played such a significant role in the development of human civilization. They had certainly been of tremendous value to him over the years, and he was pleased to have recognized their importance shortly after the End War and its devastating aftermath wiped out all other forms of long-distance communication.

For nearly eight-thousand years humans had employed pigeons to quickly relay vital information over vast distances—well before other messaging technologies were even conceived, much less developed. Both the early Egyptian and Persian empires used them to maintain close contact with their outlying districts. The legendary Genghis Khan, one of Chen's most revered and admired heroes, was also known to have relied on them as an important communications element linking his widespread empire and armies.

The twentieth century military use of carrier pigeons had been extensive during the first two World Wars. Several individual birds had actually been awarded medals for their courageous service during WWII, having delivered crucial intelligence data that assisted in securing allied victories. Hundreds of the birds were dropped into northwestern Europe during the conflict to provide resistance forces a means by which to relay timely intelligence to war planners back in England.

The renowned *Reuters News Service*—originally established in 1851 by Paul Julius Reuter—began as a long distance communications network consisting of telegraph cable and hundreds of carrier-pigeon posts. As recently as the year 2002 before the Fall, carrier pigeons were still being used as an emergency messaging service to areas in rural India cut off by natural disasters. In early 2011 the Chinese military began training 10,000 of the little birds as a back up communications network in the event an Electro-Magnetic Pulse (EMP) or other such weapon knocked out their computerized communications systems. Understanding the *liberating nature* of the free exchange of ideas and information, the Taliban of Afghanistan, along with the People's Republic of China and other censorship-minded governments, had outlawed private ownership of the birds in an attempt to limit access to "subversive" information by their populations.

With sustained flying speeds of up to fifty miles per hour over relatively long distances such as 500 miles, and with an ability to fly at speeds above 100 miles per hour over shorter distances of 100 miles or so, this amazing bird species provided Royal Chen with the means to remain abreast of the most important developments in the emerging economy. The little doves were his post-End War internet and Chen pored over their encrypted daily reports with extreme interest.

Unfortunately for Chen, most of the large landholders raised flocks of their own, and other individuals with widespread interests and influence maintained healthy populations as well. Even organized criminal gangs and pirates were known to employ them, and though he had no proof, he was certain that the criminal Sisterhood cult used them to maintain contact with one another as well.

Acutely aware of the edge they gave him in making important decisions based on breaking developments throughout the region, Chen surreptitiously hired bird hunters with bows and nets to attempt to intercept his rivals' pigeon messengers, but, due to their high rate of speed in flight, it was nearly impossible to bring them down. On the rare occasion when the hunters were successful in intercepting one, its message was guaranteed to be encrypted.

The birds' usefulness was tied to the fact that they were genetically wired to always return to their place of origin—

their home cote or nest. Most pre-End War scientists studying this homing capability concurred that they navigated using Earth's magnetic field as a map grid on which they overlay specific olfactory data and landmarks unique to their particular nesting area. The truth was, Chen didn't really care *how* his pigeons accomplished this feat, but he appreciated the fact that he could rely on them to deliver the information he needed in order to protect his empire and increase his profits and holdings in the challenging Afterworld.

* * *

BEFORE THE END War changed everything, Royal Chen, Keeper of the Gathering, had simply been Paul Chen, a promising young Asian-American grad student working on a second masters degree at UC Berkeley—this one in International Business and Economics. His undergraduate studies had been in History, specifically the history of ancient empire building and military conquest focusing on the successful careers of such greats as Genghis Khan, Attila the Hun, and Alexander the Great. From his tiny room across San Francisco Bay above a noisy noodle shop in Chinatown, San Francisco, Paul studied everything he could get his hands on regarding the profitable flow of goods and services from producer to consumer and back again in the form of revenue. The history and science of supply and demand—and the actuality of how business could be successfully conducted, empires built, and fortunes amassed *based on those principles*—were his passion. He secretly dreamed of someday amassing his own global empire using these same successful guidelines, but Fate intervened as international events quite beyond his control abruptly brought his post-graduate ambitions to a screeching halt.

The innocuous day marking the beginning of the end of twenty-first century civilization began as any other average, foggy Sunday morning on the northern California coast, but that all changed dramatically at exactly 10 AM Pacific Standard Time. The Department of Homeland Security issued a mandatory evacuation order for the greater San Francisco Bay Area broadcast simultaneously over the internet and through all public television, radio, and ancillary media outlets via the Emergency Alert System.

That morning, like many other Sunday mornings, Paul Chen had been jogging along the sparsely populated beach a mile southwest of the Golden Gate Bridge, listening to his favorite playlist and enjoying the caress of the salt breeze on his slightly perspiring skin when the eerie tsunami warning sirens began to sound. Not having sensed an earthquake, he assumed that one may have occurred elsewhere, perhaps in a similar scenario to the tsunami that caused extensive damage along the northern California coast following the 9.0 Japanese earthquake back in 2011. Whatever the reason, he stopped to check his hand-held web-browsing device and was startled to discover the mandatory evacuation warning already in effect. With the closest evacuation route heading into Marin County, Chen soon found himself unable to return to his room, and was swept up in a panicked stream of refugees fleeing north toward the entrance to the Golden Gate Bridge.

The madness he witnessed that day would forever alter his perception of his fellow human beings. Normally polite citizens, when driven by fear and desperation to escape the city, had morphed into raging lunatics who clawed their way through the swollen crowds at the expense of the weak or timid, wielding makeshift clubs and other crude weapons fashioned from materials at hand. Mob mentality and violence swept through the collective consciousness and in the pandemonium that followed, thousands were trampled, or pushed to the edge and over the side of the bridges spanning the bay—tumbling to watery deaths hundreds of feet below.

For miles in every direction, surface streets and highways were clogged with mobs of fleeing people. Abandoned cars and trucks stuffed with hastily gathered belongings were stuck in the middle of intersections, and brought traffic to a standstill. Men and women in excellent athletic condition had a distinct advantage over their couch-potato neighbors. Many who were challenged with disabilities, obesity, old age, illness, or frailty quickly perished beneath the trampling feet of the panicked crowds.

Everywhere young Paul looked, people were going berserk, attacking each other for food, supplies or weapons, or for some darker purpose he preferred not to think about. Cell phones became obsolete as circuits overloaded, isolating people from family and friends. Likewise, the internet collapsed as millions logged on simultaneously, mimicking the denial of service attacks favored by hackers.

Police, fire and EMT services were quickly overwhelmed, and even became targets of the mobs who sought their guns, tools, and medical supplies. By noon, their official presence on the streets of San Francisco was non-existent as prudent public servants changed out of their uniforms and into civilian clothes before setting out for home on foot, or to rendezvous with loved ones at a secure, predetermined location as part of their family disaster readiness plan.

Gunfire echoed from nearby buildings as Paul Chen hurried along the streets, jostled by the fear-stricken crowds, his adrenaline peaking as he avoided the bodies lying in the roadway or on adjacent sidewalks and alleyways. He covered his ears to block out the screams of women and the angry shouts of men streaming from windows and doorways as he hurried past audible evidence of bad things taking place that he ignored as best he could, talking to himself inside his head to maintain his sanity. Shocking scenes played themselves out over and over again throughout the city and on the colossal architectural wonders spanning San Francisco Bay.

Throughout the long afternoon, disoriented throngs streamed into Marin County on foot in a zombie-like state of shock. A few organized groups arrived by bicycle or motorcycle—rare individuals who had apparently prepared themselves for just such a disaster and who were well-armed and ready to repel the desperate fools who might attempt to rob them of their desirable modes of transportation. Families and friends held hands and tried to protect one another, while many individuals took whatever selfish measures necessary to make it out alive.

As evening approached and the ocean slowly swallowed the blood-red sun, Chen made it across the bridge and continued moving northwest into the Marin Headlands of the Golden Gate National Recreation Area, stopping just after midnight. Like so many others, he was desperate to get as far away from the madness as possible; the fear of what hungry people might do to him if they discovered the granola and

Kind Bars stashed in his backpack drove him deeper into the hills.

Halfway through the night, huddled beside a concrete bunker that had been built in WWII as part of an extensive system of San Francisco harbor fortifications, Paul's fitful sleep was interrupted as massive explosions erupted across the bay. The powerful shock waves and cacophony of destruction forced his hands up over his ears and his eyes riveted on the horizon, as conventional ordnance lit up the southern sky in an astounding red, white, and orange fireworks display. The attacks continued intermittently for several hours, but with the coming of sunrise the bombardment ceased, its merciful silence nearly as painful as the impact of the warheads blasting the city into oblivion.

Dawn revealed little—fog mixed with smoke made visibility impossible and the air hard to breathe. Chen was forced to climb further into the hills in an attempt to get above the suffocating smog. Just before noon, a fleeting rainstorm swept through, washing some of the grit from the atmosphere and enabling him finally to catch a glimpse across the water to where the metro skyline should have been. His busy mind screeched to a halt.

During the night, San Francisco had been leveled—her towering skyscrapers obliterated. The entire city center was now a smoldering mass of twisted wreckage from the hard rain of conventional warheads. Moving out from the epicenter, the entire Bay Area was burning, enveloped in flames from the overnight missile strikes. Raging fires spread outward in a ragged line, fueled by ruptured gas lines and wood-and-shingle house construction.

Long sections of the massive bridge he'd crossed just the day before, San Francisco's iconic landmark, lay in ruins, partially submerged beneath the waves. The Bay Bridge, too, had suffered a similar fate, and all along the East Bay, infernos devoured oil storage facilities and chemical processing plants, generating billows of black toxic smoke and scores of secondary explosions, wreaking utter devastation from the waterline to the ridge.

Realizing that he could never return to his former life in academia, the shell-shocked young man headed deeper into the coastal highlands. As the weather rapidly turned sour and the air more foul, young Chen avoided using even the back roads, and slept in thickets where he could find a bit of cover, supplementing his dwindling supplies by scavenging what little he could find from orchards and fields.

After two days on the move, he lucked upon a weathered wooden sign indicating the entrance to a Boy Scout camp. Following the winding gravel access road for five more miles, he arrived at the rustic one-story facility, breaking in through a small window in the back, where he collapsed onto a folding cot to enjoy his first proper sleep since the night of the missiles.

* * *

WAKING FOURTEEN HOURS later, Chen's first order of business was to backtrack down the access road in the pre-dawn light, axe and shovel in hand, to destroy all evidence of the camp's wooden sign. With air temperatures steadily dropping, he returned to his hideout and got busy fortifying its doors and windows with a screw gun, fasteners, and some numbered sections of marine-grade ¾ inch plywood located in an adjacent shed. In a practical demonstration of their beloved motto, the Scouts had conveniently cached the protective sheathing nearby in the event of a violent storm. Apparently "Be Prepared" was more than just a cliche.

Once the camp headquarters was relatively secure, he scoured the office, reviewing inventory lists detailing every item stockpiled by the Scouts. Rifling through an unlocked filing cabinet, he came upon a set of blueprints for some sort of below-ground storage facility. Following the directions in the plans, he searched the small cellar to find a hidden doorway ingeniously disguised as a wall-mounted shelving unit. Activating the release mechanism, the entire unit swung out to reveal a narrow stairway leading down into a survival bunker.

Constructed more than half a century earlier as a "cold war" civil-defense project in anticipation of a potential cataclysmic event such as a Soviet nuclear-missile attack, the reinforced access was similar to a bank vault door. Armed with the combination from the plans, Chen managed to gain access to the facility and flipped the light switch beside the door, which activated a battery-powered lighting system. He excitedly surveyed the surreal scene before him, not believing his astounding luck.

Stacked on sturdy steel shelves lining the walls of the reinforced structure were hundreds of dehydrated food packets, canned goods, vitamin/mineral nutritional powders and supplements, along with all manner of useful tools, supplies, and survival gear. Wrapped in black plastic and well hidden beneath a stack of olive green Army Surplus blankets he discovered a Ruger 10/22 autoloading rifle with 4x30 scope—the shelter's only weapon—along with six 25-round magazines and ten boxes of .22 caliber ammunition in air-tight, moisture-proof containers containing 525 rounds each.

From the looks of it, the shelter had been recently reno-vated and upgraded, and was equipped with a sophisticated, latest generation Nuclear, Biological, and Chemical air filtra-tion system, complete with spare cartridges, courtesy of the ongoing "war on terror." A deep rock well with a military-grade water filtration system fitted with UV, ceramic, carbon filtration chambers and a hand pump, provided a clean sup-ply of fresh water. There was even a sink, toilet, and a decent shower.

According to the blueprints, a several thousand gallon propane tank lay buried nearby to provide fuel for cook-ing, and hot water for showers and cleaning. Everything he needed to survive was stockpiled here, and while the Scouts may have been unsuccessful in saving themselves, their well-planned disaster preparations enabled a very lucky Paul Chen to remain alive and healthy throughout the forthcom-ing nuclear winter.

As he settled into what would ultimately become two years of solitary confinement, the panicked survivors above him on the planet's rapidly cooling surface scrambled about in the bleak twilight, quickly depleting all readily available food and medical supplies. The dust-choked stratosphere, filled with particles from the relatively small number of de-ployed nuclear warheads, acted as a planetary insulation bar-rier, deflecting the sun's heat and light, and causing surface temperatures to plummet further.

When the food ran out, widespread panic gripped the globe as famine and pestilence purged more than ninety-nine percent of the human population. In the end, the thing that nearly wiped out the human race was not the six-day war that killed *millions*, it was the war's devastating aftermath, when *billions* died from starvation, disease, and exposure to the elements. There was compelling evidence afterward that many who would have otherwise survived the End War and its two-year nuclear winter were subsequently murdered for their caloric value. Roving packs of cannibals became a ghoulish plague of their own in many urban locales. After they depleted the inner cities, these predators spread out, combing the upper-class neighborhoods of outlying suburban districts in bands of fifty or more, methodically searching house-to-house in their insatiable quest for fresh meat.

Young Chen's study of economies and the cycle of supply and demand provided him with a pragmatic approach to survival. Although his facility was originally designed and outfitted to provide support for ten adults for a six month period, when Chen divided the inventory into categories, he determined that he had enough food and supplies for one adult to survive almost three years. In the well-stocked survival library was a concise, well-written manual detailing exactly how to operate, maintain, and troubleshoot each of the shelter's critical life support systems.

To renew the energy needs of the bunker as well as assist long-term shelter inhabitants to remain in good physical condition, a stationary bicycle had been converted into a pedal-powered electric generator attached to a bank of deep-cycle batteries. One strenuous hour on the bike provided twelve full hours of electricity for lighting and other needs. A chin-up bar provided an upper body workout.

During his long sojourn in the shelter, Chen came to terms with the end of civilization as he knew it. The amateur radio station installed by the Scouts was equipped with a scanner designed to pull in signals from whichever channel might be operating. At first, he heard quite a bit of radio traffic coming through, though much of it was in foreign languages Chen wasn't fluent in. He spoke English and Mandarin of course and a little Spanish, and listened intently as people called for help or provided updates from their particular region of the planet. After a month, radio traffic had dwindled to a handful of transmissions per day, and ninety days into the nuclear winter, with surface temperatures planet-wide well below zero, the speakers went dead silent and remained so for the duration.

Each day as part of his routine, Chen would check the surface temperature on the remote thermometer installed by the Scouts, watching and waiting for the earth to begin to warm up. He wasn't sure exactly what he'd find alive on the surface when the freezing twilight finally ran its course, but it was his firm belief that those who did manage to survive its reality-shattering nightmare would immediately need many things—all manner of useful things—in order to get on with their lives and begin again. A prudent individual who salvaged, stockpiled, and offered to provide such things to a desperate and appreciative population would most likely be in a favored position to dominate the new world economy— that is, if he could stay alive long enough to make it happen.

* * *

THE END WAR and its gruesome aftermath was no re-specter of persons and claimed the unlucky billions regard-less of age, race, gender, sexual orientation, social status, political affiliation, or religious persuasion. Tens of millions of innocent men, women, and children died instantly from the indiscriminate and excessive use of weapons of mass de-struction and their devastating residual effects. Untold mil-lions more, who had miraculously avoided the initial waves of annihilation, slipped quietly into despair, succumbing beneath the crushing emotional weight of hopelessness and mob violence, as the sun grew dim behind ashen skies and air temperatures—even at the equator—plummeted to below freezing and remained there. Global famine and pestilence of Biblical proportions seemed to fulfill the ancient prophecies foretelling of sinful Man's pre-ordained fate at the hands of a wrathful God.

But human beings were not alone in this time of tribula-tion. All living things: beasts of the field, birds of the air, insects, fish, and plants alike, all suffered the same fate, each struggling to eke out an existence amidst the suddenly harsh, Ice-Age environment. Luckily for the survivors of every species, the worst was over in less than two years, and the skies began to clear as the sun shone through at last, gradual-ly thawing out the frozen planet and its grateful inhabitants.

When Chen finally emerged to a pale dawn two years later he was shocked to discover the coastal highland region nearly one-hundred percent depopulated. Having lived en-tirely below ground for such a long time, it required some mental and physical adjustments for him to adapt to life back on the surface of the planet. Initially, he felt exposed and vulnerable, and would retreat back down into the safety of the shelter upon hearing any noise that he could not immediately identify. Overcome by the bizarre sensation of looking at objects more than 20 feet away, his eyes gave him plenty of trouble for the first few days, being out of practice at focusing out to the farthest horizon, but they soon became accustomed to the new experience and adapted accordingly.

With the weather improving each week, Chen began to plan his journey west over to the Coast Road where he would head north and search for a suitable location to set his plan for economic domination into motion. The Scouts had compiled an extensive collection of local and regional maps and he poured over them, identifying a potentially ideal location one third of the way up the Oregon coast, but it was hundreds of miles north, much too far for him to walk or run.

Rummaging about the Scout camp garages and sheds, he found just what he was looking for partially hidden beneath an old canvas tarp: a small, motorized trail bike complete with a sturdy utility trailer. The *Rokon* motorbike—renowned the world over by explorers and special forces units for its simple reliability and tough, overbuilt components—was one of three identical units left in storage by the Scouts.

In making final preparations to leave his tiny shelter, Chen camouflaged the cellar entrance, burning the plans and memorizing the door combination in case he ever found himself back in the vicinity and in need of supplies. Towing the small trailer stuffed with food, fuel, fishing gear and camping supplies behind the motorbike, Chen carefully made his way back toward Highway 1, Ruger 10/22 slung handily across his back. He pushed steadily through the slushy, half-frozen landscape, and where the land met the sea headed north along the deserted road.

Along the way, he scrounged fuel—in the form of high alcohol content spirits—which his bike engine readily consumed as if it were unleaded gasoline. The problem with simply taking a length of old garden hose and siphoning off the plentiful fuel from derelict vehicles and gas station storage tanks was that after a few months, without the addition of chemical additives designed to condition gasoline against decay and disintegration, it eventually broke down and spoiled, becoming unusable. But ethanol was readily available in the form of vodka, tequila, gin, rum, whiskey and other high-proof liquors and it worked equally as well, if not better, due to its higher octane rating.

Heading up a desolate Highway 1 and then 101, during which time he didn't see another living soul, Chen arrived at the spot he'd picked out on the map back at the Scout camp. Nestled on the high ground above the banks of a clear-running river, he decided that this would be the perfect place to make his dreams a reality. Through the centuries, the river had formed a protected harbor and its citizens had built wharves and a curved rock jetty to hold the Pacific at bay. In a two-story warehouse Chen began stockpiling his trade goods. Anything of current or future value was fair game and he sought out all types of useful items, bringing them, one-by-one, to the large storage facility beside the aluminum-framed wharf.

* * *

AS THE PLANET warmed, the blue returned to the sky and those who survived the longest winter on record emerged from a wide variety of hiding places: barricaded basements, abandoned mines and caves, subway tunnels, high-rise apartment buildings, seaside warehouses, fortified prisons, and abandoned government complexes. Like hibernating bears awakening in spring to a surreal landscape void of familiar sights and sounds, they emerged hungry and desperate—for food, for news of others, and ready to start their lives over. Several weeks after finding his warehouse, while Chen was out searching for collectible treasures, he came across a pair of emaciated teenagers rummaging through a previously looted high-school cafeteria, apparently hoping to find something—anything—that might have been overlooked by the scavengers who'd been there years before.

During the *Deep Freeze*, as the nuclear winter came to be known, the boys had forted up together inside a mail order health-food distribution warehouse, staying alive by rationing the edible goodies they found lining the shelves, spread out along motionless conveyor belts, and stacked on silent loading docks. Toward the end of their sojourn there, their fat-free supplies ran thin and they emerged from their hideaway, gaunt and hungry. In exchange for edible canned goods—pork and beans being their favorite—Chen enlisted the pair to scavenge for him, and he soon came across and hired several more like them, enabling him to stay behind and guard his burgeoning hoard of treasures while his growing army of "diggers" searched high and low for useful things to bring him.

Once he no longer needed to scavenge for himself, Chen divided his time between beefing up warehouse security and organizing the constant stream of items brought in by the diggers. He sorted them into the basic categories of food, clothing, shelter, medical, personal hygiene, cleaning supplies, defense, tools, transport, furniture, and raw materials.

Over the ensuing months and years, Chen built an efficient organization, enlisting others to work for him in various capacities inside the warehouse complex. While diggers brought him more valuables, he incorporated people with fighting and military skills into his fledgling security apparatus. Women flocked to him, recognizing the advantages of a *lack of scarcity* as being the most compelling form of modern luxury, and many young, attractive types, looked after his household domestic needs and came to serve him in other, more personal ways as well.

Carpenters, stonemasons, blacksmiths, and other experienced craftsmen constructed an impenetrable perimeter wall and gates, and expanded his trading facilities as Chen's gathering phenomenon continued to gain momentum. After a few years, word had spread about a unique walled city— a Gathering place on the coast—where anything was available for a price. Ambitious artisans and entrepreneurs flocked to his enterprise, bringing with them the skills and knowledge Chen needed to further expand the scope of his offerings by opening up shops and providing a wide range of desired products and services. After nearly two decades, what initially began as a swap meet and open-air market, had grown into a bustling metropolis renowned throughout the region and beyond, with young Paul Chen blossoming into who he was today: Royal Chen, Keeper of the Gathering.

CHAPTER NINE

THE PEOPLE

SKYE RAVENCLOUD'S VILLAGE was located on the banks of a glacier-fed river north of Vancouver Island in Old British Columbia, Canada, several miles upstream from where the icy waterway emptied its nutrient-rich bounty into the saline waters of the Pacific. Nestled atop a horseshoe-shaped rise some thirty feet above the river's pebbled beach, two dozen communal longhouses provided their inhabitants with an aesthetic and protected settlement in which to live.

For thousands of years, this food-abundant coastal region had been a popular choice for human habitation, occasionally visited throughout prehistory by courageous seafaring explorers from as far away as the South Pacific and the Far North, but void of permanent settlers until early nomadic bands of *Paleo Indians* traveled down the west coast of North America some 14,000 years earlier. Originating in Asia tens of thousands of years before that, their ancestors followed the great bison, wooly mammoth, and mastodon herds migrating across the vast, grass-covered Bering land bridge from Siberia to Alaska at the end of the most recent Ice Age. After a several-thousand-year layover in *Berengia* due to the presence of insurmountable glaciers blocking their way south, the first land-based *Homo sapien* sojourners arrived in this bountiful place and quickly flourished.

Draining a complex web of broad basins in the Coast Mountains, the watercourse was not very long as rivers go—a mere fifty miles from its headwaters in the Pemberton Icefield to the sea, but what it lacked in length, it made up for in volume, being joined along the way by several notable tributaries. The fast-moving torrent transporting a remarkable quantity of glacial runoff was home to a number of important fish species—salmon and steelhead in particular—that hatched upstream in pebble-bottomed shallows. Upon reaching an appropriate size, the fingerlings journeyed out into the vast, food-rich Pacific to feed and mature. After a specified absence of one or more years, depending on the species, they faithfully returned to their original spawning grounds far upstream to ensure the survival of their kind.

The bustling community built on the site of ancient settlements going back many thousands of years was protected by a twenty-foot-tall perimeter palisade fashioned from stout cedar logs standing on end, their lower sections encased in a thick stone and concrete foundation. Heavily fortified gates remained open during the day, but were prudently secured at dusk, leaving only a narrow inset doorway to allow nighttime access. Four feet below the top of the wall, wide bamboo decking ran along the inside, creating a protected walkway designed for defense against external assault. Stairways and ladders, also constructed of resilient bamboo, were placed at regular intervals around the inside of the decking, providing access to the walkway above. Built into the perimeter wall, stout, strategically placed lookout towers perched another ten feet above the barricade, providing a commanding overlook of the area.

Framing the massive gates, two huge totem poles stood guard, fashioned from western red cedar specimens some forty feet in length and nearly four feet in diameter at their base. Each pole was decorated with hand-carved Aboriginal totems representing orca, raven, salmon, beaver, and eagle, and incorporating design elements depicting village myth and history. Within the perimeter wall's enclosure, traditional longhouses formed a semi-circle around a central clearing. Before the entrance to each domicile, somewhat smaller totem poles watched over clan dormitories, appropriately decorated according to individual family history and genealogy.

Tethered to posts buried near the river's edge, ancestral sea-going canoes lined the banks. Constructed from hollowed out cedar logs, their prominent prows were painted in the shapes of howling wolves or raven heads. Parked beside these were a hodgepodge of durable aluminum, plastic, and fiberglass canoes and kayaks, all salvaged from the previous incarnation of human culture and industry.

Like their ancestors before them, Skye Ravencloud's People were a seafaring culture, their survival forever linked directly to the ocean. From it they harvested a varied and abundant bounty which included four different varieties of salmon, halibut, cod, flounder, sturgeon, and dogfish, as well as sea otter, seal, dolphin, and even an occasional gray or humpback whale should the opportunity present itself. The small but versatile eulachon, or candlefish, was a silver smelt harvested by the tens of thousands for just one week per year. Prized for the rich, versatile oil that made up fifteen percent of its body weight, the sardine-sized species was particularly useful in cooking and lighting applications.

Within the warp and weft of their social fabric, Skye's People honored the competent handling of net, spear, and harpoon as sacred survival skills handed down from their ancestors. Such competency was highly esteemed in a society where the quality of the fishing season determined the level of community comfort and prosperity throughout the year. The community also hunted the deer, elk, and moose that thrived in the relatively mild climate of the Coast Mountain drainage, providing meat to supplement their seafood-laden diet and pelts to fashion warm, durable clothing and other useful items.

* * *

WHEN ANNA AND Skye first arrived at his village—or *tsinúk* as it was called in his native tongue—she received a warm welcome into the close-knit Ravencloud clan by her companion's many relatives. As word of their arrival spread, Skye's extended family gathered spontaneously beside the totem pole in front of their clan longhouse to sing the *Returning Song* in the Salish dialect. Forming a circle with Anna and Skye at the center, the older generations sang and clapped their hands to the music as the young people danced enthusiastically around the couple, twirling and spinning to the beating of drums. The People wore fringed buckskins and moose-hide moccasins decorated with bead and quill work, while the dancers adorned themselves in brightly-colored masks fashioned from cedar, and elaborate horn-and-bird-feather headdresses.

Three days later, a feast honoring Anna and Skye's union was attended by the entire village and Anna was formally welcomed by the elders and the rest of the community. Though vastly different from the culture of New Eden, Anna already felt very much at home here. The air was fresh—cleansed by the salt breeze from the nearby sea sifting through the surrounding conifer forests—and the people were friendly and industrious, quick to lend a hand or offer constructive advice. The tribal culture was a blend of traditional First Peoples' beliefs and practices, intermingled with post-modern and post-End War ways, all mixed together. Individual expression was encouraged while traditional tribal values, laws, and guidelines maintained order for the five-hundred-plus souls flourishing in this small corner of the world.

To Anna, the settlement was more than a collection of individual clans and their constituents. She found here a vibrant cultural identification, a vivid, living history connecting the past with the here and now. Elders were respected, contributing members of society, prized and honored for their knowledge and hard-won life skills and experience. Tribal lore was passed down in the oral tradition to the next generations and the stories told around evening bonfires blazed deep into the hearts and souls of their young people who listened with wide eyes and open spirits.

The powerful bond with their ancestors defined an authentic continuity and sense of place and belonging, deeper and more meaningful on many levels than that to which Anna had been accustomed back home. Here she was totally immersed in the community energy and consciousness, yet felt neither overwhelmed, nor bombarded by it. Rather, she basked in the positive vibe and love so evidently flowing among the People. Akin to a spiritually rich river coursing through her soul, the community nourished her deep-seated hunger for tribe.

The interior of the communal longhouse that she and Skye shared with the Ravencloud clan was designed with a large common area in the center and smaller apartments around the edges partitioned by dividers of bamboo, hemp and hides, providing individual family units a necessary and appropriate degree of privacy. It was a comforting and inviting living space filled with the nostalgic aroma of wood fires and communally-cooked meals. Rising beside the entrance, a totem traced the family lineage and major historical events that had occurred within the Ravencloud clan over the past century.

Anna especially enjoyed their evening get-togethers when family clans gathered around welcoming bonfires to share food, songs, and stories while young people danced and the older generation reminisced about the glorious accomplishments of their youth. She loved watching the children before bedtime dance and sing, seemingly well-grounded in their culture and full of smiles and enthusiasm. Their days were divided between assigned duties that contributed to clan and community continuity and wellbeing, and receiving various kinds of training in appropriate living and survival skills under the tutelage of a caring mentor who had mastered a specific skill set. Anna recognized the thoughtful and balanced educational regimen that enabled children here to rapidly develop into competent and confident members of their community and she looked forward to the time when her own child would be fully engaged in that process.

* * *

IN A LUSH river valley with a cascading waterfall at its far end, Hunter sat comfortably astride Sagebrush, his sure-footed dun mare who, after five years and counting, still remained one of his favorite mounts. He and Elise had finally arrived at Skye's village, and they were both relieved to have their nearly two-month-long journey come to its happy conclusion. Invited to partake in a guided tour of the surrounding area with Skye, Hunter drew inspiration from the beauty and diversity of the Coastal Mountain region and was eager to explore its riches.

The morning of their arrival, Anna was completely taken by surprise to be so unexpectedly reunited with her sister, and she experienced a volley of emotions ranging from shock and disbelief, to joyful exhilaration and tears. That the fiercely independent couple had actually made the pilgrimage to the coast—especially after seeing what they'd accomplished for themselves in the Rockies—was amazing to her. Their monumental decision only made sense upon hearing the joyful news about their baby, at which point Anna danced around giddily thrilled to have Elise back in her life and excited about the future advantages their children would now be able to enjoy together.

Until the newcomers sorted out exactly where to establish their homestead, Hunter and Elise were invited to move into one of the large communal longhouses sometimes used as guest quarters for visitors, where they quickly settled into the daily routine of village life. The enthusiastic welcome they received from Skye's many friends and relatives was a bit daunting at first, especially one evening when a lively feast held in their honor was attended by what seemed to be the entire village. Hunter had become so uncomfortable at one point that he nearly excused himself and vanished into the woods, never to be seen or heard from again. Somehow though, he managed to tough it out, and was greatly relieved when the social affair finally subsided, allowing him and Elise to withdraw to the peace and privacy of their own rooms.

A few days later, Elise had been invited to accompany Anna, and Skye's twin sisters, Lily and River, on their weekly ride to a local marketplace downriver on the coast. As they would be gone the better part of the day, Skye and several of his closest friends had offered to escort Hunter on a sight-seeing tour of a particularly pristine river valley a couple hours ride north of the settlement.

So far, Hunter was very pleased with what he had seen of this place. The landscape was green and the soil black and fertile with forested mountains and grass-filled valleys harboring clear running streams and creeks. He was impressed with the variety and abundance of wildlife, not only in the plentiful deer, elk, and moose herds that roamed the hills and valleys, but also with the rivers which ran clear and fast, and were filled with large steelhead and their smaller trout cousins that had yet to make the sojourn to the Pacific to feed on the abundance there and grow into monsters. The rainforest was profuse, with Northwest Coastal evergreens growing significantly larger than their Wind River counterparts.

Taking it all in, Hunter was beginning to relax, feeling positive so far about their decision to relocate here from their home in the Wind—which stark landscape seemed rather barren and inhospitable in comparison. He sensed that this would be a good place to put down roots and raise his soon-to-be-expanding family, and because the climate was relatively mild here, they would no longer have to fight the bitterly cold winters, or the constant high winds that the Wind River Range was infamously named for.

Already, Elise seemed to smile more often and spoke animatedly about how their son or daughter might experience a childhood enhanced by the diversity and enrichment offered through interaction with Skye's People, who seemed solid, down-to-earth, and well-established. It was immediately obvious that the community here worked and played hard, and with many shoulders to bear the workload and pairs of eyes to see what was needed, everyone seemed content and well-looked after.

* * *

RELAXING IN HIS native-style saddle, enjoying the warm sunshine and pleasant breeze, Skye Ravencloud glanced over at Hunter, pleased that his brother-in-law was having such a positive reaction to his new environment. As a man of few words, the wilderness dweller hadn't offered to share his thoughts yet, but Skye didn't require words to sense a man's mood or spirit; he could read the energetic vibrations emanating from one's aura and right now Hunter was purring like a contented feline. Which was a good thing, he reflected, because Anna was counting on Elise to settle down someplace close by, and this would only be possible if Hunter was happy here. In the short time since their arrival, the People had already decided that the two were welcome to become members of the tribe if they so desired, an honor not lightly bestowed upon strangers, however Skye realized that it was highly unlikely that Hunter would agree to move into the confines of a settlement just yet.

Without warning, the shaman felt a sharp disturbance in his own energy field—a flood of foreign emotions ranging from anxiety and fear, to anger and despair, that rippled through his body and soul in rapid-fire succession. Instantly on his guard, he recognized the foreshadowing of impending disaster and grew very still. From the surrounding forest, a raven called to him and Skye looked up, acknowledging the presence of his spirit guide in the tree opposite. The obsidian-black messenger cawed loudly three times before lifting off, fully circling the riders once before heading southwest on a beeline toward the village.

Briefly conferring with his tribesmen, Skye hastily informed Hunter that they must return to the village at once. Without further explanation, he spun his horse around and broke into a full gallop toward home. Confused about the sudden urgency of their departure, Hunter raced after the riders who were already vanishing around a bend in the trail ahead.

* * *

ARRIVING AT THE village a brutal 90 minutes later, the riders were met by an electrified crowd having just received word from Elise of a bold bandit attack on their people. Skye's uncle and village elder, T'lmuk, grasped the young shaman's arm and peered deeply into his searching face to gravely announce, "Your wife and sisters have been kidnapped!" As Skye, Hunter, and the others listened with accelerating concern, he repeated Elise's story about a gang of cutthroats who had ambushed the quartet on their return ride home from the market, kidnapping Anna, Lily, and River with Elise barely escaping with her life.

Visibly upset, Elise emerged from the longhouse still dressed in her wet clothes and wrapped in a wool blanket. She began recounting the details of the ambush on the old railroad bridge, how after wounding two of the attackers, she barely escaped by leaping from her horse off the side of the bridge into the swiftly flowing river. Not long after the attack, as she crawled from the icy waters, a group of passing travelers had graciously offered to escort her back to the village.

Holding her close, Hunter expressed concern for her wellbeing and for that of their baby, and was quickly reassured that both were fine. Greatly relieved, he pressed her for detailed descriptions of the bandits and any other relevant facts that she could recall. With only sketchy impressions of the assault and Elise's escape, Hunter, Skye and several others—two of whom were engaged to Lily and River—made hasty preparations to go after them, knowing that they would have to move quickly if they hoped to have any real chance of success. Elise, who assumed that she would be accompanying the rescue party, was shocked when Hunter insisted that she stay behind for the sake of their baby growing in her womb.

Far more concerned for Anna, who was a month further along in her pregnancy than Elise, she quietly argued to be included, but ended up staying behind rather than waste precious time openly challenging Hunter's unyielding point of view. Not being afforded the opportunity to freely follow her instincts went strongly against Elise's nature. She naturally would have chosen to take action rather than wait and worry back at camp, and Hunter's unprecedented enforcement that she stay behind was not only surprising and awkward, but deeply troubling.

With the entire village looking on—their collective emotions a warring mixture of disbelief, hope, fear, and anger—the rescue party hastily gathered food, weapons, and other necessary provisions before mounting fresh horses and speeding through the massive gates at a gallop. Heading southwest toward the scene of the ambush, they arrived hours later at a rusting railroad bridge where they dismounted and began scouring the area for sign to determine the direction the kidnappers had taken.

Hunter could see from the trampled earth where the bandits had waited in the forest beside the road near the bridge abutment, with their horses and wagon tethered nearby. Glancing over the railing into the swift-moving waters below, he was grateful that Elise had been able to fend off her attackers and escape into the relative safety of the river which had quickly whisked her downstream and out of harm's way. He fought to control the anger welling up inside him as contempt for the kidnappers threatened to consume his soul—the rage roiling just beneath the surface of his self-controlled facade.

Noting the dried blood splattered across the railing and bridge decking, he smiled grimly, certain that here, one or more of the bandits had tasted brave Elise's blade. Three months pregnant and she could still offer a notable accounting of herself. He was proud of her and grateful that his woman and their child were safe, but he feared for Anna and the twins, imagining the anguish that Skye and his tribesmen must be experiencing.

Mounting up again, Hunter's adrenaline-charged mind and body bristled with singleness of purpose as he and Skye raced away, leading the determined rescuers on their desperate chase. Somewhere up ahead, Skye's loved ones were at the mercy of brutal criminals who had cruelly separated them from all they held dear. With hearts united in a black desire for revenge, the posse rode the cowards down like an impending storm of vengeance aching to be unleashed upon the luckless souls of the fleeing outlaws.

Now several hours behind the kidnappers, the rescue party pressed on as the evening sky darkened and daylight failed them. They continued forward well after nightfall, slowly picking their way along the road by torchlight until weariness and their flagging horses forced the men to pitch a lean camp to wait out the remainder of the night in fitful sleep, ready to resume the chase at first light.

When the fading night sky finally gave way to a bleak, overcast dawn, the group struck camp and urged their rested mounts forward at a loping canter, desperate to make up as much time as possible without wearing out their horses. Soon the forested track bisected a well-traveled east-west roadway angling downhill toward the sea still a few miles due west. Here, the wagon tracks were easy to distinguish and the men guided their horses toward the coast with renewed purpose. Ahead, the sullen sky rapidly filled with dark rainclouds rolling in from the Pacific, and by mid-morning, the winds had increased. Swollen thunderheads rushed by overhead, threatening an imminent downpour.

As the morning progressed, Skye Ravencloud rode on with a deepening vengeance pervading his normally serene countenance—black thoughts as dark and troubled as the day chipped away at his sense of justice and humanity. Up ahead, the three women he most loved in this world were in the hands of ruthless barbarians willing to risk everything to ply their detestable trade in human flesh and he was determined to bring his wife and twin sisters back safely, whatever the cost. His fellows were similarly resolved—especially Walker Dan and Paints-His-Face-Red—who were betrothed to the twins with longstanding plans to be wed at the fullness of the autumnal equinox. Being so closely attuned and connected to the captives, Skye perceived every nuance of their fear and anxiety in full measure, and did well to keep his emotions at bay, lest he succumb and become ineffectual in their rescue.

Much of his frustration was directed inward, disappointed with himself that he had failed to foresee this event or somehow prevent it from happening. The *gifts* bestowed on him during his vision quest were not fully under his control, but rather, were more similar to a channel of knowledge that seemed to come from somewhere beyond himself, providing insight into specific situations and circumstances.

* * *

ALL MORNING AND well into the afternoon, the posse rode hard and when the thunderstorm finally unleashed its turbulent energy upon them, they doggedly kept on, oblivious of the wind and rain buffeting the highlands. However, at the height of the storm they had no choice but to seek shelter beneath a shallow rock overhang edged with boulders, as the already powerful winds increased even further, and gale force gusts snapped large tree branches like twigs, demanding that saplings bow down in worship before their merciless onslaught. Above in the thick maelstrom, ominous tendrils hung down from the black ceiling in dangling wisps like embryonic tornadoes awaiting the opportunity to hatch. Noticeably absent were the usual countless numbers of seabirds, that had wisely sheltered elsewhere to escape the violent weather system.

As the dangerous winds and rain finally began to subside, the region was blanketed in a patchy mist and the riders ventured back out onto the road, urging their animals forward as fast as they dared on the treacherously muddy track. A short time later, a towering black oak materialized out of the fog ahead, marking a fork in the road that forced the waterlogged band to rein in. Pausing at the junction, they sought a clue that might direct them which way to go, but the deluge had washed away all traces of horse or wagon tracks in the mud. Time stood still as each man weighed the consequences of choosing the wrong path.

Easing his Appaloosa alongside Hunter's bay Mustang, Skye looked to the heavens as the storm continued to wind down. Fine droplets of water trickled down his face as the mists were transformed into a light drizzle. With the sky partially clearing to the west, steam rose from the necks and flanks of the soaked horses that appeared beset and bedraggled from the toll of enduring arduous miles assaulted by wind, rain, and mud. Waiting quietly as the group weighed their options, Hunter remained stoic, though inside he seethed, certain that the group would now be forced to split into two groups, each taking separate routes to cover both possible paths.

Unable to physically determine which direction the kidnappers had gone, the Native shaman beside him closed his eyes and traveled inward, smoothly entering a light, trance-like state in a matter of seconds. On the *inner road* he read the sign, following the trail, and could see in his mind's eye that the bandits with their wagon had taken the left fork. Through years of experience he'd learned to fully trust this subjective form of intuition and opened his eyes with certainty.

"This way!" he called out, immediately urging his horse to the left as Hunter hesitated, uncertain about Skye's decision while the others followed him at a gallop. With increasing anxiety, he watched them disappear into the lingering mist, quelling the urge to scream out his frustration at the top of his lungs. Conflicted, yet unwilling to sit in the drizzle doing nothing, he took off after the others. Hunter hoped his host knew where the hell he was going, but logically was unable to resolve how Skye could possibly be certain that his choice had been correct. Hunter's rational mind was not yet willing to fully embrace the reality that Skye was somehow navigating by some inner spiritual compass.

The mystery, had Hunter been able to embrace it, was easily explained by understanding the connection between Skye and his raven spirit guide, which enabled a transfer of images directly into the shaman's consciousness. As Skye opened himself and asked for guidance, visions flashed across the stage of his mind like a full-color motion picture. Scenes witnessed by the raven community which included crows, jays and even some birds of prey, were held in common within their collective consciousness, and came into

Skye's view, vividly showing him the way. His feathered brethren had seen everything from the skies above, or safe from the storm in adjacent forests, as the kidnappers passed beneath them with their wagon filled with captives, speeding west toward their seaside destination. Within Skye's spiritual reality, what *one* saw, *all* had seen.

This commonly misunderstood phenomenon, part of a greater communal intelligence, was easily observed in flocks of birds as well as in schools of fish and herds of animals. This 'One-Mind shared consciousness' explained the ability of animals to instantly turn and change direction as one, even when their group might consist of several hundred or even several thousands of individuals.

* * *

THE KIDNAPPERS RODE hard for their rendezvous point at the old wharf, their captives bound, blindfolded, and safely secured inside the jolting horse-drawn wagon. They covered the last twenty miles of roadway at a furious pace, determined to outrun the menacing offshore downpour steadily moving in to meet them, and keenly aware of the reward awaiting them at the end of the trail. Time was of the essence, not only because of the approaching storm, but especially since one of the women had managed to escape. If she had survived her dive into the river, she would no doubt raise the alarm among her people as soon as possible and fierce men would come after them, deadly determined to win their women back.

Early that morning, lookouts had spotted the four potential targets at the open market, curiously lacking the accompaniment of male escorts. Notifying the kidnappers, the gang quickly arranged to ambush them on their return ride home. When surrounded on the bridge, the outnumbered women bunched up and drew blades as the close quarters and rapid attack inhibited their ability to access their bows. As the men charged forward from both ends of the bridge blocking their escape, three of the females were quickly tackled from their horses and overwhelmed, but the one who escaped had viciously slashed at her attackers before standing up on top of her saddle and leaping off the side of the bridge into the fast-moving water below.

Gringo had been surprised at the unexpected bravery and fighting skills demonstrated by the pale-faced, dark-haired one. The gang's previous victims had been subdued without much of a fight at all, but this particular woman had managed to inflict several savage wounds on two of his boys with her blade before making her escape.

Close enough now to taste the salt air of the sea, the gang spurred their weary horses, urging them onward to beat the incoming storm. Looking behind him, Gringo dropped back and shouted to Sal, the most severely-injured member of the group, who had suffered two vicious slash wounds, courtesy of the dark-haired she-devil.

"How you doing, compadre?"

"Not too good, Gringo," Sal spat between clenched teeth, " I think I'll be needin some stitches pretty soon, I reckon."

In spite of drinking the opiate tea and being fitted with a makeshift tourniquet and sling intended to immobilize his arm and stop the bleeding, the younger man winced each time his horse's hooves hit the ground. The fact was, the deep wound to his tricep was a much more critical injury than his comrades had led him believe. Though his partially severed arm was tied off and bandaged up in blood-soaked strips from an old shirt, thin rivulets of bright arterial blood steadily trickled off his elbow to the roadbed below.

"We'll be there soon, kid, and you can get that thing looked at."

Gringo noticed how pale Sal had become. *Tough luck,* the hardened outlaw leader reflected. Gringo knew enough to expect that the wound would get infected, and if so, the boy would likely lose the limb. *If he don't die from blood loss first.* A faint smile appeared on his pock-marked face. He couldn't help but find the dark humor in Sal's predicament. *Ain't too much work for a one-armed kidnapper these days. But boy, I sure could use his boots.*

He mentally claimed first dibs on the kid's nearly new black cowboy boots. Sal had taken them off a well-dressed traveler he had sniped from ambush a couple of weeks back and Gringo had been coveting them ever since. He decided to hang back and remain close by so when Sal passed out from blood loss and fell to the road, Gringo could pounce on him quick, before the others. That way, he wouldn't have to pull rank to appropriate them: Law of the gang—if a man went down, he was fair game and whoever got to him first had rightful claim to any and all of his worldly possessions.

CHAPTER TEN

THE VOYAGE SOUTH

HALF A MILE offshore, the sailing vessel *Windsong* raced down the coast, a fine salt spray breaking over her bow as she sliced through the white-capped chop, thirty-knot winds freshening her sails, canvas swelled and lines taut. At her helm, Lars guided his prize through the hazardous waters, confidently negotiating underwater rock formations with the help of his able-bodied lookout perched gingerly atop the head of his ship's dragon prow.

The sky at the waterline was a few shades lighter than the waves, while above in the blue expanse, high cirrus wisps flew inland before the stiff westerly breeze. The coastal cliffs were tall and sheer—slate and beige outcroppings peppered with bird droppings and topped with dark-green vegetation. Farther south, an ominous storm front invaded the shore replete with spectacular black-and-white thunderclouds building and billowing high into the stratosphere.

The surrounding waters teemed with life as species fed upon species, symbiotically entwined in the complex ecology of the maritime food chain. At the top were orca—killer whales—the largest of the dolphin species with adult males growing as much as 30 feet in length and weighing in at over 16,000 pounds. Living in loose family groupings of up to 40 individuals called *pods,* they preyed on basically whatever happened to pique their culinary interest at the moment. A tasty meal of fish, shark, squid, seal, walrus, sea lion, bird, turtle, otter, whale, or even the occasional swimming bear or moose was always on the menu. The one entree they didn't seem to favor was man, as there was not one recorded incident of an orca actually attacking a human being, though it was highly unlikely that recipients of such an encounter would live to tell the tale. In the airspace above the waves, flocks of sea birds whirled and swooped, gorging themselves on plentiful ocean fare before returning to nourish their young in nests among the cliffs.

Nine feet above the deck, young Jessi straddled the head of the dragon prow like a pro rodeo rider, balancing effortlessly between its ears while her sharp eyes scoured the water ahead for trouble. At the helm, Lars piloted his wood-and-canvass mistress purely by instinct, his busy consciousness immersed in the events of the past couple of weeks. The young escapee from the trawler remained an enigma full of mysteries.

As far as he could determine, Jessi was fearless and physically willing to do any dangerous thing, yet she remained secretive and self-contained, rarely volunteering information about herself, such as where she came from, or how she came to be aboard the slaver's ship. She answered his interrogatives in one-or two-word sentences, if at all. He managed to deduce that she had been raised by her mother in an all-female community of some kind, however she refused to disclose its name or location, stating simply that he could drop her off anywhere on the coast and she would be able to find her way home. When he dug deeper she clammed up, ignoring further attempts to pry out an answer. When asked about the bad men in the boat and the other women held there, her countenance darkened and she offered a monotone response indicating that her revenge was forthcoming and it would be sweet.

After several tense days and nights anxiously expecting the motor vessel's return, Lars had agreed to transport Jessi to the mainland, to a small settlement down south he knew about, though his heart certainly wasn't in it as he was worried about her safety. Provisioning *Windsong* for the voyage, he loaded another firearm with extra ammo in the event they were set upon by slavers or pirates and found themselves forced to fight their way through.

Seated between the dragon's ears, Jessi enjoyed the feeling of the salt breeze as it caressed her scalp. Running her fingers through her close-cropped hair she smiled. A day earlier she'd spontaneously chopped off her long tresses. Her short hair felt good—very liberating somehow.

With her eyes fixed on the sea ahead, her thoughts drifted to her mother, Alena, and her childhood friend, Alibi, both of whom, she assumed, remained imprisoned on the trawler. She shuddered at the thought of their continued abuse, but held out hope that their trio would soon be reunited once she was able to send word to the Sisterhood of the situation and of the captives' expected whereabouts. Overhearing bits of conversation between members of the crew, Jessi knew exactly where the slavers were headed.

Because the two women bore the *warrior's mark*—the scarlet tattoo between their shoulder blades that every Sisterhood fighter was honored to bear—the slavers were determined to deliver them to the infamous Royal Chen, Keeper of the Gathering, who had recently placed a 1,000-credit bounty on all such tattooed women. Although Jessi expected to someday carry the mark as well, she was still too young. Her full initiation would not occur until she reached the age of sixteen, and she had two more years to wait. Her own fate, had she not escaped, would have been transportation to the auction block at the Gathering to be sold to the highest bidder—in her mind, a fate *far worse* than death.

Choosing the warrior's path required much dedication and sacrifice—relinquishing the commonplace goals of finding a mate and raising a family. Many of the women and girls liberated from bondage by the Sisterhood chose to remain at the former monastery that their founder had christened *Wolfhaven,* to become fighters. Others stayed on as non-warrior members of the community, as it was a safe, supportive sanctuary in which to begin the healing process. Some of the recently kidnapped women who were rescued chose to return to their families, but for many others—after suffering years of cruel captivity—it was much too late for that.

Jessi knew from personal experience that the lawlessness of the post-End War era condemned many powerless souls to an abusive, life-shattering existence. Children were abandoned or sold into slavery by parents unwilling to assume responsibility for raising them in a troubled, uncertain world. Orphans found their way into brothels and work camps. Young women and girls especially, but also many young boys served as sex slaves for the best years of their youth, while in the forced labor camps overseers worked slaves of both sexes as if they were beasts void of basic human rights, and made their already pitiful lives a living hell.

As an early teen, Jessi's mother Alena had ended up in just such a place. She told disturbing stories of beatings and abuse by bad men who derived pleasure from forcing innocent souls physically weaker than themselves to do their bidding. Used as cheap labor at a migrant farming operation owned by a despicable man and his cruel sons, Alena had spent her early teens in bondage, traveling from place-to-place throughout the year.

From Old California to Washington's Yakima Valley, she and her fellow laborers had worked on farms, vineyards, and orchards—planting in the spring, cultivating in the summer, and harvesting in the fall. In winter, the master and his sons relocated their crew south to the outlaw towns, where the young ones and the women were pimped out until spring, when the wagons were loaded and they returned to the road. Alena was only fifteen when Jessi was born and the child would have been sold or traded somewhere along the line had it not been for the Sisterhood.

When Jessi was ten-years-old, her mother had told her the story. One early morning in mid-autumn when she was picking apples with baby Jessi in a wicker basket at her side, an oddly-dressed woman she'd never seen before stepped out from behind a tree. Alena stopped picking fruit to stare at her. The stranger wore all black and was armed with a bow, arrows, and crossed swords in a scabbard on her back. A menacing-looking wolf-dog stood quietly at her side as the woman casually caressed its thick fur with her gloved hand. Looking directly into Alena's eyes, she smiled, and together with her canine companion, melted into the morning mists as silently as ghosts.

Down at camp headquarters the cruel master's guard dogs began to bark. Moments later, an armed cavalry, more than one-hundred-women-strong, materialized out of the fog, encircling the modest hillside orchard. Alena grabbed Jessi and climbed into the uppermost branches of the tree to seek refuge within its foliage and gain a vantage point from which to observe the unfolding event. Moments later, gunfire erupted at the bottom of the hill near the tents and lunch wagon. As the sun burned off the morning haze, she could see her master and his four sons huddled down there, using the wagons for cover. They fired rifles at the riders who raced their horses around the wagons in a dusty circle, whooping and trilling in a celebratory cacophony of jubilation.

Scattered throughout the orchard, some 30 hired hands made their desperate stands. Armed only with the whipping canes of their loathsome profession, they were no match for the vicious wolf-dogs who seemed to appear out of nowhere to violently tear out their throats. The well trained and disciplined female force quickly overwhelmed their enemies, with half of the slavers dead in the first few minutes of the assault. At the wagons, the master and his sons spent all of their precious ammunition in a desperate bid to survive. One-by-one, three of his sons fell mortally wounded, pierced through by black-fletched arrows that easily found their deadly mark. Finally, the master and his only remaining son threw down their weapons and surrendered, pleading for mercy, but none was forthcoming. The longstanding cruelty they had inflicted upon their slaves was to be repaid in full measure.

Alena described how the abusers—both dead and alive—were stripped naked and tied spread-eagle to trees.

The same bamboo whipping canes they had used to discipline their captives were distributed among the newly liberated slaves who took turns savagely beating their oppressors in a frenzied venting of bottled-up rage. Afterwards, their mutilated bodies were hoisted into the fruit trees and a flag emblazoned with the warrior's mark was raised overhead as a warning to all who might think to benefit from the enslavement of others.

Rejoicing in her freedom and having no other family or home, Alena elected to remain at Wolfhaven to become an initiate—eventually receiving the warrior's mark of the Sisterhood Alliance and the accompanying expert training in the martial and equestrian arts. Baby Jessi grew to young womanhood in that close-knit community of females, nurtured and loved by everyone who knew her—and she, in turn, pledged her loyalty to her communal family.

"How we looking, Jessi?" Lars called out, breaking her reverie. They were heading into some shallows directly ahead and he needed her full attention on the task-at-hand.

"All clear, Captain" she shouted over her shoulder, her blue-green eyes scanning the sea for trouble. Since her escape and rescue ten days earlier, she'd been on her guard, even around Lars, though neither his words nor actions had yet given her cause for alarm. It was just that he was a stranger—a *male* stranger at that—and she had never really been around men. By virtue of having been raised in the Sisterhood's protective enclave, Jessi had been spared much of the world's harsh and dangerous realities until three weeks ago when everything in her storybook world suddenly changed.

It had happened on the return journey to Wolfhaven following a buying trip to a horse ranch where the Sisterhood purchased most of their mounts. Late in the afternoon, while crossing a low-slung wooden bridge across a rain-swollen river, one of the sections had suddenly given way, plunging Jessi's wagon, horses and all, into the fast moving current.

While the wagon's wheels were dashed to pieces on the rocks, the horses—still harnessed to the tongue—splintered off from the cargo box which had remained intact. Clinging to the buoyant boat-like box, Jessi was carried many miles downstream before the river spilled out into a small bay where the river met the sea. Bruised and pummeled by the fast-moving current banging her raft against the rocks, she was shaken but not seriously injured, and ended up spending the night alone on the beach at the river's mouth, huddled next to a roaring driftwood bonfire.

Being out alone at night didn't bother Jessi as long as she had fire. As a bright nine-year-old Sisterhood cadet, she'd mastered the fine art of making fire from scratch years ago using diverse materials under a variety of conditions. Her fire-building skills enabled her to maintain her composure throughout the long night, and she was comforted knowing that sooner or later the sun would rise and her sisters would travel downstream in search of her.

In the morning, she awoke to the unnatural sounds of what turned out to be a ship's loud engines and men shouting epitaphs. She was shocked to see a rusty, steel-hulled vessel anchored just offshore, its longboat resting on the rocky beach a quarter mile away, and a dozen well-armed ruffians rapidly closing in on her camp. Their long hair and beards were braided and decorated with beads and feathers, and their baggy clothing was loose and ragged like a torn sail flapping in the wind. Possessing only a staff fashioned from a piece of driftwood to defend herself, Jessi was quickly chased down and overcome.

With her hands and feet bound with ropes, she was roughly bundled into the longboat and hustled back to the motor vessel's captain. After being stripped naked and paraded around on deck to be pawed at by the jeering crew, Jessi was taken belowdecks to the captain's quarters and tethered to his bedpost with a braided leather strap attached to her ankle. There she remained for the better part of a week, barely clothed and subject to the liquored-up captain's every depraved whim.

Two days into her ordeal, Jessi had become aware that there were other women on board, though she never caught a glimpse of them or found out who they were until the morning of her escape.

"There's big money in them tats, Carson I tell ya true!" Carson's one-eyed first mate spoke plainly to the barrel-chested bosun. The two longtime friends had paused in the passageway belowdecks just outside the door to the captain's quarters. As the ship's bosun, Carson was in charge of the ship's crew, and beholden only to Captain Drake. Carson and Char had become friends as young men during their Merchant Marine days back before the End War. Two years earlier, when Carson signed on to be Captain Drake's bosun aboard the *Mt. Shasta,* he appointed Char as his first mate and put him in charge of what he did best—crew discipline.

"More loot for the crew?" Char asked his friend, skeptical about the shares being divided equally, as was promised. Char was becoming increasingly suspicious of Captain Drake's honesty. "A better price means a better split, am I not right Carson?" the first mate winked his one eye and the bosun smiled, shaking his head in a noncommittal gesture. "Supposed to be that way…"

"Well, them two witches's got the mark and I mean to get my share of the overage when we deliver 'em to the Gathering!" Char stated it emphatically. He was unhappy with the way things had been going lately aboard the slave trawler.

"It'll all come out in the wash, Matey, don't you worry." Carson patted his old friend's shoulder and they continued walking toward the companionway. Their discussion referred to the additional bounty offered for "witches" caught bearing the Sisterhood tattoo. Two of the women bore the mark which represented additional value. The Keeper's bounty guaranteed that they would fetch a higher price, and Char just wanted to be sure he received his share of the extra credits.

Tethered to the captain's bed, Jessi had overheard their conversation and was surprised that there were other Sisterhood women aboard the ship. It turned out that Jessi's mother and Alibi had also been captured and were being sequestered in the crew's quarters at the opposite end of the boat. Afterwards, Jessi occasionally overheard the muffled sounds of their mistreatment through the creaking cabin walls. Filled with a black hatred for all abusers, she reaffirmed her pledge of revenge for the hundredth time, promising herself that the sadistic bastards would soon answer for their crimes—she just prayed to be present when they did.

"Storm ahead!" Lars called out, again bringing her back to the present. He observed the clouds rapidly moving inland ahead of them, relieved that the front would pass through by the time they reached their destination, perhaps leaving a saturated coastline and a few waves, but nothing to be very concerned about. Comparing the horizon against his chart, he figured that in another hour or so and they would arrive at their destination below Tipping Rock—really not much of a settlement—just a dock, a warehouse and other storage buildings, and a small horse stable and corral. The last time Lars had visited a few years back, it had been occupied by a trader and his family who specialized in supplying passing ships with pure spring water from a nearby artesian well, and fresh eggs, milk, fruits and vegetables provided by local farmers.

* * *

THE MIST CLEARED along the coast as the spent storm clouds dissipated above the waterlogged band of rescuers who had paused on a barren knoll overlooking the Pacific. Hunter peered through his binoculars at the small settlement down below comprised of a couple of weather-beaten structures dominated by a rusting warehouse and attached outbuildings. A dilapidated wharf spread out along a rocky shoreline that formed a natural harbor protecting the tiny hamlet from the sea.

Angling carefully down the muddy road to the bottom, Hunter, Skye and the others switched back several times until coming to a halt next to the tin-roofed warehouse. In the adjacent stable they found a stagecoach-style wagon parked in the center aisle, still dripping puddles from being out in the recent storm. A dozen spent horses were busy munching scattered hay; wispy columns of steam rose from their wet backs like ghostly gray fingers reaching up into the cobwebbed rafters above.

Recognizing animals that belonged to the kidnapped women among the bunch, the posse dismounted and fanned out to encircle and check the remaining buildings. Following Skye into the dim warehouse, Hunter found a lamp on a hook near the door, lit it and held it aloft, allowing its soft, yellow light to illuminate the morbid scene before them. In the center of the room a bootless young man lay slumped onto his side, unconscious and near death. His skin was as white as bleached bone as a result of blood loss from the several fresh blade wounds to his arms and back; Hunter determined that he was very likely one of the bandits Elise had wounded before making her escape.

Skye knelt and checked the luckless outlaw's vitals. Barely alive, Sal was semi-conscious and fading fast, his pulse weak and irregular, breathing shallow. Placing his palms on the dying man's forehead, Skye closed his own eyes and opened to the channel within. Almost immediately, vivid images began to flash through the shaman's consciousness, motion picture-like experiences from the bandit's recent memory.

He saw the struggle on the bridge with Elise, the overland ride to the coast, the rainstorm sweeping in from the sea, and the arrival and departure of a vessel equipped with a noisy engine belching smoke.

The stream of images began to fade and dissolved to black. Skye opened his eyes, knowing that the youthful bandit's departure from the physical plane was imminent. He leaned in close to within inches of the boy's face who suddenly opened his eyes, a desperate, pleading look in them.

"Help me," he rasped, his grasping hand securing a vice-like grip on Skye's arm.

"Where are they taking the captives?" Skye demanded. "Where is the ship headed?"

The dying bandit opened his mouth to speak but nothing came out. Skye leaned in to whisper, his mouth at the man's ear.

"Tell me where they are taking the women and you will find peace." Skye turned his head, his ear almost touching the man's lips.

Young Sal was desperate to believe the stranger's words. He had been raised by his granny, an Italian Catholic who had filled his early years with the lash and fear of the Lord, Death and the Devil. Summoning all of his remaining strength for one last hope of redemption he whispered, "Ga...ther...ing..." His final breath barely completed the last syllable. With a terminal spasm, Sal's body stiffened—dead eyes rolling back in his head—and he was gone.

"Look what we found in the hayloft."

Skye and Hunter turned to see Skye's two future brothers-in-law, Walker Dan and Paints-His-Face-Red, flanking a wrinkled, white-haired man with a withered arm.

"Says he takes care of the animals and watches over the place whenever the captain and his crew are away on *business*."

Hunter looked him over, noting the fresh contusions welling up on the frightened man's face. One of their lookouts suddenly rushed in with news of a lone sailing vessel approaching from the north. Red and Dan quickly dragged the old caretaker into a darkened corner of the building where he was secured to a post, hogtied and gagged for later interrogation. The posse readied their weapons and spread out, positioning themselves to spring from ambush and take the pirates by surprise in a crossfire. Hidden behind crates, beneath stairways, and within the dock infrastructure itself, the nine watched the mystery ship approach, mentally preparing themselves for battle.

*　　*　　*

STILL HALF A mile offshore, Lars searched the soggy coastline with a pair of finely engineered marine binoculars, methodically sweeping the surrounding terrain and worn-out docks and buildings for any sign of life or movement. He had expected to see some people about and at least a boat or two, but the place appeared to be strangely deserted—unlike the last time he'd docked here. Now it looked abandoned, like it had fallen into disuse. He scrutinized every inch of the landfall, but in spite of his careful efforts, entirely missed seeing the lookouts posted throughout the small hamlet, hidden among the docks and rundown buildings of the former cannery. The sea was running high with a heavy incoming tide, and testy onshore winds blew fresh across *Windsong's* starboard bow, giving Lars very little latitude when adjusting his course to avoid shallows or obstacles directly in his path.

He called out to Jessi to haul in some jib to reduce their speed as *Windsong* entered smoothly into the little bay like a graceful swan, gliding across the gray, choppy waters. Maneuvering his ship alongside the dock, he barely avoided grazing a fully-submerged shrimp boat. His mind was in turmoil, preoccupied with thoughts of Jessi. In spite of her assertion that she was capable of taking care of herself, he didn't want to simply drop her off alone and leave her to her fate.

Over the past couple of weeks he had grown rather fond of the young woman with the big chip on her shoulder in an older-brotherly kind of way, and didn't want to see her run into any more trouble before she could reconnect with her people—whoever they might be. He realized that she was tough, high-spirited and courageous, but as recent events had shown, the world After the Fall could still be a very dangerous and heartless place with evil men lying in wait like ravenous wolves to devour the weak and unsuspecting.

Of course he'd tried to reason with her, but in her usual unapproachable and uncompromising fashion, Jessi had remained stubbornly silent, refusing to engage in any dialogue on the matter. Lars had decided that upon landing he would make one final effort to dissuade her from her course, hoping that she would reconsider remaining with him at least until they could arrive at a properly established settlement on down the coast where her chances of survival would be better.

* * *

CRADLING HIS CROSSBOW in his arms, Hunter waited as the single-masted craft drew closer. It was of curious design, unlike any he had seen before. While the hull and rigging appeared to be of standard sailing form, the bow reminded him of a Viking ship, adorned with the curved neck and head of a dragon. On the foredeck, a young deckhand moved about, readying the lines for arrival, while at the helm, a tanned and athletic mariner with red-blond hair and beard and wearing sailcloth dungarees, eased the vessel smoothly into position beside the dock. While still a few yards out, the deckhand dropped a couple of rubber fenders into place along the side and jumped across to the dock as the craft gently made contact, securing the bow line to a brass cleat.

Moving toward the stern, Lars stepped down onto the dock with a coiled rope in his hand. Seeing a blur of motion in his peripheral vision, he reached for his sidearm too late. The attackers were upon him in a flash and he went down hard with no chance to make a stand. His thoughts flew to Jessi as he was wrestled onto his stomach and pinned. Suddenly a shotgun blast ripped the decking, sending splintered bits of wood flying everywhere and bringing the short-lived melee to an abrupt halt.

The scrappy fourteen-year-old stood on *Windsong's* foredeck, her feet spread shoulder wide and a stainless steel 12-gauge in her hands.

"Take your hands off him or die!" she barked, chambering another round.

Immediately releasing Lars, the posse spread out and trained their weapons on her, but no one was willing to cut the young teen down. Jumping to his feet, Lars drew his .45 and backed up toward his ship, planning a hasty retreat.

Rapidly analyzing the fluid situation, Hunter was shocked that the young deckhand had turned out to be female. Based on her swift and unexpected defense of the ship's captain, Hunter was now uncertain of the present circumstances. During the initial slow-motion moments of the standoff, his thought process flipped through a series of presumptions and possibilities. He first labelled Lars a pirate in the business of trafficking captives and surmised that the girl had been forced to work on the ship as well as perform other less honorable duties as evidenced by her healing bruises and the obvious bite marks and hickeys fading on her neck. However, the ferocity with which she had come to her captor's defense made no sense, thereby introducing the element of uncertainty in the minds of Hunter and the balance of her would-be rescuers.

As no one seemed willing to take the first shot, Skye interpreted this as a sign that the strangers were of honorable intent and not the conscienceless enemies he'd initially assumed them to be. Addressing Lars with an occasional sidelong glance toward Jessi he explained, "We are on the trail of a gang of kidnappers who abducted three of our women." He told them about the dying kidnapper, the wagon and horses, the caretaker and other physical evidence proving that the bandit crew and trawler had recently been through here.

Upon hearing Skye's story, Lars immediately lowered his weapon and offered an explanation of his own presence in this place. "I know the ship you speak of. The slaver's boat pulled into my harbor up north a couple of weeks back and Jessi here managed to jump ship." He briefly described his run-in with the slave vessel, Jessi's escape, and the female captives still trapped aboard their slave boat.

Sensing the man's integrity, Skye lowered his weapon and the others followed suit. Making a quick calculation in his head, Skye offered, "They are headed to the Gathering in the south, to sell our women at the slave auction." He was well aware of the fact that the Gathering was a month's ride down the Coast Road, having travelled there a couple of times on village trading expeditions. With the fullness of the moon a mere eight days away, there was no possibility of arriving in time for the Moontide Festival on horseback. Eyeing *Windsong*, he looked to Lars with a hopeful expression on his face, "Is it possible for you to take us there?"

* * *

The Gathering... Lars knew something of that place—everyone in the northwest did. He'd been there several times a few years back while he was a teenager. His father, Sven, had sailed down there on occasion to trade, and Lars and his older brothers, Zeke and Thor, would go along to help, while the younger twins remained at home with their mother, being too small to be of any use and too much trouble aboard the boat. There were too many responsibilities and no one had time to look after toddlers.

Lars knew the route down the coast well, but hadn't planned on making that trip anytime soon, the memories of that place still being too painful to disturb. Looking at Skye and his band of desperate men and knowing both the extent of their anguish and the plight of their loved ones, Lars felt himself give in, and in spite of his better judgment, agreed to take them. Later that evening, as the reality of his decision hit home, Lars wondered if it wasn't all a big mistake, but then perhaps it *was* time to revisit his past—he simply wasn't sure that he was emotionally prepared, or even willing for that matter, to come face-to-face with those demons just yet.

CHAPTER ELEVEN

MANY QUESTIONS

WHY DID THIS terrible thing have to happen? Elise mulled over the disastrous events of the past twenty-four hours, her heart and soul vexed beyond comprehension. The ambush at the bridge and the kidnapping of Anna and the twins had immediately sent her into a tailspin of self-doubt and regret. Her torment was further exacerbated when she was excluded from riding to Anna's rescue with the others. Hunter absolutely forbade her participation, something that had not once occurred in their five harmonious years together. *Never had he imposed his will on her in this way...*

From the very beginning, their relationship had been based on mutual respect and admiration, and as such, Elise considered it on a higher plane than most others she'd witnessed in this life. Both she and Hunter were equal contributors to their common livelihood and mutual happiness, but today the man she so admired and loved had stepped over the line "for the baby's sake," of course. *Damn all men and their over-protective tendencies—and damn the manner in which genetics and human development over eons of creative selection and adaptation had determined the male and female sexual and reproductive roles!*

129

Elise had no problem accepting the fact that women were entrusted with the childbearing responsibilities for the species and because of that, they were generally looked after and protected by the men in their lives and the community at large. In safeguarding pregnant women, men acted simply to protect their loved ones and—on a more genetic level—took whatever reasonable precautions were necessary to ensure the continuity of the human race. Knowing this did nothing to alleviate her deep sense of frustration at being left out of the rescue.

Down through the annals of human history, countless generations of women had worked and fought alongside their men, bearing and looking after their children as they went. Commonsense precautions during pregnancy were prudent to ensure the safety of mother and child—but to regard pregnancy as if it were an illness or disability was absurd and Elise wasn't the least bit inclined to agree with it.

* * *

THE POSSE ESCORTED Jessi back to the village and arrived two days later. Although the young girl had wanted to go off on her own, Skye ordered her to be taken back to his people so she could be looked after until suitable arrangements could be made for her repatriation. Upon their arrival, the People gathered to hear news of Anna and the Ravencloud twins. They were encouraged to hear about Skye and the others meeting Lars, and about their proposed voyage south aboard *Windsong*, the strange-looking Viking ship from the north. Everyone was curious to meet this girl who was in some way involved in the unfolding drama.

The way they gawked at her and asked questions only made Jessi withdraw further into her shell. Uncomfortable beneath their withering scrutiny and attention, she thought only about rejoining her people down the coast. After a lengthy discussion among the tribal elders, they decided that because of her youth, it was out of the question to allow Jessi to travel home alone. Instead, they offered to escort her, or at least send word to her people of her whereabouts so they could come collect her, but she remained vague, refusing to provide any specifics as to who her people were, or where they might be contacted. Unable to arrive at a suitable resolution of the matter by nightfall, the council decided to sleep on it and re-approach the problem on the morrow with a fresh mind and perspective.

* * *

JUST AFTER MIDNIGHT, with a bright, three-quarter moon gracing the star-flecked sky, young Jessi moved stealthily through the sleeping settlement keeping to the shadows of buildings and fences while making for the tall perimeter wall on the forest side of the enclosure. The night was cool with temperatures in the high fifties and a ten knot breeze blowing in from the ocean driving wispy tendrils of spent rainclouds before it. She was comfortable in a snug wool sweater, cap and stockings, and deerskin trousers and moccasins—all gifts from Lars, her benevolent rescuer. Her humble belongings were stuffed into a sealskin knapsack carried on her back, its one wide strap passing over her shoulder and diagonally across her chest.

As grateful as she was for the gracious hospitality offered by Skye's People, Jessi was desperate to get word to
the Sisterhood as soon as possible, acutely aware that time
was running out. If she ever hoped to see her mother or Alibi
again, she had to get a message to Star before it was too late.
Even with the trawler's head start, there was still a chance
the Sisterhood could intercept the smoke-belching slave boat
before it reached the Gathering.

Kneeling in the shadow of a low-roofed shed, Jessi listened intently, well aware that at this late hour, alert village
guards would be on the lookout for anything unusual. Hearing a snuffling sound nearby, she froze, her hand moving to
the double-edged skinning knife at her side—the very same
blade she had accidentally cut herself with when she first
met Lars. It had been another generous, practical offering
from her red-haired savior.

Barely daring to breathe, her night eyes picked out a
gliding, ephemeral shape materializing out of the darkness
ahead and coming her way. The village dog drew near, then
stopped, suspiciously sniffing the air and emitting a low,
throaty growl. All of a sudden, it brightened up, apparently
recognizing the scent from the sleeping furs Jessi had borrowed. A wag broke out and a smile seemed to appear on the
dog's face as the girl reached into her pocket to withdraw
a bit of venison she'd saved from dinner, stashed away in
preparation for her escape. Rubbing the friendly pup's ears,
Jessi moved off through the shadows toward the palisade.

Reaching the imposing barrier, she checked for lookouts
on the walkways above, and seeing none, made for the closest stairway. Creeping to the landing, she crouched on the
bamboo floor, surveying her surroundings in the moonlight.

It was late, and at this hour most people were fast asleep in their beds, but she was certain that guards were posted somewhere nearby, watching over the settlement from the shadows. She was counting on the fact that their attention would be directed *outside* the compound, beyond the perimeter wall, and not focused within its borders.

Slowly standing, she peered over the top of the logs into the semi darkness beyond. Seeing nothing amiss, she crouched down to withdraw a short section of braided leather lariat from her knapsack—a little something she'd pilfered when no one was watching. Without warning, a gloved hand clamped tightly over her mouth and a strong arm grabbed her around the waist, pinning her own arms tightly to her body and her body up against the logs, effectively rendering her helpless to draw her blade or fight back.

As Jessi struggled violently, twisting back and forth in a vain attempt at escape, she heard a woman's calm voice whisper softly in her ear, "Do not fear." She instantly became still and turned her head to see a shadowed face just inches from her own. Jessi's eyes widened as she recognized her: dark hair, pale white skin, piercing green eyes—she was not of this place and recalled that the woman's younger sister was among those kidnapped from the village.

Earlier, around the evening campfire, Jessi had listened to Elise's story with interest, impressed to hear how she fought off her attackers and raced back to the village to raise the alarm. Hers was but one action in a long line of independent decisions resulting in Hunter, Skye, and the others riding to the captives' rescue—and the close call at the dock where Lars had nearly been killed by mistake.

"Listen to me, Jessi. I understand that you don't want to be here, that you want to go home."

She leaned in close, face-to-face, a kind voice speaking in a low whisper. "I, too, wish to get away—to help save my sister, Anna, and her husband's twin sisters from the kidnappers—but I don't know the way."

She loosened her grip on the girl, maintaining light physical contact with her hands. Peering into her eyes she implored, "If you promise to guide me to this place they call the Gathering, I will outfit you with a horse and provisions which are yours to keep upon our safe arrival there."

Jessi weighed Elise's words and their far-reaching implications, and finally said, "If I agree to show you the way we must go at once or it will be too late."

A look of relief broke over Elise's face and she released the girl. "Okay," she whispered, "we leave at daybreak."

* * *

THE TWO RIDERS sped south along the rugged Coast Road, hoofbeats diffused by the thick morning fog rolling in from the sea. On both sides of the narrow passage, trees and boulders materialized out of the mist like ghostly apparitions, only to quickly vanish back into the swirl as if they never were. The air was cool and damp with tiny droplets clinging to horse and rider, and dripping steadily from damp leather tack. Above in the leaden sky, rain-filled clouds obscured the sun, offering scant light or warmth to comfort the troubled pair in their desperate race against time.

Winding steadily through gently rolling hills along the extreme western edge of the continent, young Jessi led the way within muffled earshot of heavy surf crashing onto the driftwood-littered beach far below. Bundled against the chill in a thick woolen sweater and trousers complemented by a fine pair of riding boots and travel cloak, courtesy of her newfound benefactor and companion, Jessi focused on her primary objective of reaching the nearest messaging station as soon as possible.

There she could send word, alerting Star and the Sisterhood of the present plight of her mother and Alibi—kidnapped by bounty hunters and en route via motor-trawler to the Keeper of the Gathering. She knew of a small fishing village with possible messaging capabilities a few miles south and despite the low visibility factor, charged forward, determined to pare down the distance as quickly as possible without taking undue risks.

Following a safe distance behind Jessi's flashy Paint gelding, Elise relaxed into her Mustang's loping gait, gliding through the fog poised comfortably atop the gorgeous buckskin mare whose legs seemed an extension of her own body. A firm but gentle hand defined the natural horsemanship technique which Elise instinctively employed. Its mastery was born of endless hours in the saddle and honed over a period of more than two decades, until horse and rider were no longer servant and master, but co-creators and partners in the ebb and flow of the ride—willing participants within a mutually rewarding relationship in which each understood what was expected of the other and was eager and willing to provide such.

Snug inside her warm travel garments, Elise was fraught with inner turmoil, a troubled heart spoiling her normally positive outlook. Anna, Lily and River had been snatched four days earlier and whisked to the coast where they had been passed off to flesh traders in a motor-driven boat. According to Skye's people, they were now on their way south to be sold at the Moontide slave auction just six days hence. Hunter and Skye were currently sailing down the coast in pursuit aboard *Windsong* with Lars, but were at least one full day behind the slave boat, which, unlike the sailing vessel, was unhampered by the tides, or the direction and strength of the wind.

Elise had wrestled with her decision to leave Skye's village against Hunter's wishes, believing in her heart that she had done the right thing. At three-months pregnant, she was aware of her need to be careful and not take unnecessary risks for the baby's sake, especially still so close to her first trimester, but sitting around the village worrying about Anna only made matters worse. Besides, she proved that she could take care of herself, pregnant or not, by fighting off the kidnappers at the bridge and escaping into the rushing waters, and was no worse for wear because of it.

She was also an accomplished equestrian and an experienced wielder of blade, spear thrower, and crossbow—the latter of which Hunter had introduced her to five years earlier. In Elise's mind, she had no choice; she was compelled to take action to help save her family, but hadn't a clue as to where to begin looking for Anna until Jessi's arrival had solved her dilemma.

Observing the competent manner in which Jessi handled her horse, Elise was convinced that there was more to the mysterious young Jessi than met the eye. Striking out together was a natural fit, though she was certain that if it occurred to Jessi that she'd be better off alone, the girl would be gone in a flash. Luckily, at the moment they needed one another and they both knew it. The daunting challenge that would ultimately determine the quality of both of their lives from this point forward, was how to arrive at the Gathering in six day's time. Charging ahead through the mist, one thing was certain in both rider's minds—if there ever was such a thing as a miracle, they could truly use one now.

* * *

SLAVERY—FROM THE earliest origins of the human saga its festering wound had been an insidious, crippling scourge upon Humankind. The physical ownership and control of one human being by another was the most reprehensible of all social injustices still plaguing the human race. The fact that a rumored slave auction was held every Moontide Festival at the Gathering disgusted and angered Elise to her very core.

Prior to the End War, slavery had been officially abolished across the globe, yet in every hemisphere it had survived and even flourished in one form or another. Its misery could be discovered in the seedy back streets and alleyways of red light districts, and hidden deep within misogynistic religions and repressive, male-dominated cultures throughout the world.

The double standard it represented gnawed at Elise's sense of justice and equality. Her father, Colonel Adam Planchet, had been an old-school constitutionalist, raising his children to believe that every individual, no matter how humble or seemingly disenfranchised, was endowed with certain inalienable rights—minimally life, liberty, and the pursuit of happiness. Yet, many were denied those rights by individuals of wealth and power who, through brute force or cunning, dominated the ruined lives of others for their own pleasure and personal gain.

Throughout history, human nature seemed to dictate that those with wherewithal and privilege were compelled to rule over their less fortunate fellows. The highborn lived in luxury while the poor scratched out a desperate existence far from the comforts or security enjoyed by the rich. It had always been so. The present was no different, except that today there was no social or cultural safety net, nor any semblance of an official mechanism in place to protect the weak and innocent from those who were less altruistically inclined. Within the social and political realities twenty years After The Fall, the oppressed could either submit to their slave masters or band together to throw off the yoke of their bondage.

CHAPTER TWELVE

THE SISTERHOOD

IN A POORLY-lit back room on the second floor of a rundown farmhouse-turned-brothel, an obese man covered in sweat was busy showing a new arrival the ropes. He loved this part of his job the most—honing a new girl's skills to ensure that his clients wouldn't be disappointed when they dropped by for some carnal entertainment. Over the years, he'd known dozens like her: submissive waifs forced to whore away their best years to bring him the finer things in life.

She was a fairly typical example: a half-starved teen with not much fight left in her who had wisely chosen the path of least resistance quickly, submitting to her new master before Dejan was forced to raise a hand to her. He preferred not to beat a girl into submission, but then, the stubborn ones provided their own unique blend of sadistic gratification as he steadily increased their discomfort until they ultimately surrendered their wills. They all did, eventually. As he watched this new one drift in and out of consciousness, he realized that she was overly sedated by the "medicine" he had administered earlier to ensure her smooth break-in period.

She had arrived on his doorstep two days ago, delivered by a flesh trader who claimed to have found her somewhere down the coast hiding in a ruined barn, starving and alone. Dejan could care less who she was or where she came from; to him she was simply fresh meat—no more, no less—and his regular customers were always ready to sample something new.

The girl moaned, eyes fluttering, and he slapped her sharply across the face in an attempt to rouse her, but alas, it was no use. The dose of opiate he'd given was obviously too strong; he should have considered her low body weight—and now she'd probably have no memory of the things he'd taught her today. *Dammit.* Not pleased, he shoved the semiconscious girl aside and stood up. *Next time I'll forgo the medicine, then she'll pay attention to my lessons...*

Pulling on his trousers, Dejan eyed his reflection in the full-length mirror, smugly fancying himself quite the stud, though the dozen or so girls sequestered in his house of sorrows would find that characterization well beyond humorous. They constantly joked behind his back about his shriveled privates, corpulent belly, and pale, flaccid skin covered with dense, gorilla-like hair. Their current favorite nickname for him—*dickless fat man*—would have gotten them all strangled or worse if he ever found out.

Pushing his bulk down the hallway, he called out for Megan, the house matron, who came running to do his bidding.

"Take the new girl and clean her up," he ordered, "Give her something to revive her—I want her presentable and in service later tonight."

"Yes, Master, right away" Megan replied, her eyes downcast and head bowed in a demonstration of respect not present in her heart. "Kyla, Fran, come quick!" She called for two level-headed girls in their late teens to come help gather up the new girl. "Wonder what damage he's done this time, the pig!" she hissed to them under her breath, appalled at the condition of the half-starved thing. The girl needed someone to nurture her back to health—not pump her full of dope and dick. *Men are disgusting beasts,* Megan declared to herself, *carnal creatures that enjoyed treating women like dung.*

Like her younger counterparts, Megan was in bondage here as well, but as she was nearly thirty—beyond the age desired by most of the customers—her life in the last couple of years, at least, had become nearly bearable. But the compassion she harbored for her younger charges stemmed from her years spent in similar torment. She was intimately acquainted with the humiliating nightmare of their lives. To be a slave was a tragic enough horror, but to spend the best years of one's youth being used and debased without consent by anyone having enough credits to pay the Master's price was a psychological and spiritual death beyond comprehension. No wonder so many of them had attempted suicide. Megan, herself, had tried it several times when barely a teen, when she was first pimped out by her dead mother's boyfriend—but that was lifetimes ago now.

Descending the wide staircase to the ground floor, Dejan plodded down the broad central hall, exiting the rear of the building through the unlocked screen door. Standing on the edge of the steps in the balmy night air, Dejan let out a sigh of relief as his pungent yellow urine stream splattered the carefully tended flower beds ringing the veranda. His cursory glance at the sky failed to appreciate the brilliant, multi-colored stars strewn randomly across the velvet heavens—like precious jewels unwittingly spilled from a thief's tattered treasure bag. Heading back inside the house, Dejan intended to rustle up something to eat and check on Dar, the barrel-chested bouncer employed to act as muscle in the event of trouble in the brothel.

Passing by Dar's duty station on the way to the kitchen, Dejan noticed him missing. *The shiftless bastard is probably off dozing somewhere. Damn, he'd better not be upstairs sampling my wares!* Dar had specifically been warned to keep his hands—and any other parts of his anatomy—off the merchandise. If Dejan caught Dar messing with his girls again, by God, there'd be hell to pay. Furtively mounting the stairs as quietly as possible considering his bulk, he smiled, hoping to catch the lazy turd doing something stupid so that he could humiliate him in front of the girls. Dejan padded down the hallway, peeking into each room as he went, oblivious of the impending storm about to descend upon his sordid little corner of the universe.

* * *

LYING IN QUIET concealment in the darkness beneath the trees a few feet beyond the veranda, a dozen black-clothed warriors watched as the repulsive figure re-entered the house, the screen door slamming loudly behind him. Around front, a second team of assassins waited in the shadows while archers took up positions along the tree-lined approach road and half-a-dozen menacing canines crouched quietly beside their handlers in hushed anticipation of the ambush soon to shatter the tranquility of the pleasant summer's eve. The Sisterhood fighters had moved quietly into position an hour earlier, bound by a solemn oath to liberate their enslaved sisters and mete out justice to their abusers. Surrounding the farmhouse, they awaited the imminent arrival of a prominent regional overlord and his entourage, who—according to the fighters' pervasive spy network— were planning an early-evening visit to this so-called House of Pleasure.

House of Pain, House of Suffering, and House of Misery, Star bitterly reflected—but that all-too-familiar bedtime story was about to come to an end. The sinewy, twenty-seven-year-old Sisterhood founder went over the battle plan one final time with two of her most experienced assault leaders. Ticking off the sequential elements of the attack one-by-one to make certain that all was ready, they confirmed that each fighter was at her battle station and knew exactly what to do when the order was given to begin the assault.

A successful sortie tonight would be an important step forward in the campaign to liberate all women and children held in bondage throughout the region. It was a tall order to be sure—some said an impossible pipe dream—but Star believed in her life's mission, and hundreds of like-minded others had joined her cause, supporting the blossoming clandestine organization she had simply named *The Sisterhood.* Reflecting on the principal events and major developments of the past decade, she was amazed and pleased at how far their movement had come in the ten years since its very humble beginnings.

* * *

AS FAR BACK as her years had memory, Star had known the brutality of being *forced.* Forced to fear and forced to hide. Forced to flee with her parents into the high country when the slavers first came to their village, abducting as many women and children as they could get their hands on. Men who stood up to them had suffered excruciating deaths, begging, in the end, for the sweet release of oblivion. Women who refused them were made examples too horrifying to describe.

Star grew up on the run, hidden away in remote places, spending her early years learning to live off the land—knowing when to sneak down to the towns and settlements along the coast to scavenge for scraps and leftovers from fields and gardens. From a young age, her Ottawa-Scots father had instructed her in the survival arts of shelter building and weapon making, tracking game, hunting and fishing, and how to trap animals for food and pelts during the long, cold winter months. She learned to gather wild foods, grow and harvest plants and herbs, and ride and care for horses—mostly from her mother who had been adopted from Thailand as a baby back before the End War changed everything. The family trio tanned hides and made buckskin clothing, scavenging various useful items—such as steel and iron tools and reusable implements—from decomposing ghost towns long-since abandoned along the river, or crumbling into ruin beside the fearsome Coast Road.

Shortly after she turned fifteen, Star's parents were killed in an unprovoked bear attack. Her father died trying to save her mother, though neither managed to survive the savage mauling by a berserk male grizzly that suddenly appeared out of nowhere just after spring thaw. In the aftermath of the unimaginable tragedy, the badly hemorrhaging predator, suffering severe wounds of its own inflicted by the valiant human fighting for the love of his life, dragged itself into a nearby thicket to die.

In a numbed state of disbelief, her mind and emotions clouded by shock and operating on autopilot, Star laid the lifeless bodies of her parents, side-by-side, on a stacked-cedar funeral pyre as had always been their wish. In the south-facing meadow next to the cabin, as their earthly remains surrendered to the orange flames, the smoke of their offering rose high into the night sky, dissipating on the westerly wind, and for the first time in her sheltered life, Star found herself alone.

Huddled in her parents' big bed with Sadie—the young wolf-dog mix that her father had found abandoned beside a frozen stream when it was just a pup—vivid memories of her life, from earliest childhood to the present, flashed through her mind, robbing her of much needed sleep. Throughout the restive night, as she drifted in and out of present time, the pain of her tragedy wove itself throughout the random memories of her past, amplifying Star's fears of an uncertain future that threatened to overwhelm her broken heart.

As the pink eastern sky announced the dawn, Star met the new day with what determination and courage she could muster. Approaching the fallen beast, she proceeded to skin out the huge bear's carcass with her father's sharpest knife— the same blade that he had plunged into the animal's chest again and again before his own life was finally quenched in the bear's crushing, teeth-lined jaws. She went about her task with singleness of purpose, as if engaged in some subconscious attempt to redeem the irreplaceable loss the beast had caused her, the process itself being therapeutic as well as practical in nature. Beyond the symbolic meaning found in defacing her parents' killer by removing its blood-stained pelt, the future fashioning of the tanned hide into useful items such as clothing or sleeping furs exemplified the teachings of her parents in honoring the natural world in which they lived.

Throughout her upbringing, Star's parents had empha-sized the importance of conscious living in a reverent, in-tentional manner so as not to waste or neglect nature's gifts when offered. As if it were a final gift from her father, she worked the bear's pelt both in his honor and in some high-er sense, far beyond the reach of her present awareness, in appreciation of the bear as well, for its sacrifice, however unwillingly, on her behalf. While the rawness of her im-mediate grief and loss would not allow her to view these symbiotic elements until after having processed the experi-ence over time, she would eventually come to realize that everything—even such a devastating tragedy—happened for a reason, and if embraced as an opportunity for growth, could be employed as a catalyst to transform one's life for the better.

When she finished hours later, Star split the skin down the backbone and dragged the bramble-covered halves to the creek to begin rinsing them, using a rounded canoe paddle to remove stringy strips of flesh. She scrubbed the hair side using her mother's homemade peppermint soap, and rinsed the dirt and blood out of the thick fur over and over until it was clear of foreign matter and debris. Hauling the two halves of the pelt to the funeral pyre's ash pile, she erected racks of strong, flexible bamboo and tightly stretched the wet hides across them. Beginning with her mother's scraping blade, Star methodically removed all remaining bits of flesh and fat from the skin. With a sharp, specially designed cutting tool, she thinned the high spots, being careful not to slice through the soft, uncured pelt.

Once the halves were scraped and thinned, she cracked open the bear's skull with a rock and removed its brain, placing the slimy organ into a large pot, to which she added urine to concoct the tanning solution required in curing the hide. After thoroughly mixing the brains and urine with her wooden paddle, Star applied several coats of the gooey paste to the skin side, working the mushy solution deep into the fibers with her paddle and kneading it with her hands like bread dough. After allowing the halves to dry overnight, she pounded them repeatedly with her paddle, re-kneading the skins with her hands before repositioning her support poles to form a semi-circle. Re-draping the skins over the newly formed frames, she started a slow-burning, green-wood fire to smoke-cure the pelts, making sure that the damp wood would smolder, emitting smoke constantly throughout the entire procedure.

With the all-day tanning process underway, Star turned her attention to Sadie, who was feeling a bit nervous and neglected. Greatly comforted by her canine friend's companionship, Star sliced thin strips from the grizzly's now-skinless carcass and sat cross-legged in worn buckskins, cradling the wolfish young female in her lap. Enjoying the warmth and closeness of her human pack-mate, Sadie greedily gobbled down the tasty bits of bear flesh, content for the time being to be the center of Star's attentions. Her smoke-blackened cheeks streaked with dried tears from the night before, Star gently stroked Sadie's soft, thick fur and took stock of her situation, weighing her options with a heavy heart.

A careful review of her predicament made the difficult decision to abandon the familiarity of this high country painfully obvious. Glancing about the clearing where she'd spent the last several years of her life under the watchful eyes of loving parents, Star made peace with her fate and began mentally preparing to embark upon her solitary sojourn, seeking something as yet undefined, driven by a longing she could not put into words. *It was certainly not community among the flatlanders that she craved*—Star knew better than that—but there was nothing left for her here in the remote beauty of these mountains, nothing but loneliness without any real prospect of future human companionship.

Compelled by circumstance to move on, and inspired by a longing to discover a new and different land to call home, the determined young woman formulated her plan, acutely aware of the dangers awaiting her in the wide, wicked world below. Though it was a difficult choice, it was a chance she would have to take, knowing that remaining here she would be slowly driven mad by her solitary existence. Beyond these fields and forests she would be at risk at all times and if she expected to survive long as a woman alone within the unforgiving social parameters of the post End War landscape, she would have to remain vigilant. Furthermore, she must maintain total secrecy and stealth, certain of her fate should she be discovered by ill-intentioned strangers who would not hesitate to capture and use her for whatever dark purposes their black hearts might contrive.

Father, who had often traveled beyond these borders to procure items that his family was unable to produce themselves, had warned her always of the dangers down in the towns, sheltering Star and her mother from direct contact with the outside world. As she came of age though, Star had become an expert huntress and equestrian. She sometimes accompanied her father dressed as a boy, though she always remained well-hidden from sight in a nearby wood or field while he ventured alone into a village or market to trade for necessities. Through the books he collected and stories he told, Star learned to read and write and became familiar with science and math and the warlike history of the human race. Living so close to the land in a semi-nomadic lifestyle, had instilled in her a host of practical survival skills, developing a deep, intimate relationship between her and the natural world in which she was immersed.

Following the minimalist example of her parents, Star packed with care, selecting only the most essential items for her journey. Loading the stalwart family mule and her father's big, gentle gelding with an assortment of practical gear, she saddled *Windcatcher,* her pretty six-year-old Paint mare with bold white and copper markings and flashy white mane and tail. With Sadie at her side, Star led her entourage south through the backcountry, carefully avoiding settlements and roads.

After several weeks in the wilds Star stumbled upon an ancient, vine-covered monastery constructed almost two centuries earlier of native stone and timbers, well hidden in a lush valley ringed by steep, redwood-forested hills. The hermitage was quite rundown and overgrown, having been long-since abandoned by an obscure order of vintner monks, decades before the End War wiped all memory of this place from the maps and consciousness of the Old World.

Rummaging through the sprawling estate's vast, dusty chambers, Star came to a doorway leading up into a tower attached to the side of one of the buildings. Poking around in its loft, she discovered an iron-bound trunk hidden behind a sliding wooden panel. Jimmying its rusting latch and lifting the lid, she was surprised that it contained a set of seven books entitled, *The Most Important Lessons in Life* by Zen Master Muri Kyoto.

In the front of the first volume was a line drawing of a female Japanese martial arts master firing a short bow at a stationary target while poised astride a galloping horse. The book went on to describe how to ride and shoot with precision, even detailing the required horse-training procedures. Each volume provided in-depth explanations of additional necessary skills one must master in order to become a true ninja warrior.

Folded up between the pages at the end of volume seven was a hand-drawn map with an X marking the location of an unspecified treasure. Star followed the map with its pictographic directions to a trap door in the floor of one of the winery buildings, that had been hidden beneath a large wooden hutch. Jostling the heavy piece of furniture aside, she pulled open the hatch, revealing a dusty stairway leading down into a cool, dark basement. Fetching her lantern, she mustered her courage and slowly descended the steps, peering apprehensively into the eerie shadows with her father's deadly skinning knife clutched tightly in her hand.

Following the map's directions, she proceeded down a narrow corridor to a small, shelf-lined room. Stepping inside, she found what she was looking for: a small access panel leading into a vast storage room filled with hundreds of large barrels. Guided by her map, she made her way between the third and fourth rows of oak kegs, counting to fifteen and stopped. Prying open the wax-sealed lid she held up her lamp and looked inside.

There, wrapped in dark green cloth were three bulky bundles secured with leather laces. She retrieved them, one-by-one, and placed them atop an adjacent barrel. With her hands trembling with excitement, Star unwrapped the first bundle and was amazed. Inside was a beautifully crafted composite bow, it's waxed and braided bowstring wound carefully around the polished wooden staff.

A cleverly made leather quiver filled with a dozen exquisitely constructed practice arrows lay nestled beside the bow. Inside a false bottom in the quiver's base, she found two dozen, razor-sharp tips ingeniously designed to screw into a threaded fitting on the front end of the shafts. She could change out the heads on the arrow shafts from practice to hunting tips simply by unthreading the one and replacing it with the other.

Re-wrapping the weapons, she opened the second bundle and found inside a beautiful curved dagger in a bound-metal sheath, attached to a thick leather belt. Its hilt was crafted from some type of bone or antler, and engraved with scrimshaw-like drawings of runes and magic symbols. Alongside the dagger was a similarly engraved metal scabbard housing two wickedly curved, razor-sharp swords. They were longer than the dagger but shorter than a full-sized sword, and the scabbard was made to be worn on the back like a backpack with the crossed hilts protruding up behind one's head.

Replacing the gleaming blades, Star opened the third bundle and was surprised to find several pieces of black clothing made from some type of stretchy material she had never before seen. There were snug-fitting legging-type pants, two pairs of black socks, a sleeveless tunic, a long sleeved shirt, and a hood with eyeholes cut out of it. At the bottom of the barrel she found footwear—a pair of slippers with a grippy rubber sole and black leather lace-up boots with the word *Vibram* in raised yellow letters on the bottoms.

Stripping off her travel-stained garments, Star tried on the strange outfit and found she could get into everything easily enough, but she wasn't used to the stretchy snugness of the fit. Collecting the weapons, she gathered her things, making her way back into the corridor and up the stairs to ground level. In the main hall of the manor house she stood before a large, cracked mirror, heavy with dust and wiped off the glass surface with her sleeve.

Staring at her reflection, she was shocked. She looked quite amazing—like a warrior from a storybook her father had read to her as a child. Strapping on the dagger at her waist and pulling on the twin scabbards with the curved swords, she found it hard to believe that the intimidating figure in the mirror could be herself. She attached the quiver to her dagger belt, picked up her bow, and looked again— this time with the black hood pulled down low. Suddenly overcome with inspiration, Star raised her face to the heavens and howled like a she-wolf! Sadie appeared and barked menacingly until Star pulled off the hood and kneeled down to reassure her dog friend that she was not a scary stranger.

Standing there in the empty hallway before the damaged mirror, Star experienced a soul-stirring epiphany; in a flash of color, light, image, and sound she understood that something deeply significant had occurred within her. A wonderful warmth coursed throughout her body and a peace rose up, permeating her soul. She recalled the lifelong encouragement of her parents and how they insisted that she could become anyone or do anything she put her mind to. After finding this magical place with its books and other treasures, Star knew that she could never return to her old persona— her perception of herself was now irrevocably changed. Knowing that *she* was the warrior in the mirror made her feel incredibly empowered. She pledged that from this day forward, she would never again allow anyone to intimidate her, or threaten her life or freedom.

* * *

THE SUDDEN CALL of a nighthawk against the back-drop of the evening's cricket chorus brought Star fully back to the present. A lookout had spotted the approach of the overlord and his entourage. Star turned and whispered some-thing to one of two young runners at her side, dressed all in black like the others, and watched as young Emily sped off down the line to pass the word to the archers to ready their bows. Racing along the forest floor, swift and silent as a wood elf, Emily was thrilled to be along on this, her first actual mission. She was a Warrior's Apprentice 1st Class—a young warrior-in-training who had already passed her rigor-ous stealth and physical agility exams with flying colors.

Star leaned over and whispered into her second messen-ger's ear and Lindsey dashed off toward a clump of greenery near a low shed that served as the horse stables. In moments, a ladder was silently raised against the building, and three black-garbed fighters scrambled soundlessly onto the slight-ly sloping roof, vanishing into the shadows of the overhang-ing boughs.

Well-hidden beneath the trees, Star gazed up through the branches at the stars scattered against the heavens and picked out the Big Dipper brightly positioned in the clear night sky. Above the sounds of crickets she could make out the beating hooves of the approaching riders well before they came into view. Seven men in all, they rode three abreast across the narrow roadway with one rider in the center, and three more taking up the rear. The riders pulled up to the house in high spirits, smiling and joking among themselves as they tied their horses off to a split rail fence. One man in particular looked to be their leader—tall and thin with a clean-shaven face—rather unusual in this era of full beards.

As the eager men approached the front steps, Dejan re-appeared in the doorway, grandly welcoming them with a flashing smile and ingratiating mannerisms, promising them all an especially good time.

"My lovely beauties await you, my friends!" he gushed, "and tonight for your personal enjoyment *we offer fresh talent!*"

He shook hands with his important visitors, paying special attention to the tall one—practically fawning over him as he ushered the group inside.

Subduing her rising anger with tremendous effort, Star seethed at the casual manner in which the visitors approached their upcoming mistreatment of the women imprisoned in this dark place. She felt the pre-battle rush of adrenaline release into her bloodstream—*the time for vengeance had arrived.* She would feel no remorse for what was about to take place. These callous men were here of their own free will, to knowingly use and abuse these imprisoned young women and girls without a second thought as to the violation of their human rights or dignity.

What enraged Star most was the *hypocrisy* of it all. These same men would never have allowed anything untoward to happen to their own wives, sisters, or daughters at home, but here in this place, anything was acceptable, regardless of the anguish their patronage caused. It was their support of such places, and the support of men such as they all over the region that kept the brothels in business. But Star and her Sisterhood were on a mission to burn them all down.

Raising her face to the night, Star paused, taking in the beauty of the moment before inhaling a deep breath of jasmine-scented air and releasing it in the haunting *solo* of a hunting she-wolf. Materializing from the shadows, dozens of silent warriors accompanied by their bristling wolven companions rushed the house alongside their leader—a deadly flood of Justice pouring in through doors and windows to utterly obliterate those who, by their indefensible actions and activities, had positioned themselves as unrepentant enemies of all Womankind.

CHAPTER THIRTEEN

THE COMING STORM

THE TEAMS COMPETITION will be fierce again this Moontide, Elliot Greyson reflected, ruminating over his continuing string of bad luck at the Gathering's sanctioned fights. He stood at the wide picture window in his study overlooking the gently rolling apple and cherry orchards surrounding his rambling brick manor house. It wasn't just the loss of winnings that bothered him—the loss of prestige among the landholders over the past year was embarrassing—and it was beginning to wear on Elliot's nerves. In addition, he'd lost three of his best athletes in the past two moons alone, seasoned fighters all. One died from an illegal strike to the back of the neck and two others had been so seriously injured that they would likely never return to competition.

His thoughts drifted to his arch-rival, Stephan McClellan, owner of a substantial English walnut plantation twelve miles downriver. Stephan's stable of fighters lately always seemed to come out on top—as if they could do no wrong. McClellan was Elliot's sworn enemy and had been so for the past five years, ever since Rachel, Elliot's beautiful, cold-hearted ex-wife, had jumped ship straight into McClellan's bed.

"Bitch," Elliot spat the words aloud, the veins in his neck bulging—he hated her more now than ever, even after such a long time. He swallowed hard, hating McClellan, his former best friend, even more for taking Rachel in. He knew their attraction wasn't love, but rather jealousy and spite on both their parts that brought them together and kept them that way. As a result, Elliot had become the laughingstock of the landed community and he hated her for it. Staring out toward the distant hills, he saw only the memories of their betrayal acted out across the stage of his mind. *Enough!* he told himself, tearing his thoughts away from the past. *Now is the moment in which I live. One day my revenge will manifest and it will be sweet indeed.* He swore his silent promise for the thousandth time.

Turning to more pressing matters, Elliot Greyson sat down at his desk and went over the year-to-date balance sheet. He was operating in the red again and hated it, but all of the Grand Houses were obliged to accept credit to remain afloat until final harvest in the fall. Luckily, the fruit had set well this spring and the trees promised a bountiful harvest—unless another disaster struck them like last year when a late-killing frost had descended out of nowhere. Elliot and his crews had struggled through two desperate nights of damning sleet, doing what they could to protect the tender fruit blossoms, but they ended up only salvaging half of what had promised to be a bumper crop.

At least he had his livestock operation to fall back on. The sheep and cattle brought in enough steady credits throughout the year to keep him afloat, but just barely. *Curse Royal Chen and all bloody moneylenders!* he thought. Elliot was borrowed to the hilt and needed a massive harvest this year in order to set things right. He took another deep breath and tried to calm himself.

Just then, Mara, his attractive mulatto housekeeper, passed by his doorway and he traded his furrowed brow for a quick smile in her direction. It was like a mask in a theatrical performance worn to disguise his true frustrations. He felt it was vital that he keep his financial woes a secret. Any perceived problem might be interpreted as weakness by the others who were waiting in the wings for an excuse to swoop down and divide up his land and possessions among them.

* * *

THIRTY MILES SOUTH of the Gathering, on a grassy, tree-dotted knoll overlooking the Coast Road, Stephan McClellan sat atop his pure-white stallion watching the late afternoon sun dance upon the shimmering waves of the Pacific. Stationed at intervals around the flanks of the hill, two-dozen mounted bodyguards kept a watchful eye over their 33-year-old master, ever mindful of the oath of his enemy sworn to kill him. Positioned slightly behind and to either side, McClellan's two lieutenants remained silently alert, intently surveying the southern horizon with binoculars.

Balanced on their master's glove-protected left hand was perched a strikingly marked female Peregrine Falcon named *Tuuk*. As the fastest members of the animal kingdom, Peregrines were excellent bird hunters. The men waited quietly in the warm sunshine, the freshening onshore breeze rippling through the dry, foot-long grass at their horses' hooves. All eyes scanned the skies in anticipation of the arrival of the afternoon carrier pigeon on its direct flight north to the dovecote at Royal Chen's seaside fortress.

The instant the pure-white dove appeared over the ridge top, McClellan swept off the falcon's hood and raised his arm, pointing skyward with his free hand. Blessed with a remarkable visual acuity, Tuuk's eyes zeroed in on the approaching messenger, and as McClellan raised his arm to release her, the streamlined carnivore flew straight up into the sky, her powerful four-foot wingspan allowing her to rapidly gain altitude. As the smaller bird passed beneath her far below, Tuuk made a sudden pivot and plummeted earthward, hurtling fearlessly toward her prey.

Glued to his field glasses, McClellan was transfixed by the raptor's technical ferocity, the evolutionary perfection of form and function, resulting in a unique blend of physics and flight that allowed her to attain speeds upward of two-hundred miles per hour. Diving on her prey from above, Tuuk collided with the unsuspecting messenger, crushing it in her terrible black talons. Plucking the little white dove from the blue as a frog's tongue snaps up a fly—a few downy feathers that floated lazily to the ground were the only evidence of their midair collision. Returning with her limp prize, the penultimate aerial predator soared gracefully across the grassy hillock to land lightly on McClellan's outstretched arm.

With his right hand, he removed the tiny message tube from the lifeless pigeon's leg. Passing Tuuk and her kill on to one of his lieutenants, McClellan opened the small container, unrolled the rice-paper scroll and read the encoded message with keen interest:

Car amb by M at Des Bay. 10 W and C wgns lost,
4 k, 20 w. 2 att k, 1 c.
Bro 3 att by S, 5 K-h, C tak, prop brn, 14 slav lost.
T via alt rte.

McClellan pondered how to best use this timely and valuable information. One of Chen's caravans had been ambushed at Desolation Bay by "M" who would be Madsen, the bold highwayman and self-proclaimed anarchist who had been wreaking havoc up and down the Coast Road, seemingly hell-bent on conducting his own private revolution. With ten wagons loaded with wine and cannabis hijacked, these valuable commodities would very shortly be at a premium. It must have been quite a fight with four dead caravaners and twenty wounded along with two attackers killed and one captured and headed to his doom after certain excruciating interrogations by the Keeper had stripped every dark secret from his soul. *I'd hate to be in his shoes right about now,* McClellan thought, knowing something of the ruthlessness of Royal Chen.

Brothel Number Three had been attacked and torched by "S" the clandestine society known as the Sisterhood— an outlaw alliance of female warriors trained in the martial arts and devoted to the liberation of all women and children held in bondage, and the punishment of their abusers. They had recently attacked another of Chen's pleasure houses, strung up its five employees, and "liberated" the women before making off with the profits, referred to as "chens." The Keeper had recently placed a thousand-credit bounty on their heads for disrupting his business, but he demanded they be delivered alive; dead they would only bring one-hundred chens, hardly worth bothering with. McClellan figured that The Keeper would probably double the reward upon hearing news of this latest attack.

"T" was tribute, or interest paid to Royal Chen that took many forms and divergent pathways back to the Keeper—it could be in the form of credits, commodities, goods and services, or even in human beings.

Rolling up the scroll, McClellan reinserted it into its tiny container as one of his men handed him a replacement bird. Carefully fitting the container to the leg of his replacement dove, McClellan released her into the air where she circled overhead once before speeding north toward the Gathering. The eyes of the winningest landholder in the region followed her until she became but a speck, finally disappearing into the distance.

Turning his horse to descend the hill, McClellan's mental machinery rivaled the velocity of the bird of prey as he considered the many implications of the timely message. He couldn't help being excited about finally intercepting one of Royal Chen's personal communications. It had taken over three years to master the art of falconry just to arrive at this point. By acting on the information gleaned from this one poorly-encoded report, McClellan could quickly realize a small fortune. He smiled. *The entire operation had taken him less than five minutes!*

* * *

TWO MILES OFF the coast, in the dark belly of the noisy trawler, Anna Planchet lay curled up in a fetal position, a tattered blanket wrapped loosely around her weary form.

Beside her on the uncomfortable steel floor, twins—Lily and River Ravencloud—lay in troubled sleep, one or the other emitting an occasional moan, or muttering something unintelligible under her breath. They were crammed into the filthy hold like sardines, along with more than three-dozen captives like themselves, all huddled together out of necessity, and attempting, without much success, to secure some much-needed rest.

Anna was wide awake and hungry. She cradled her tummy in her hands, instinctively protecting her growing baby hidden within her womb. At four-and-a-half-months along, she was beginning to show and was desperate to keep her pregnancy a secret for as long as possible. *How many days had they been imprisoned inside this miserable, smoke-belching boat?* Since their capture she had tried to keep track of time, but in the near-darkness, with the constant yaw, pitch, and roll of the ship making her ill, it was nearly impossible to know. Overall, the voyage had been a nightmare.

For long periods of time they made headway at a steady forward speed and eventually would slow down, coming to a stop at a dock somewhere along the coast. At each new rendezvous the ship took on additional captives, usually just one or two, but sometimes more. At one particular stop, six teens and a young woman in her mid-twenties were added to the lot. The hold became overcrowded, with only room enough for half of the women to lie down at a given time so they took turns sleeping in shifts.

The mood belowdecks was pure misery—a mixture of shock and fear blended with disbelief and despair. Of the forty-odd captives thrown together in the odious hold, none had expected their lives to end up like this—being ripped from their homes and loved ones, and destined only for a life of slavery. While most were in their early- to mid-teens, there was a smattering of older women, perhaps eighteen to twenty-five, and a couple of others in their early thirties.

Since coming aboard, proper personal hygiene had been nearly impossible to maintain as there was only enough fresh water for two ladles per day, per person, morning and night, and proper shower or toilet facilities were non-existent. They were afforded a black rubber bucket to go in when necessary and a tin pail for drinking water that was filled twice a day. Precious food took the form of one pitiful meal, usually some type of tasteless gruel over maggoty rice—hardly the nourishing diet required to provide for the growing life within Anna's belly.

But that was not the worst of it. Each evening at dusk a pair of drunk slavers would unlock the door and hustle off a captive or two to the upper deck to serve as evening entertainment to the eight-man crew. Sometime after midnight the men would return the poor wretches, clothes in disarray, eyes red from crying, and smelling of strong drink. Anna could see the despair on their faces, violated souls forever impacted by the bestial treatment they'd received at the hands of the drunken crew. So far, Anna had narrowly escaped a similar fate, being positioned by the twins farthest away from the door. So far, they had been successful in hastily covering her in rags and crates to avoid detection by the crude lechers seeking their next victims.

One evening however, as the crew members unexpectedly pushed their way to the back of the hold in search of something new and un-sampled as yet, it appeared that they might discover Anna hidden there. Quickly improvising, the twins created a distraction by pretending to fight—scratching and screaming at one another and pulling at each other's hair. By drawing attention to themselves they were awarded their own humiliating turn above decks. Afterwards, Anna promised that as long as she lived, she would continue to honor their selfless sacrifice on her behalf.

Anna's thoughts turned again to her family, providing her a glimmer of hope amidst the suffering and despair all around her. She could feel them out there, searching, and she believed that Skye, the love of her life, along with Hunter and the twins' fiances, would leave no stone unturned until the women they loved were safely returned to them.

In the confusion on the bridge, Anna didn't see what had happened to Elise, but later, had overheard two of the kidnappers remark on the surprising fighting skills of the "dark-haired one that got away." Knowing Elise and the others as she did, Anna was certain that her compatriots were doing everything in their power to come to her rescue—and that certainty gave her and the Ravencloud twins the strength and hope they needed to stay alive.

CHAPTER FOURTEEN

CROSSROADS

JUST PAST NOON on the third day out, Jessi and Elise reined in on a rocky knoll overlooking the endless horizon, where baby-blue sky met indigo sea. A steady onshore wind buffeted the heights, driving gray storm clouds inland toward the far-off Cascades and dispelling the morning fog to reveal a collection of ramshackle buildings below. The modest fishing village had grown up beside a clear, rushing river that originated in the Coastal Range and emptied into the Sound. It was typical of many small seaside settlements found up and down the coast. Boats of various shapes and sizes were tied up at a long, narrow dock, or anchored offshore in the little jetty-protected bay. Along the shoreline, fishing nets lay stretched out on bamboo frames to dry in the sun.

Heading down the trail toward the tiny hamlet, Jessi was relieved to see the white flag with a red sunburst fluttering above the dovecote atop the weathered, two-story cannery, denoting the town as an official messaging station. Participating communities up and down the coast accepted doves from as many remote dovecotes as possible. While no station housed birds from everywhere, they tried to stock doves from the surrounding dovecotes, which might be located anywhere from fifty to several hundred miles away.

The idea was that one could send a message to the station nearest the desired destination, and the stationmaster there could remove the tube from their bird and place it on another, in order to send the message on its way to a station further along the line, until it ultimately arrived safely at its final destination. Of course, not all messages arrived according to plan. Storms, predators, and many other possible factors could affect the health of the carrier pigeon and the success of its mission. Nevertheless, Jessi was relieved to have found what she'd hoped for here—a potential way to get word to Star about the plight of Alena and Alibi.

Walking their mounts through the town's single street, Jessi and Elsie looked into storefronts for signs of life, their nostrils filling with the familiar scent of fish oil mixed with wood smoke and salt air. On the weathered dock, a middle-aged man with a full salt-and-pepper beard cleaned fish, throwing the heads and guts into the water as a raucous bevy of seabirds hovered at arms length, diving down with eager beaks to scoop up the tasty morsels before they sank to the bottom where waiting crabs and lobsters would make quick work of them.

A dozen other men were busy mending nets, or hauling provisions and catches to and from the boats and the rusting cannery. As the travelers rode into town, young boys paused to stare until the graybeard barked at them about getting back to work. Resuming their duties, they cast curious glances toward the two mysterious riders, speculating about who they were and what they might want.

Dismounting at the street-side entrance to the old cannery, Jessi rummaged through her saddlebags, producing a shiny nickel-plated revolver from her sealskin knapsack. The snub-nosed .38 special wasn't much good at a distance, but up close and personal it would do what was required of it without much of a recoil. Lars had gifted it to her from his private collection on the island and she'd practiced enough to be fairly accurate with it in a pinch. Stuffing the gun into her waistband, she covered the pistol grip with her borrowed cloak.

Watching her young guide with interest, Elise pondered the girl's ability to handle herself should they happen to run into any real trouble. Her own faithful dagger was readily accessible, strapped handily to her thigh, and at her side hung a quiver stuffed with deadly bolts. Slung casually across her back rested the crossbow that Hunter had made for her, ready to be cocked and loaded in a matter of seconds.

As they approached the front steps, a tall, muscular man appeared in the doorway, blocking their path—a shortened double-barrel shotgun resting casually in the crook of his arm. His long, black dreadlocks were tied back into a thick bundle, and his weathered skin was the color of aged harness leather. Filling the doorway, he looked them over with a sweeping glance and raised a large palm in greeting.

"Peace to you and welcome to Trinity. May I be of service?" Gideon spoke in a polite, yet formal manner, referring to the name of the seaside settlement and getting right to the point. As the town's official Guardian, appointed by the thirty-odd fishermen, their families and crews who called Trinity home, his job was to patrol the settlement, keep the peace, and defuse trouble *before* it had a chance to manifest.

"Peace on your town," Elise began, palm raised in response to his universal gesture of friendship, "we seek both to send a message and to secure passage south on a ship, if such is available." She glanced up toward the dovecote from which gentle coos and the fluttering of pigeons could be heard.

Gideon noted her finely crafted weapons, steady demeanor, and the obvious confidence in her voice. *Two females on the Road alone. Not a place for the weak or faint-hearted, to be sure. And the younger one—early teens from the look of her.* Something told him that Jessi could probably hold her own in a scrap. Looking over their fine animals and outfit, Gideon became even more curious. *Sisterhood? Perhaps...* His intuition told him that whoever they were, the travelers were definitely not damsels in distress.

"A message to where?" he asked, his direct gaze searching their faces for the truth.

Elise looked to Jessi who hadn't told her where the message should be sent.

"Eureka," the girl replied, her voice steady and return gaze direct and unflinching.

A woman suddenly appeared from somewhere in the back, looking the strangers over while conferring with Gideon in hushed tones. She faded backward into the shadowed room, giving Elise a hard stare and touching her finger to her lips in a gesture of silence. Gideon turned toward the travelers with a masked smile and invited them inside.

"You are welcome here. Your message can be sent, but there is just one scheduled boat heading south. How far down are you going?"

"To the Gathering" Elise replied, side-glancing Jessi, careful about saying too much to this stranger after the sign they had received from the mysterious woman.

"You planning on being there for the festivities?"

They both nodded yes and he did a quick calculation in his head, well aware of the distance to the Gathering and the timing of its events. The next Moontide Festival was eight days away. He knew it was physically impossible for these two riders to make it there on horseback—it was too far to ride. Without passage all the way down on a ship there was just one other option, but that was hit or miss, and even if they made the connection, the trip was chancy at best.

"How are you planning on paying?" he asked, looking expectantly first to one and then the other of his unlikely visitors, curious to see what they had to offer.

"We have books," Elise went to her saddlebags and pulled out a beautifully illustrated hardcover volume on *North American Natural History* wrapped in a stitched eel-skin book cover and handed it to him.

Gideon's eyes widened as he accepted her offering. Books were rare trade items, especially important books like this one in good condition. Most of those still in existence were hoarded, locked up in private collections by people of means and rarely glimpsed in common circulation. While they were universally accepted as trade items, they were unusually hard to find.

"Your message we can handle, but regrettably, two ships sailed yesterday for the Gathering and there is but one vessel going south, but only as far as Grays Harbor at Aberdeen."

Jessi let out an involuntary sigh at the news, relieved on one hand to be able to get word to Star about her mother and friend, but crestfallen regarding the transport situation. Without catching a boat ride, there was no way to reach the Gathering north of the old Oregon-California border before the Festival took place. Elise was deeply disappointed as well, desperate to arrive there before Anna and the Raven-cloud twins vanished forever. Discerning the depth of their concern from the looks on their faces, Gideon offered an unexpected alternative.

"You could arrange passage to Aberdeen—horses and all—aboard *The Swan*, disembark there and head east, two day's ride, and catch the train down. It doesn't run on a regular schedule, but you might get lucky." Gideon waited for their reaction.

"Did you say *train?*" Elise queried, not sure that she heard him correctly. She glanced at Jessi in wonder. Nodding his shaggy head, Gideon's eyes twinkled as he began to explain.

* * *

FORTY-FIVE MILES east of Aberdeen, Washington, the rusty north-south train tracks ran parallel to the old I-5 roadbed from just below Seattle to San Francisco Bay. The old Burlington Northern rail line had lain dormant for over twenty years until recently, when lifelong friends, Kent James and Bartholomew Brown, had changed all that. On one of their routine scavenging trips to the outer districts, they had discovered an 1867 steam locomotive in a dilapidated round house museum amidst the ruins of a small town, approximately midway between Old Vancouver, B.C. and the Gathering on the coast. Covered in dust and rotting tarps, it had once been lovingly restored to original working condition, and then packed away—oiled, greased, and preserved for posterity by a long-deceased organization of devoted volunteers.

For the two twenty-five-year-olds, it was the perfect find. Kent had always loved to make things go; as far back as he could remember he'd been fascinated with machines of all shapes and sizes. Contraptions with engines intrigued him the most. Electric, gas, or steam, it didn't really matter, as long as it possessed a functional motor that could turn a flywheel or generate some form of transferable power. His father had been an old-school tinkerer, the garage always cluttered with one project or another—parts and pieces spread out all over the floor on tarps or atop the big wooden workbench. He'd inherited his impressive tool collection from his dad who had passed away ten years after the End War.

Kent's friend and business partner, Bartholomew "Barty" Brown, was a risk-taking daredevil with an insatiable curiosity and a utopian vision of the future. Barty wore the hats of locomotive engineer and business manager, while Kent served as chief mechanic and operations troubleshooter. Their individual abilities and aptitudes perfectly complemented one another, dovetailing into the complete skill set needed to make their transfer company a reality. Combining letters from their first names, they formed *Bent Rails Transfer,* and from the very beginning, business had boomed. As word spread about their enterprise, the number of passengers and amount of cargo they shipped steadily increased.

Forward-thinking nineteenth- and twentieth-century railroad engineers originally designed the nation's track beds with rock berms generally set above the surrounding landscape. As a result, a relatively small percentage of the north-south track had suffered serious damage from fallen objects over the years, though to be accurate, sections running through cities at street level and those heading up and over mountain passes didn't fare quite as well.

Kent and Barty, with the enthusiastic support of many new fans and supporters in the towns and villages along the way, spent their first several months organizing local efforts to clear away all brush and debris, allowing them to replace worn out ties and bent rails along the old I-5 corridor. The eventual result was an obstacle-free stretch of track just over 800 miles long from Seattle to San Francisco that the old steam engine could cover in about 24 hours at seventy percent output, or 32 miles per hour.

The same distance by horse would take six arduous weeks or more under the most ideal of traveling conditions. Of course, the nature of Bent Rails Transfer's services required them to make many stops along the way to pick up and unload passengers and cargo, and to regularly replenish water and wood supplies. Therefore, in terms of actual timetables, the train could usually make the roundtrip journey approximately every four to six days—or longer if repairs were needed.

Barty had devised an ingenious system of filters, pumps, and hoses to provide the steam boiler with plenty of clean water, cleverly designed to draw from trackside-rivers, creeks, and ponds, wherever and whenever water was present. They did make some notable structural modifications to the front of the locomotive as well, most obvious of which was the addition of a crane-like hoist mounted on a swing arm directly behind the cowcatcher out front, useful in removing heavy objects, such as fallen trees, from the tracks.

The stout locomotive pulled a total of twenty-seven cars including: a tender fitted with a U-shaped water tank and stacked with hardwood for the firebox, a flatcar loaded with spare rails, ties, and iron spikes—handy, should they have to conduct track repairs along the way, several each of passenger cars, cattle cars for livestock, and boxcars for cargo, with the obligatory caboose bringing up the rear which the partners had outfitted as their living quarters.

Security wasn't initially a huge concern, since nearly everyone who found out about the train service was overjoyed at the modern convenience it represented for shipping goods and passengers from the Seattle area to San Francisco Bay. Most folks marveled at the opportunity to ride the rails at a time when traveling on foot, horseback, or by rare horse-drawn wagon, were the exclusive means of land-based long distance transportation.

In the beginning, it was all fun and games for Kent and Barty until an amateur pack of wannabe train robbers blocked the tracks on one of their early runs south from Seattle in a misguided and unsuccessful highjacking attempt. Though the logs they used for a barricade ended up being easily crushed by the engine's steel wheels—the partners subsequently deputized half-a-dozen young sharpshooters to ensure the security of passengers and cargo. The deputies— four men and two women in their early-twenties—were overjoyed at the unique opportunity to live and work aboard a train, and offered their services in exchange for room and board and a modest monthly allowance—their true motivation being the simple thrill and excitement of riding the train.

Commandeering and outfitting the foremost passenger car as their bunkhouse, the squad took up strategic window positions throughout the train, and posted a couple of lookouts on the roof, fore and aft. Each marksman was armed with a rifle or a shotgun, and was willing to use them. In addition to their security duties, the young hotshots assisted in the loading and unloading of cargo, and ensured a sufficient supply of hardwood for the firebox and water for the boiler.

Before long, two brothers on the team, Nate and Will, suggested naming their much-envied security force the *Steam Punk Rangers*, a term loosely borrowed from a rare graphic novel series from their dad's treasured comic collection that they had grown up reading. The group agreed to the moniker, and proceeded to import the stylized Steam Punk subculture, manufacturing their own unique uniforms—with no two alike—and dressing in the stereotypical goggles and boots of the genre. In keeping with their chosen theme, each member of the Rangers modified their weapons and clothing, continuously embellishing their outfits with all sorts of unusual and interesting items.

Train perimeter defenses were beefed up as well, with clever drop-down railings covered in rusty concertina wire which could be hoisted up to the roof and out of the way when loading or unloading, and lowered again when it was time to embark. Anyone attempting to jump the train with the railings in place would be instantly inhibited by the deadly razor wire, scientifically designed to discourage large, tough-skinned farm animals from rubbing up against it. Its barbs could effortlessly penetrate the flesh of any human being foolish enough to test its effectiveness.

Concerning fares, Bent Rails Transfer accepted nearly any valuable item in exchange for a ride and tried to be flexible and accommodating. Split dry hardwood was always appreciated, as a constant wood supply was required to fuel the furnace, that in turn, super-heated the steam boiler, so passengers could always exchange firewood for passage. Of course, the little ceramic tiles known as *chens* were a preferred means of exchange since they could be easily stored and transported, and were accepted as legal tender just about anywhere in the region, making them particularly valuable. Almost anything else of value was also accepted, and in legitimate charity cases such as transporting the aged, destitute, sick, or injured, fees were often waived altogether.

Today the train was running south through central Oregon, skirting the foothills west of the Cascades. Taking on passengers and cargo at the Overland Road crossing just south of the Portland wastelands, it was heading to the little town of Curtin where most of the cargo and passengers would be unloaded at the old State Road 99 roadbed. Following State Roads 99 and 38 west was the most direct route to the Moontide Festival at the Gathering.

From Curtin, the train would continue south through northern California, passing through the Sacramento Valley, until arriving at the end of the line just above San Francisco Bay. There the crew would disengage the engine and fuel car in the switchyard, reverse direction in the roundhouse, and take on cargo and passengers heading north. Of course, they would make as many unscheduled stops in between as needed. Although they'd only been operational for a few months, Bent Rails Transfer was already generating a brisk business among some of the bigger suppliers, especially at this time of the lunar cycle around the full moon, when the Gathering celebration would attract crowds from all over the region.

At the north end of the line below Seattle, near where old I-90—referred to as the Northern Overland Road—bisected the tracks, they started the journey all over, again loading wagons filled with supplies onto flatcars, and winching them up the ramps using block and tackle and a series of small cable winches known as come-alongs. Horses, mules and assorted livestock were loaded onto cattle cars for the trip where they were content to be shut in with fresh cut hay to munch on. The slatted sides of the cars provided adequate ventilation and there was plenty of comfortable straw bedding and sawdust on the wooden floor.

Today the wagons were loaded with a wide assortment of goods and commodities heading to the Gathering festivities, including barrels of beer and wine, smoked fish, and jerked meat, along with reed baskets stuffed with plenty of fruits and garden vegetables. Trappers loaded bundles of finely tanned animal hides and pelts; everything from grizzly bear and mountain goat to elk, moose, and deer hides. They even had an assortment of finished products such as deerskin clothing, moose-hide moccasins, belts, and hats. Previously, the box cars had been filled with lumber from a mill above Sacramento, casks and kegs from vineyards in Napa Valley and Santa Rosa, along with assorted fruits, nuts, and hay bales from orchards and ranches farther south—all of which was destined for the Gathering.

* * *

SEATED IN THE rearmost passenger car, Jessi and Elise marveled at the smoothness of the ride and the speeds at which the train traveled along the tracks as it made its way clickety-clack down the line. Mile after mile they stared out the windows in amazement, thoroughly entranced by the experience, happy to have made the connection with the train after a wind-blessed voyage from Trinity to Aberdeen. With their horses and gear secured in one of the livestock cars, they took their seats amid the broad assortment of other travelers in the surprisingly comfortable accommodations. There were families with children, couples and individuals, as well as a number of traders and what appeared to be an entire athletic team on their way to the Moontide sporting events.

Out of habit, Jessi and Elise discreetly scanned the passengers for anything unusual, noting the presence of a railroad guard posted halfway down the car, seated at a window with a lever-action Winchester rifle resting handily across her shoulder. She was not the only armed rider aboard the train. It was common practice these days that most everyone traveled with weapons blatantly displayed, both as a deterrent against potential violence and to facilitate easy access in the event they were suddenly needed. Stout staffs were prevalent and most adults carried some sort of fighting knife or sword. Handguns were commonly worn on a gun belt at the waist like wild-west gunslingers, or secured inside a waistband or shoulder holster, while long guns were routinely seen among mounted sojourners in scabbards attached to saddles.

Bows of various designs were as common as firearms, and while crossbows were unwieldy and sometimes difficult or awkward to load, they were a deadly accurate weapon and highly prized. Short recurved bows were very popular among women and young people of both sexes due to their light weight and ease of pull. Arrows were greatly valued and fletchers and craftspersons specializing in almost any type of weapon, were respected and well paid.

Firearms of every caliber and persuasion were plentiful and it was no wonder: prior to the End War there were more than 250 million guns in the United States alone. Pistols, rifles, and shotguns were easy to come by, but ammunition was an extremely scarce and precious commodity. With pre-End War factory-made rounds all but depleted in less than a decade, manufacturing cartridges from scratch was an exacting science requiring very close tolerances.

Producing gunpowder was simple enough if one had the raw ingredients of sulfur, charcoal, and saltpeter—all available from natural sources, but not necessarily found in the same vicinity or easy to procure. The Chinese had accomplished it hundreds of years prior to the Industrial Revolution, but in the world after the Fall, it was a rare individual who went to the trouble of making black powder, regardless of its value as a commodity. Factory-made bullets were highly desirable, but priced well beyond the reach of all but the wealthiest of individuals. Therefore, firearms were common, but having more than a few bullets on hand was extremely unusual.

Soon after taking their seats, Jessi noticed that the windows of the passenger car directly ahead were curiously blacked out, and access to its doorway was blocked by a thick curtain drawn across the entrance. Once the train began moving, a pair of women in their early twenties exited the doorway and took up positions in front of the curtain, obviously posted there as guards. They were dressed in well-fitting travel clothes with woodland cloaks and tall leather riding boots over leggings, and armed with scimitars and bows with arrow-filled quivers at their sides.

Jessi whispered something in Elise's ear and walked forward to engage them. After exchanging formal greetings, the trio conversed in hushed tones after which one of the guards escorted Jessi through the curtain into the car beyond. Elise waited expectantly, not sure what to think, curious, yet becoming increasingly worried the longer Jessi remained out of her sight.

Half an hour later, her young traveling companion re-emerged from the forward passenger car and returned to her seat, a look of subdued excitement on her face. Leaning close, she whispered to Elise that she had arranged a guide to help them get into the Gathering. Elise's eyes begged an explanation, but Jessi just smiled, saying that she would explain everything upon disembarking the train.

"Don't worry, Elise," Jessi whispered earnestly, "everything is working out better than I had hoped. Those women are well acquainted with situations such as ours and are more than willing to help us out."

More curious than ever, Elise sat cloaked in her thoughts, processing this new information with keen interest. Just who were these women Jessi had spoken with, and why would they want to get involved in her problems? Could they be members of the infamous Sisterhood Alliance? Elise had heard stories about them and was sympathetic to their cause. Feeling stronger than ever about her initial assessment of Jessi and her abilities, she wondered who Jessi *really* was, beyond her appearance of being an unfortunate teenage girl on her own. The young guide was mature beyond her years and knew more than she was willing to reveal at the moment. She wished that Jessi would open up and begin to trust her.

Elise agreed that things were working out surprisingly well. The mere fact that they were riding south on a *train* of all things, and would arrive at the Gathering in time for the Moontide Festival was beyond amazing to her—something she would never have considered possible. Adding the fact that Jessi had rather easily made a connection with the group of well-armed and provisioned women in the passenger car ahead, who were also on their way to the Gathering *and* were willing to be of assistance, greatly increased the possibility of success in locating and liberating Anna and the others before it was too late.

Elise felt fairly certain that Anna, River, and Lily were probably already at the Gathering, and was concerned about how her younger sister was holding up under the stress. Surely Anna had to know that her family would come after her, and *that* certainty would encourage her to remain strong despite the deplorable situation she found herself in. On top of everything else, the fact that Anna was pregnant added a tremendous strain on an already overwhelming situation. *Hang on, Anna,* Elise willed her thoughts to her sister, *we are coming for you.*

She knew that Hunter and Skye would have arrived at the Gathering by now as well, unless storms had disrupted their voyage. She was a bit apprehensive about her upcoming confrontation with Hunter, as he had expressly forbidden her from participating in the rescue operation, but she was at peace with her decision and would deal with his considerations when the time came, drawing encouragement from her belief that everything would work out as it was meant to. Their love was strong and not in question. The important issue was freeing Anna and Skye's sisters and anything beyond that would have to wait.

* * *

SEATED QUIETLY NEXT to Elise on the fast-moving train, young Jessi stared out the window, watching a bounding herd of pronghorn antelope vanish into the distance, spooked by the train's passing—an experience they were no doubt unfamiliar with in this post-End War day and age. Observing the dust cloud trailing their retreat, her thoughts were on her mother and Alibi, as she sent out prayers for their safety, hoping against hope that she would arrive in time to prevent their upcoming executions at the foul hands of Royal Chen.

While the uninformed held the Keeper in high regard, his crimes against humanity, especially against women, were well documented within the close-knit community of the Sisterhood, who had been engaged for years in all-out assault on his string of brothels scattered throughout the region. While most people revered the man, Jessi knew of his darker side from stories told by the direct victims of his abuse. She shuddered to think of her mother's forthcoming treatment at his hands.

Thoughts of her own bestial assault by the trawler's drunken captain made her feel ill, and she was repulsed by the mere thought of ever being manhandled like that again. Luckily for her, the captain had been so liquored up most of the time that he could barely perform. Instead, he had blamed her for his impotence, beaten her, and withheld her food as punishment. Though she knew she'd been emotionally scarred by the ordeal, she tried hard not to allow it to completely overshadow her worldview. Such experiences tended to warp one's outlook on life, even to the point of harboring a permanent hatred for the opposite sex.

Although her upbringing hadn't included a father figure, Jessi understood that not all men were animals. Men like Lars, and others like Skye and Hunter, appeared to abhor such acts of violence against anyone, especially those physically weaker than themselves, as most women and children were. However, she was also cognizant of the fact that there were still many abusive men who would never change, men who were comfortable with their selfish lifestyle that brought harm to others; it was these individuals whom she considered to be her blood enemies worthy of death.

This included not only evil *men*, but certain of their accomplices as well. There were women she'd heard about—traitors to their gender who assisted the slavers in their work—they, too, must be prevented from ever harming another soul. For the world to become a better place, a safe place in which to grow up and reach adulthood, where people were allowed to be free to live happy, fulfilled lives, there must be an end to the violence of misogynistic men and the women that empowered them to remain that way. Jessi was certain that if making the world a better place required that a few evil people die—unrepentant bastards who intentionally made life on earth a hell for so many innocent others—then so be it.

CHAPTER FIFTEEN

DREAMTIME

FROM A CLEARING deep in the glade, drumbeats filled the summer night like the heartbeats of lovers, intoxicating the dancers and driving them out of their minds and into their bodies. Twirling and weaving in reckless abandon, they circled the roaring bonfire beneath a clear, star-filled sky hosting a radiant, nearly full moon.

Balanced on the edge of this revelry, Star sat cross-legged on the welcoming earth, catching her breath as dozens of her sister-warriors whirled past, swaying with outstretched arms, or embracing one another in the joy and release of the sultry celebration. Writhing to the rhythm of the drums, their glistening bodies moved in and out of shadow in the flickering glow of the wavy orange flames.

Perceiving a familiar presence, Star turned to the dark-eyed beauty kneeling beside her. Barefoot, with skin like burnished bronze, and adorned with multiple gold earrings and bracelets expressing her Gypsy heritage, the glowing, twenty-three year old Amaranth was not only an accomplished warrior and weaver of magnificently wrought textiles, but for the past three orbits of the sun she had been Star's most trusted companion and confidant. Leaning in close with a serene smile on her flushed face, Amaranth presented Star with a goblet of sacramental tea made from steeped psilocybin mushroom caps sweetened with honey.

Accepting her offering, Star sipped reverently from the flask, honoring the Goddess of all Creation. As the pungent, earthy liquid enveloped her taste buds, she closed her eyes, focusing within on a bluish point of pulsating light. This glowing beam soon morphed into a purple-red energy flow, scrolling sacred geometric patterns across the inside surface of her eyelids.

Her spirit-mind-body buzzed with excitement and bubbling joy as wave upon wave of affection flowed from the Earth Mother beneath her, rising up through her whole being in a cleansing, nurturing baptism of love. The trees surrounding the clearing seemed pleased with the night's effusion as well, appearing to cheer the celebrants on, their boughs waving playfully in the evening breeze—their leaves rustling in syncopated rhythm to the drums, whose tempo and volume rose and fell, forming complex, organic patterns as if imbued with a soul of their own.

Opening her eyes, Star stared into the flames. The fire itself seemed alive—a living, breathing entity dancing in erotic abandon. Hungry tongues of flame eagerly licked the seasoned hardwood fuel, igniting pent-up hydrogen gas trapped within the carbon fibers to mingle with oxygen and be released as light and heat energy. Mesmerized by the cosmic beauty of the moment, Star admired its majesty, reverently acknowledging its magic.

Fire was unquestionably one of Life's most fundamental and beneficial allies. When guided to good and careful use, it could tame and cleanse the darkness, ward off winter cold and hungry predators, and warm both heart and hearth alike.

187

However, if one got in its way, or allowed it to get out of hand—even for a fraction of a second—there were few more potentially destructive forces on the face of the Earth. Star closed her eyes again, her thoughts like bursting revelations weaving in and out of the drumming, the dancing, and the powerful sacrament...

Fire—one of four essential elements—together with water, air, and earth—a balance. Its constant presence was recognized on a primal level throughout one's lifetime, one's human incarnation, bringing warmth, comfort, protection, purification, and illumination. In the nuances and symbolism of language—the fire of curiosity burned in a child's eyes. The fires of passion welled up from within a lover's loins initiating the beginning of the human journey—in the instant of conception and formation of the zygote—to the end of one's days, when the spent human shell was wholly consumed in the funeral pyre that finished it...

As the flames rose higher, Star began to see in them the burning strongholds of her enemies. Brothels—dark places of torment where her sisters suffered under the lash of evil men bereft of a heart. Soulless ghouls who preyed upon the flowers; men, and even colluding women, who would never see the beauty, or the connectedness of the creation as Star perceived it this night.

Suddenly, the space around her changed and she was surrounded by the sights and sounds of flames and screams as high stone walls surrounding her began falling in a surreal slow-motion vision of destruction on a massive scale. She watched in horror as helpless souls were swallowed by teeth-lined earth-mouths gaping open beneath the crowd's trembling feet. She could taste and smell the smoke and dust, and the roasting flesh of the burning victims all around her.

And then, as suddenly as it appeared, her vision vanished, and she was back in the clearing with her sisters, and the drums—the dancing maidens twirling, spinning, and laughing. Staring at the scene around her as if she'd seen a ghost, Star realized that the death and destruction she had just experienced were not really happening in the present moment, and she began to relax, allowing the drumbeats and chanting to wash over her like healing waves, caressing her center and melting away her fears.

Amaranth slid in beside Star, wrapping her arms around her companion's neck, and leaned in, resting her chin on Star's shoulder. She breathed in the sweet smell of her—skin, hair, and breath—earthy, flushed and sweaty from so much dancing and celebration. Star turned her head slightly to gaze into Amaranth's wondrous liquid eyes and was suddenly lost in them.

All at once, the clearcut distinction of exactly where Star ended and Amaranth began was blurred by the sacrament pulsing through their brains and bloodstreams, and they became liberated from their usual separateness, transcending the isolation of self to merge into a higher dialectic of consciousness.

Falling back onto the soft, welcoming earth, cocooned in one another's embrace, Star felt as if the entire universe was speaking to her in an intuitive language beyond the stunted symbolism of words—rather in a direct transference of knowingness from the living Earth beneath her, the plants and trees of the forest surrounding her, and the celestial bodies in the heavens above. The moon shone down, radiating an irrepressible, seductive energy that streamed into her open being, whispering its secrets directly to her sensitized heart of hearts.

Suddenly, in a flash of blinding white light, she knew every answer to her most intimate and immediate existential questions. Peering fearlessly into the deepest place within her being, she felt the white-hot glow of neurons forming at the top of her skull and her seventh chakra exploded open, bridging the limitlessness of the cosmic consciousness with her own.

In an orgasmic rush of color, light, sound, and emotion, Star abandoned her pulsating physical form there on the ground and raced up toward the moon as an astral body—a teardrop-shaped being made of thousands of eyes. With 360-degree vision, she saw and was one with the entire cosmos as wave upon wave of energy pulsated through her being, washing over her wide-opened soul. And then, as unexpectedly as she'd exited her body, Star was slammed back into it, rocked by the powerful magnitude of the experience, and filled with a remarkable degree of wellbeing that she had never known was possible.

Leaning over her heavily tripping companion, Amaranth placed her pursed lips over Star's partially opened mouth and shotgunned a powerful funnel of sweet-smelling cannabis smoke directly into her lungs. Inhaling deeply, Star held in the potent mixture, exhaling slowly as the mellowing effect of the THC-laced gases invaded her cerebral cortex, causing her entire body to relax into a complete state of peace. Lying there together beside the fire beneath the grandeur of the Milky Way with the whole wide universe looking on, the two blended into one, celebrating their love without any sense of self-consciousness or inhibition.

※　※　※

SKYE RAVENCLOUD SLEPT, or more specifically, his body was asleep, yet his mind was wide awake delving the mysteries of the spirit world. He was participating in a lucid dream—at least he believed himself to be dreaming, though the vivid intensity of the experience rivaled any waking moment he'd ever known.

He was hunting—searching the darkness for persons dear to him whose identities were not readily available to his subconscious mind. They were in trouble and it was terribly important that he find them before it was too late—his fleeting memory of who they were was but a partial recollection at best. Though he couldn't remember the *who*, he clearly understood that time was running out.

As he raced through an endless maze of underground tunnels, torches mounted on the walls were spaced far enough apart so as to force him into stretches of utter blackness between them. He ran blindly through these sections, expending every ounce of energy, refusing to give in to fear or fatigue in spite of the burning in his calves and thighs that protested his every stride down the cold stone corridors— darkness and light, darkness and light, darkness and light, *ad infinitum.*

As he ran, he gradually became aware that the tunnel was beginning to deteriorate behind him, its ceiling, walls, and floor cracking and crumbling into smaller and smaller bits until the dust filled his nostrils, sticking to his skin and mixing with the sweat streaming down his back like rivers of blood. Glancing behind him as he sprinted, he glimpsed the floor at his heels falling away into a black abyss. Light from the torches ahead became steadily dimmer until finally extinguishing altogether just as a doorway abruptly opened at the far end of the collapsing tunnel, filling the disintegrating corridor with precious light.

The faster he ran, the more rapidly the tunnel collapsed behind him and it began to dawn on him that he would never make it to the doorway before the floor fell out from beneath him. At the last possible moment, he leapt forward, palms down with arms outstretched, legs trailing behind him as he rocketed down the corridor two feet above the vanishing floor, exiting through the opening into the blazing sunlight just as the vivid dream segment disintegrated into nothingness.

The next instant he found himself exiting a black cave in the side of a steep cliff face and soaring high above a brilliant blue sea surrounded by dozens of giant ravens as large as buzzards who seemed to be escorting him somewhere important. They called to him as they flew, one or another occasionally veering close to stare into his soul with obsidian eyes, saying nothing, but speaking into his mind using thought pictures, projecting abstract scenes of fire, destruction, and mayhem populated by hundreds of upturned faces, their eyes wide with terror and mouths open in muted screams.

After what seemed an eternity, he glanced back to discover a wall of seawater as high as the clouds bearing down on him, its leading edge curling forward, top and bottom, like a gigantic foaming mouth, laughing in joyful anticipation of swallowing him. Turning back around he was surprised to find his feathered escort gone. Now alone, he was no longer flying, but plummeting earthward at a dizzying rate of speed. Just before impact, Skye awoke and sat upright, staring about the room, sweat pouring from his skin and breath coming in ragged gulps—his racing heart pounding audibly in his chest.

CHAPTER SIXTEEN

A QUESTION OF BALANCE

SEATED CROSS-LEGGED on *Windsong's* gently rising and falling foredeck, Skye Ravencloud closed his eyes and concentrated on his breathing, determined to dispel his inner turbulence, more pronounced since his disturbing dream the night before. *Breathe in, breathe out.* He mentally whispered the mantra to the wind, offering himself to the spirits and seeking their guidance in this time of great testing. Slipping easily into that place of inner peace wherein his mind could disengage from the warring emotions seeking to overwhelm his being and drag him down into the depths of despair, he recognized the soothing voice of Utek, chief shaman of his tribe, who spoke to him from beyond the grand illusion of death:

Just BE with it, young Ravencloud…

The lifelong tug-of-war between being responsible for what had been entrusted to him on the one hand, and letting go all attachments on the other, formed the dynamic ebb and flow of Skye's human incarnation; a balance not easily achieved or maintained, especially when it came to protecting those he loved. Relaxing further into his breathing, he felt the combined suffocating weight of fear of loss and anger begin to lighten and dissipate, releasing his essence to once again resonate with the healing rhythms of the vast universe around him.

With his auric energy field re-calibrating, Skye centered his thoughts on the Way of the Shaman as passed on by Utek, his childhood mentor. Before withdrawing into that profound and mysterious state *between lives*, the wizened holy man had guided him through the shamanic initiation rites culminating in a vision quest during which Skye, at the age of twelve, learned the secret of channeling his animal spirit guide, mitkuni'ku—the raven, who thereafter provided him with valuable knowledge and insight drawn from the unlimited resources of the spirit realm.

Regardless of outward circumstances, Skye was aware that to be effective in this mission, his life must remain in balance—his spirit centered—or the subsequent lack of harmony would warp out of control and his essence become lost in the maelstrom of the surrounding chaos. He opened his eyes and above him in the blackness, the heavens glittered with countless stars. He looked on in wonder as mysterious scintillating specks of light flashed on and off—like slow-motion strobes bobbing through the night air and across the tops of the swells and beyond. In the myths and legends of his People, the sacred knowledge spoke of the connectedness of all things in the cycle of life, death, and rebirth—the Great Mystery.

While his gifts were unable to fully pierce the veil of the future to see what was to be, Skye felt a peace about the outcome of their quest with an intuitive certainty that he and his brethren would find Anna, River, and Lily, and bring them safely home again. Exactly how it would all play out would soon be revealed, for according to their gracious benefactor, Lars, the new dawn would bring them to the shores of the Gathering. Sensing a presence, Skye turned to discover Hunter standing against the mainmast, his face half covered in shadow.

"How are you feeling, brother?" he asked the quiet mountain man, conscious of the other's shaky sea legs.

Hunter let out an audible sigh and offered a weak smile, "Much better, thanks."

Taking a seat on an oak cask filled with thick coils of anchor chain, Hunter silently reflected on the challenges of the past week. He had never before been on the ocean; canoeing and kayaking on rivers and lakes were the extent of his previous watercraft experience. Shortly after boarding *Windsong*, his body found it difficult to adapt to the constant rolling motion of the swells, becoming queasy at first and then helplessly seasick. After suffering through one night of hellish agony, Skye had placed Hunter on a regimen of ginger tea and activated charcoal which, after forcing down a few mugs of the potent mixture, began to have the desired effect, alleviating the worst of his symptoms. By the second evening, Hunter's condition had stabilized, but he still felt a bit weak in the knees when the wind shifted and the chop became more pronounced. While his equilibrium never fully returned to normal aboard ship, he dealt with it as best he could without complaining, his usual silence concealing his physical discomfort.

As they drew closer to the Gathering, Hunter's frustration increased, simmering just beneath the surface. While grateful that Elise had escaped the kidnappers, he was enraged that Anna and the Ravencloud sisters had not. His understanding that they were presently scheduled to be sold at auction downgraded his faith in human psycho-social evolution to a new all time low. Injustice in the world remained—just as it had since the beginning of recorded history. Regardless of what cataclysmic events might take place on earth, from an End War that nearly wiped out the species on a planetary scale, on down to ruthless bullies threatening the very existence of the physically vulnerable, a certain segment of the population was bound and determined to rule over their fellows by force—simply because they could.

This self-destructive aberration affecting Mankind's long-term survival was the original reason for Hunter's self-imposed exile immediately following the End War. With humans nearly extinct, he was done interacting with his fellows—he considered himself to be much better off as far away as possible from the influences of others. When Elise unexpectedly entered his life, she gave him a reason to reconnect with his own humanity, but that connection did not include—nor did it engender a greater love for, or acceptance of—humankind in general.

As the dawn threatened to the east, he looked out across the gray rolling swells toward the mist-filled horizon, only able to guesstimate where the land met the sea. Looking up and gauging the progression of the waxing ivory orb that illuminated the awakening skies above, he reckoned one more day before the moon would achieve her fullness, aggressively drawing the surface of the ocean toward her in the rhythmic lunar cycle of magnetic attraction.

The rapidly approaching confrontation at the Gathering loomed large upon Hunter's psyche. Ironically, he found himself once again pulled into a fight not of his choosing, through events forced upon him by circumstance—obligating him to come to the aid of Anna and Skye's sisters, which of course, he was more than willing to do. At least this time Elise was well out of harm's way, and in going on this mission he was not alone, but had newfound allies in Lars, Skye Ravencloud, and Skye's two tribesmen, Walker Dan and Paints-His-Face-Red—all men of honor and courage who would walk into battle and give their lives if necessary to rescue their loved ones—a familiar scene played out entirely too often down through the blood-stained mists of human history.

Soon the mettle of their little troupe would be tested, the results but a tale from the distant past, to be told around the evening fire, when lulled into tranquility by one's favorite foods surrounded by family and friends in a walled village on the banks of a rushing river far to the north. Deep within his being, Hunter was troubled by the events about to play out on the morrow. Taking into account all that had happened since arriving on the coast, he was entertaining serious second thoughts about having migrated to this grand Pacific Northwest—this supposed enlightened land of the New-World Renaissance.

* * *

THE FOLLOWING DAY, Lars passed the helm to Skye in order to take the daily sighting with his sextant, an instrument of navigation passed down to him by his father, used for centuries to determine one's relative location at sea. Marine navigation since the Fall was much more challenging than during pre-End War times. No longer having benefit of the Global Positioning System (GPS) satellite array, present-day mariners were forced to revert to mechanical navigation systems used for hundreds, or even in some cases, thousands of years prior to the electronic revolution.

A competent mariner himself, Lars possessed all of the necessary tools of his trade, including an extensive laminated nautical chart library collected from the offices of harbormasters and pilfered from the pilothouses of rotting shipwrecks lining the coastal harbors. He even owned a dogeared copy of the Marine Almanac from the year prior to the End War.

Lars' father, a renowned master cabinetmaker who designed and crafted upper-end custom interiors for the luxury boatbuilding industry, taught his three older sons celestial navigation at an early age. On weekends aboard the family-owned 42-foot sailing yacht *Wanderlust*, Lars and his brothers were required to plot a course on a nautical chart to any one of a series of offshore islands predetermined by their father. Using a sextant and marine chronometer, they charted their course throughout the voyage, marking down their location on the chart. Lars had inherited his father's sextant, ship's compass, and marine chronometer, salvaging them from the disastrous storm-caused shipwreck that had destroyed his family and nearly cost him his own life. Whenever sailing aboard Windsong he used the tools daily out of habit, ever conscious of their emotionally charged origins.

Since the End War, in addition to no longer receiving GPS satellite signals to help guide one's course, neither were there atomic clocks automatically communicating via satellite to adjust quartz chronometers, keeping them accurate to within a tenth of a second per day. Nor were there annually published nautical almanacs outlining the relative positions, minutes, and altitudes of the 57 celestial bodies so helpful in determining longitude as a navigational aid. Gone, as well, were up-to-date tide tables and all of the other modern conveniences to make maritime navigation easy.

Nowadays, if one wished to actually arrive in reasonably close proximity to a predetermined destination, proficiency in the theory and practical application of "old-school" nautical navigation instruments, systems, and technologies was required. Referring to charts of the Pacific Northwest coastline and offshore islands was helpful, though Lars couldn't absolutely rely on their accuracy, since changes to the coastline caused by seismic and meteorologic activity over the past twenty years had wrought their own particular brand of havoc upon them.

Standing on *Windsong's* foredeck at high noon, Lars held his sextant at eye level and peered through the 3X telescopic lens, sighting the horizon where the ocean met the sky directly beneath the sun using the horizon mirror. Releasing the instrument's index arm, he adjusted the index mirror until the sun's reflection came into view directly above the horizon. Swinging the sextant carefully from side to side on its axis to ensure that the sun was positioned correctly in the mirror, he engaged the index bar clamp, turned the device sideways and noted the degree of angle on the graduated scale of the arc. Returning to his cabin to fix their position on his chart, he took into account the height of his eyes above sea level and the exact time of day in formulating the correct mathematical equation.

Whenever the sky was clear and the sun visible, Lars conducted the daily noontime exercise out of habit when aboard any vessel, a cardinal rule ingrained in him by his father. In addition to sighting with the sextant, when cruising the coastline within sight of land, he referred to National Oceanic and Atmospheric Administration (NOAA) Pacific Northwest coastal charts to identify landmarks used to determine his distance from shore, location in the water and proximity in relation to other objects, both hidden undersea and visible above the surface.

As a rule, whenever sailing along the coast he charted a course to stay about a mile or so offshore—deep enough to avoid the undersea hazards closer to land. Here, off the coast of central Oregon, the water was dark blue with the ocean floor several hundred feet beneath them. The weather was typical for this time of year, with occasional thunderstorms, but mostly it was sunny and dry in the afternoons with morning fog rolling in from the sea quickly burned off by the noonday sun.

Relieving Skye at the wheel, Lars noticed something moving off their starboard bow, quickly recognizing a pod of a dozen or so bottlenose dolphins crossing between the offshore islands and the mainland—their gray dorsal fins and whale-like tails glistened in the afternoon sun. They would cross his bow close enough to hear the spent air exhaling from their cranium-mounted blowholes. As they intersected the ship, the pod veered off course and disappeared, reappearing a few moments later to breach in her bow wake. Hunter and the others went forward to watch them galavanting through the whitecaps, surfing the wave generated by *Windsong* as she pushed through the gentle swells at a steady twenty-two knots. After several minutes, the pod veered east toward the coast, humans and dolphins alike having enjoyed their carefree, insouciant display.

Raising his marine binoculars toward a collection of dark clouds looming on the western horizon, Lars felt the wind shift a few points and made an appropriate adjustment to the jib boom to keep the luff out of the mainsail. Weather permitting, they would be closing in on their destination, two-thirds down the Oregon coast a few hours from now. He couldn't help but wonder what they might find when they arrived at the Gathering. It had been several years since he'd sailed this far south, and he steeled himself against the repressed memories that this section of coastline always seemed to invoke. With a growing anxiety in the center of his chest, he pushed back the skeletons of his past and stood fast, focused on the task at hand.

Determined that their rescue attempt meet with success, Lars felt confident in the strength of character and determination of his four passengers. As far as he could tell, all were men of integrity—members of a Native settlement north of Vancouver Island, all but the woodsman, Hunter, who had been effectively subdued by motion sickness for most of the trip. Spending this emotionally intense time with his guests made Lars proud to be part of their noble effort. In the last few days he'd taken the opportunity to gently delve their hearts and minds, and was honored to know that good people such as these still walked the earth, dedicated to the realization of a better world.

With the Gathering's harbor looming ahead, it wouldn't be long before their rescue plan was set in motion. Upon their arrival, Lars understood that his new friends must infiltrate the Keeper's bastion—his walled fortress protected by a legion of well-armed and highly trained troops—and once inside, they would be required to take back their loved ones by force of arms. In spite of his well-intentioned postulate for success, Lars couldn't completely ignore his foreboding that they were on a collision course with destiny. Furthermore, in some disconnected portion of his being, the cliff-dwelling mariner had not quite reconciled the fact that he was actually in the process of sailing his precious mistress directly into potential disaster, and could very well lose everything he had come to cherish, including his very life.

* * *

TWO HUNDRED MILES south of the Gathering, in the lavish master cabin of his modern, Hong Kong-style, eighty-five foot long junk-rigged sailing vessel, *Sea Witch*, Venerable Wu read the encrypted message with a thinly disguised smile, inwardly gloating over the most recent report from his favorite niece. Holding the thin rice paper over the oil lamp's soft yellow flame, he allowed it to burn almost to his fingertips before dropping the final bit out the open porthole into the rolling sea. He laid back on his futon and relaxed, stroking his thin white beard, pleased with the progress the girl had made in such a short period of time.

It had scarcely been two months since her arrival up north, yet already, May Ling had maneuvered herself into position as Royal Chen's number-one concubine. She had even moved into the living quarters next to the Keeper's private suite. Excellent! Wu must remember to send a special gift to Lien Hua, May Ling's acclaimed pillowing instructor.

Sensing a slight shift in the vessel's heading, Wu reached for the braided silk cord hanging down above his head. A moment later, a liveried servant wearing a crisp white uniform knocked discretely on the door and stepped into the room with head bowed, awaiting his master's orders.

"Inform the pilot I wish to see him."

"Yes, Your Excellency, right away." The man bowed again and backed out the door, closing it quietly behind him.

Wu stretched his shoulders and winced, reaching up to pull the cord again. The bowing servant returned and Wu ordered, "Send down my masseuse."

"Yes Your Excellency, right away."

The Red Dragon Triad chief's muscles were stiff from boar hunting in the Marin Headlands the day before leaving on this voyage and felt he could benefit from the ministrations of Chow Li, the most renowned massage practitioner in all of New Chinatown.

There soon came another knock and two teenaged boys entered the cabin, one carrying a folding massage table, the other leading a wiry, elderly man by the hand. The white-haired gentleman walked with an unusual ambling gait, a kind of half-bent-over shuffle-step with his eyes tightly shut. Sightless from birth, Chow Li was the founder of the exalted Chow Li Massage School for the Vision Impaired.

For more than forty years he'd been teaching massage therapy, and hundreds of his students—each vision-impaired like himself—and otherwise doomed to a life of misery and deprivation within the especially unforgiving social landscape of the Afterworld—were now gainfully employed and well-looked after as live-in masseuses in the more well-to-do households throughout the Bay area and beyond.

Venerable Wu's mother had sworn by Chow Li and many years earlier had encouraged her son to experience the man's exceptional healing hands for himself. One session was all it took for Wu to become Li's thankful patron. Wu had offered generous financial support to Chow Li's school and granted him special social status and protection, enabling the master healer to freely come and go as he pleased without fear of being harassed by the notorious youth gangs, or anyone else who might otherwise elect to prey upon the vulnerable older gentleman. To Wu, Chow Li was a living treasure, and woe unto the unlucky soul who might dare contrive to bring him harm.

The pilot arrived as Li's helpers were setting up, and Wu asked the uniformed officer when he expected the *Sea Witch* to arrive at the Gathering.

"Early morning the day after tomorrow, Sir, perhaps eight or nine AM." The man waited stiffly, head slightly bowed, always uncomfortable when called down to the master's cabin. He checked his breathing and exhaled, wishing to be back at the wheel.

"Excellent, Pilot, see that we arrive on time..." Wu paused, "and our three honorable guests, how are they faring?"

Pilot Chan's stomach turned at the mention of the unfortunates strapped naked to bamboo poles and dangling inches above the surface of the ocean off the stern of his ship.

"They are still breathing, Sir, as far as I can tell, but probably not for much longer." He swallowed hard and wished to be back in the fresh air and away from Sadistic Tyrant Wu, who had somehow come to own Chan's entire universe.

"Well done, Pilot. Hold your course and mind the shoals, we don't need any mishaps such as that dung-magnet predecessor of yours was prone to collect."

Wu referred to former pilot Hang's predisposition to drive the ship into stationary underwater objects while underway.

"Yes Sir," the pilot stammered, "I mean, no Sir. No mishaps, Sir."

"Good. That will be all."

The nervous officer backed out the door into the corridor and breathed a huge sigh of relief, practically running up the stairs to the main deck. Pilot Chan checked the wind and returned to the wheel, glad to relieve his First Mate at the conn. Just thinking about the former pilot and the nature of his demise made him quake with fear. May the gods protect me from the wicked Master Wu and his unusually inventive punishments!

As Li's assistants completed their set up, Wu chuckled at the terror he struck into the hearts of common men. It wasn't that he enjoyed being the persona of evil, he just understood the principles of control, and played his part well so that he had no need to worry about assassins around every corner. Wu's security apparatus, thought to be ubiquitous, was feared by all.

By simply convincing the population, along with his many enemies, that his eyes and ears were everywhere, Wu was able to maintain a social environment of relative peace and tranquility—much better for business that way than in a world steeped in chaos and uncertainty. Unfortunately, every once in a while it was necessary for Wu to present the public with an especially brutal demonstration of his ruthlessness, to remind them that no one was exempt from his justice. The three naked men lashed to poles were such an example.

The trio were members of a smalltime criminal gang, guilty of petty crimes and simple assaults mostly, along with a few amateur burglaries and such. Wu had known about the crew for months, but in port four days ago he'd had them rounded up and tied to upright posts that were hinged to the stern of his ship. Hundreds thronged along the waterfront to witness the men's humiliation as each received thirty vicious lashes with a seven foot cane.

Afterwards, they were lowered into the sea once very ten minutes for thirty seconds—the caustic salt water soaked into their tender wounds and the dunking nearly drowned them. Even worse, a pair of male bull sharks had appeared not long after their first dunking, drawn by the fragrant scent of blood oozing from the miserable trio's wounds. Seeing dark fins slicing through the water encircling the boat's stern, the terrified ne'er-do-wells shrieked and cried out for mercy, knowing that they would be utterly defenseless when lowered again into the blood-chummed sea.

Moments before they were scheduled to be dunked again, Wu appeared on the aft deck and interceded, asking the restive crowd whether they thought the men deserved mercy. He feigned surprise at their overwhelmingly negative response.

"No mercy!" they chanted, "No mercy for the criminals!"

Wu raised his hands in resignation and shrugged as the pleading men plummeted into the Bay. This time, their poles were raised the instant before a shark was upon them, the shrieking outlaws dangling just inches above the thrashing predator's teeth-lined jaws.

After several near misses, the criminals were hoisted to just above the waterline and secured. Fully exposed to the elements, they had suffered there for the past four days without food or water—their pale, cane-striped flesh blistering in the afternoon sun.

Wu relaxed on the massage table as the sightless master worked his magic, his knowledgable fingers kneading Wu's sore muscles and releasing the standing waves of energy trapped there. Aahhhhhh, heavenly! Wu smiled to himself, going over May Ling's report in his mind. Things up north were moving ahead quite nicely and Wu looked forward to his semi-annual visit to the Gathering where he might see for himself how everything was lining up.

The value of May Ling's information far exceeded what he had hoped for. Royal Chen was rapidly losing control of his empire as well as his own mind, and he didn't even know it! Constantly stoned on opium, Chen was becoming increasingly unbalanced and disconnected from reality. Wu couldn't be more pleased. He had been personally instrumental in introducing Royal Chen to the pipe a little over a year ago through a secret ally who was also in Chen's spy ring and on Wu's payroll. The double agent fed Wu valuable intelligence while passing phony reports to Chen about Venerable Wu's unflinching loyalty to the Keeper. By turning him into an opium addict, Wu was hoping that Chen's hand would falter more quickly so that his own inevitable takeover of the Gathering could be hastened. According to May Ling, it was all coming true, and much faster than Wu could have possibly imagined.

CHAPTER SEVENTEEN

DECEPTION

THE SHABBILY CLOTHED flesh trader with greasy hair and dirt under his raggedly chewed fingernails waited nervously in the half-light of the shadowed portico, flanked by members of Royal Chen's personal guard. In the spacious room ahead, through a wide stone doorway, two manacled women crouched on all fours upon marble flagstones, their backs exposed to the Keeper's inspection. Chen walked slowly around them, scrutinizing their identical scarlet tattoos. He bent forward to look more closely at them, tracing the familiar sign with his finger—a winged triangle within a circle with an all-seeing eye in the center above an inverted cross.

Noting the puffy redness of the surrounding skin, Chen pressed down lightly and the terrorized girl barely suppressed a whimper. Chen smiled—a fresh ink job without a doubt, though not a bad counterfeit. His face was composed and revealed nothing of his thoughts. Chen had to concede that although the artist lacked intelligence, he definitely displayed talent. The tattoo was an exact replica of the symbol he'd examined on numerous flags and ceramic tiles left behind by the criminal cult at the scene of their crimes against his interests.

Stepping back with aplomb, he waved the captives off with his hand. They were immediately hustled away toward the slave quarters to be evaluated for suitable placement prior to beginning lives of servitude—just another pair of luckless innocents to disappear into one or another of the many diverse enterprises encompassing the Keeper's far-reaching entrepreneurial interests. Turning toward the alcove, he gestured to his guards, summoning the waiting trader into his presence.

The fawning bounty hunter came shuffling forward, half bowing and looking about the vast room in wonder, while doing his best to avoid Chen's piercing gaze. He had never before met the Keeper, or been to his palace, and was authentically awed to be granted an audience with the most powerful personage in the New World.

"What is your name, trader?" Chen asked kindly, looking him over in masked disgust.

"Lyman, Your Excellency, Lyman Klooj, at your service." He attempted a gracious bow, but nearly lost his balance, being somewhat tipsy from the strong drink he had hastily consumed in a last-ditch effort to counteract his fraying nerves.

"Well done on capturing this pair of dangerous criminals!" Chen praised, at which the man looked up and smiled into the Keeper's face. "How exactly did you manage it, if you don't mind my asking?" Chen waited expectantly for the answer, already knowing that whatever this sodden miscreant brought forth from his sewer hole of a mouth would be a ridiculous, bold-faced lie.

A week earlier, Chen had received word, via carrier pigeon, that two more Sisterhood witches had been captured, in addition to the pair already en route via ship from the north. The trader responsible for this worthy act would be arriving with the criminals in a couple of days to collect the two-thousand-credit bounty. A day later, a curious message arrived from an informant, casting doubt upon the authenticity of the bounty hunter's claims. Chen immediately dispatched a low-profile fact-finding team that included one of his most accomplished interrogators to the scene to delicately inquire about the matter in order to clarify the facts in the case. What they discovered was quite illuminating and Chen couldn't wait to meet the unwitting buffoon responsible for the blatantly transparent ruse.

Klooj's mind raced as he gauged Chen's reaction, relieved to see that he had apparently accepted the tattoos as genuine. His partner in crime, a misshapen dwarf named Brak, was a gifted ink artist who came up with the scheme some weeks ago, promising Klooj half the bounty if he would simply transport the captives north and collect the reward. Bad luck for the two young women who were simple working girls—bar maids kidnapped from a flop house outside of Cato City in the seedy South Bay district.

"Well, ya see, your Worthiness—" Klooj cleared his throat. "I sort a found out, through the grapevine, that two suspicious young females was travelin' alone through the territory where I stay, and so I got me some boys together, and we tracked 'em down, surroundin' 'em in a remote fishing village where we trapped 'em in a bathhouse along the Coast Road down south aways." He waved his arm in the general direction of the famous thoroughfare. "They put up quite a fight, yes sir, you can tell it by their bruises and all, and what with their fancy warrior training and such, but me'n the boys—" Klooj narrowed his eyes and lowered his voice dramatically at this point in his carefully practiced narrative, "—we knows a thing or two about danger ourselves." He nodded his head slowly and smiled, "and so we handily overpowered 'em after a bit of a fuss."

Klooj drew himself up, puffing out his chest and continued. "Well, we could see by their tats that they was, indeed, two of them ones with the rewards on their heads, and so we kept 'em locked up until we could arrange to deliver 'em here."

Klooj glanced up at the Keeper and smiled, wiping beads of sweat from his brow with the back of his filthy sleeve, a sense of relief washing over him as he ended his wildly embellished tale. Lowering his eyes, he waited, trying not to fidget and praying for Chen to hurry up and pay him so he could get the hell out of here and back to his regular life. *Just need to collect my credits and be gone,* he reassured himself, fighting the dizziness from the drink and the stress caused by his ruse, his heart palpitating wildly in his chest from the effort. He smiled again, softening his eyes in his best "kindly old gentleman" expression, inwardly repeating the mantra that everything was going to work out, and not to worry.

"Well done, indeed!" the Keeper extolled. "You have performed a great service to me, for which I am eternally grateful. Now, Trader Klooj, allow me to present you with *your* reward."

Chen clapped his hands and a pair of liveried male servants instantly appeared from the wings, placing an intricately engraved wood-and-copper chest on a low side table. The Keeper gestured for Klooj to open it and the man stepped forward, fingers clumsily undoing the clasp. Lifting the lid, his smile froze and he went chalk-white as the blood drained from his face. Inside the chest was Brak's head with his eyes plucked out and replaced with what appeared to be his testicles—his severed penis dangling from bloodied lips stitched tightly around it with thick, black sewing thread. Klooj dropped to his knees in horror as the Keeper approached.

"Ignorant dung eater!" Chen screamed, his face purple with malevolent rage, "You thought you could trick *me*?" His voice reached a shrieking crescendo as he kicked the terrified man in the groin.

"Thought you were bold enough to come into *my* house and cheat *me?* Worthless turd licker!"

He aimed a blow at the prevaricator's fat head and landed a kick against his ear.

"Now you will suffer like your shriveled midget accomplice here, and the screams of your torment will serve as a worthy deterrent to anyone foolish enough to attempt to outsmart me!"

Chen's guards grabbed the man by the arms as he lay collapsed in a blubbering heap, and dragged him sobbing from the room. As he went, the stricken grifter let out several high-pitched shrieks and began to babble on about how it had not been his idea, that that he was only the errand boy, and that he didn't realize that anything was amiss—it all being "just a terrible, regrettable misunderstanding…"

But his dramatics were of no use. Klooj was doomed and he knew it, convinced that the final moments of his earthly existence would be excruciatingly painful beyond all description. And although his recent perception of reality had been heavily obscured by delusions of grandeur and had missed the mark altogether regarding the outcome of his trade, this time, unfortunately for him, his estimation of his immediate future was remarkably accurate.

*　*　*

HOW MUCH DID one person need? The elderly Asian gentleman sat at his workstation posing the rhetorical question to himself. *How much is enough?* Hung Su quietly closed the ledger and stood up, placing the slender, leather-bound volume on the bookcase behind him where hundreds of similar ledgers lined the surrounding shelves, identical, but for the color coding and unique Roman numerals imprinted on each volume's spine.

Turning back around, he placed his fountain pen into the half-filled inkwell built into the top of his Spartan mahogany desk and dropped a freshly penned, five-page financial report into a worn leather briefcase before making his way to the coat rack next to the exit to gather his things. Donning his warm cardigan against the chill night air, Su made a final visual survey of the round, high-ceilinged room—its windowless walls lined with bookshelves and its space outfitted with seven identical workstations.

Extinguishing the final oil lamp, he pressed lightly against the massive steel-alloy door that had been salvaged some years earlier from a commercial bank vault in a far-off city long since abandoned. Balanced on three industrial strength hinges, the door swung noiselessly open as he walked through it, and automatically closed behind him with a distinctive metallic clank. Spinning the large black dial on the outer surface of the door, first one way and then the other, Su sealed the repository until morning, when he would return again to open the archives, marking the beginning of another productive day.

At the end of the hall he turned, heading down the staircase to street level where he acknowledged the security detail awaiting him at the bottom. Turning east, they followed the cobblestones leading to the Keeper's private residence high in his nearby mansion, one guard three paces ahead and the other the same distance behind Su. It was an evening ritual that Su had carried out precisely at the same time each day for the past decade and a half. At the Keeper's standing request, Su always hand-delivered *the tally*, or more formally, the Gathering Daily Report, or GDR, which listed by category, every single transaction that had taken place in the previous 24 hours. This included not only *local* business affairs, but transactions involving Chen's interests across the entire region based on reports arriving throughout the day via carrier pigeon.

Although there were six junior bookkeepers employed by Royal Chen, as Chief Accountant, only Hung Su knew everything. In his head he had memorized more facts and details about the Keeper's possessions, wealth, and accounts receivables than all of his business partners, closest associates, and personal confidants combined—though it wasn't any wonder, since their relationship had existed nearly from the beginning. As a young man, Paul Chen had arrived here shortly after the Dark Times and began hoarding needful things to trade for future items of value, and Su—already well past middle age—had arrived shortly thereafter and began keeping ledgers of account for everything Paul Chen owned, or was owed, right down to the last tea cup and chopstick.

As Chen's wealth began to accumulate, Su became indispensable, freeing Chen's attention to concentrate on increasing his holdings and consolidating his gains. Through the years, Su had watched young Paul Chen gradually morph into *Royal Chen, Keeper of the Gathering* to become one of the most well known and respected architects of the post End War society—achieving near legendary status among the far-flung population. Chen's public persona was one of refinement and civility, a benevolent *champion of the people* who provided an economic framework designed to enhance everyone's quality of life.

Residents from communities located up and down the coast, and many farther inland, made the Moontide Festival pilgrimage as often as they could, affectionately referring to Royal Chen as the *Keeper of the New Civilization* for hosting the festivities on *neutral* ground. The highly popular Moontide Festivals coincided with the full moon and lasted three days. Day One was a day of preparation and preliminary activities, Day Two was the Festival itself, and Day Three a winding down and recuperation day marked by the striking of tents and the return home of contented folks. Because the festivals revolved around moon cycles, there were thirteen events per year, not twelve as one would expect if based on Gregorian calendar months.

Throughout the three-day events, attendees enjoyed a myriad of enjoyable entertainment, everything from musical and theatrical presentations on twelve stages throughout the venue, drumming circles, dancing, various types of participatory gaming and contests, as well as the very popular horse races and professional fights in the arena. Of course, all forms of alcohol and various other potent psyche-altering substances were generally available, either through officially sanctioned outlets or via the less regulated black market distributors.

Su found it humorous that smugglers and dealers who thought they were operating outside the law were actually distributing Chen's products without realizing it. True black marketeers and anyone else who bypassed the standard channels by representing a financial network that excluded Royal Chen were quickly ferreted out and eliminated by Gathering Security Chief, Von Hammer's ruthless intelligence apparatus.

Over the years, a bustling community had grown up around the Gathering's shadowed walls, supporting a year-round population of a couple thousand souls, mostly shopkeepers, food venders, attendants, service personnel, and their families. During the three-day Moontide events, the population swelled to ten thousand or more and the venue stayed open 24 hours a day. The rules of the Gathering were few and irrevocable: no weapons, no fighting, and no trading outside the proper channels, period. Those caught doing any of the above risked being banned from participation for life. Above all, the Keeper required his tribute, his single percentage of each transaction, for that was the way it was ordained and there could be no getting around it.

Everyone was welcome to trade their goods and services without regard to age, gender, ethnicity, sexual orientation, political persuasion, or religious affiliation—free to enjoy the unique sense of community and belonging for which the ever-evolving venue was known. Chen's creation was a clearinghouse, providing the remnants of humanity with more than merely a functional economic framework in which to barter and conduct business. More importantly, it served as a transformational cultural phenomenon, allowing people to come together to meet and mingle as they partook of the fruits of their collective labors. While the population admired Royal Chen's seemingly altruistic inclinations, Hung Su understood that the Keeper's apparent benevolence was merely a pragmatic solution contrived in order to fulfill his insatiable appetite for wealth. Royal Chen didn't "care" about the people, but his greedy soul simply understood that the attendees would trade more if they felt positive about their relationship with the Gathering and it's founder.

Prior to its establishment, individuals and communities were forced to go it alone, hoping to randomly come across others with whom to trade who happened to possess the things they needed, but could not provide for themselves. Over the years, nearly everyone in the region had come to rely on the Gathering for the many valuable items that were unobtainable elsewhere, things they couldn't now imagine living without. The fact that Royal Chen had personally conceived, founded, established, expanded, and operated the enterprise—extracting just a single percentage of every transaction for his trouble—was universally accepted as a small price to pay for the overwhelmingly positive benefits that his creation offered.

For one thing, within its high stone walls people felt safe, which, in this day and age, was a rarity. From the beginning, it was deemed neutral territory—neither traders or attendees were allowed to possess weapons inside the perimeter. Within its boundaries, Chen's security forces kept the peace, allowing traders and attendees to go about their business without fear of being robbed, or worse. In fact, during the

Gathering's entire history there had never been a single murder or robbery committed on the premises.

Once, several years back, a small band of outlaws had attempted to infiltrate the crowds with a plan to rob Chen's treasury of its kiln-fired discs. When Von Hammer, chief of Gathering Security had learned of the scheme, he arrested the entire group and had them stripped, and hung upside down from the rafters of the arena during the festival's popular gladiatorial event, after which they were fed alive to Chen's giant dogs. Since then, nothing had disturbed the orderly exchange of goods and services, except perhaps a rowdy patron or two guilty of imbibing a bit too much alcohol—a readily forgivable offense as long as no one ended up seriously hurt as a result. Chronic troublemakers unable to control their own excesses ended up outside the walls—permanently.

Accommodations for overnight guests were numerous and varied. There were rooms for rent in the alcoves above the ground-level stalls and shops, and camping was allowed in a large field next to the arena where occasional horse races were held. Here visitors erected tents and makeshift temporary dwellings during mild-weather months. Winter brought its own unique set of challenges, but the coastal weather rarely dumped much snow west of the Cascades, and if it did, it was usually only enough to dust the earth, making it seem appropriately holiday-esque.

Trading tended to slack off during the colder months, especially after the frenzied activities of the fall harvest concluded, with many communities settling in for the season, enjoying their stockpiled provisions exchanged during the autumnal abundance. Through the years, even during really bad weather, the gates remained open daily for everyday trading—the basic philosophy being that traders and buyers would always have access to the Gathering no matter what.

Nearing Chen's mansion, Su looked to the eastern horizon for the moon and felt a slight constriction in his chest, his anxiety level beginning to rise a bit, though he purposefully kept any evidence of his concern from his face. With the start of the three-day Moontide Festival commencing in the morning, he anticipated a sharp increase of frenzied activity in the office, generating greater than usual stress among the six junior accountants with whom he shared the modest space. Subconsciously adding to his concern, he had just today become aware of the rumored imminent arrival of Venerable Wu within the next day or so.

The Bay Area strongman's longstanding plans for replacing Royal Chen on the throne of the Gathering were nearing fruition and Su found himself feeling somewhat exposed and vulnerable—trapped in the middle. Several years back, he had been approached by Wu through an intermediary, who offered him a generous—though necessarily surreptitious—employment opportunity. Although he was morally opposed to the concept of disloyalty to one's employer, Su was ultimately a realist and considered it expeditious to cover all potential eventualities. Thus he had ended up agreeing to periodically provide copies of Chen's top secret financial reports to Wu. Now that the end of Chen's reign was drawing nigh, Su hoped his longtime cooperation would pay off and that he would be allowed to retain his auspicious position at the top of the accounting heap.

Arriving at the Keeper's residence, Su was ushered into a magnificent, book-lined study where Chen sat at an ornate, Louis XIV-period desk. With lowered eyes and a nearly imperceptible bow, Su placed the summary report directly into Royal Chen's waiting hands, and, without a word passing between them, turned and exited the room, escorted as always by his security detail.

Exhaling in relief, Su made a beeline for his favorite pleasure parlor where one of the expert young goddesses there would work her magic on his old stiff joints with her marvelously trained hands. Su tried not to think about the duplicate copy of the very report he had just handed to Chen secreted away inside the false bottom of his briefcase. As always, sometime during his massage visit the report would be removed, though Su never actually saw anyone take it. That was fine with him, because as far as Su was concerned, the less he knew about the sinister machinations of the seamy world of espionage, the safer he would be.

CHAPTER EIGHTEEN

WHIRLWIND

IN THE DEEPENING dusk just after sunset, two armed men waited at the base of the stone perimeter for the exact right moment to infiltrate the inner sanctum of the Gathering proper. Posted as the lookout, Hunter scanned the shadows for guards as Skye tossed a coiled rope over the wall, pulling back until the padded grappling hook caught the top cap's lip and held. Climbing quickly up and over, Skye waited for Hunter to join him before dropping to an open balcony and scaling the adjacent rooftop to rapidly rappel down the other side.

Beneath ghostly wisps of scattered clouds drifting raggedly across the star-pocked heavens, Hunter dropped lightly to the ground beside his shaman friend and the pair made their way cautiously along a shadowed footpath between close-packed buildings. As they had anticipated, the streets were deserted, the crowds having flocked to the sports arena for the popular tournaments in full swing there. Seeking a particular set of stairs leading to the basement level of the complex, they bypassed several shadowed openings until finally locating the one they were looking for.

Gingerly descending the narrow stone steps, Hunter welcomed the return of his equilibrium, relieved to be back on solid ground after suffering through the voyage plagued by a debilitating motion sickness he had no possible way of anticipating, having never before been to sea. Hours earlier, their four-man rescue team had split up, with Lars shuttling Hunter and Skye to a deserted beach a few miles north of the Gathering in the tender, and subsequently dropping Red and Dan further on down the coast below the Gathering so as to have them appear to arrive at the festival from some place down south.

As Hunter and Skye slipped over the wall and into the auction facilities, their compatriots Red and Dan had already blended in with the milling crowds of regular attendees, ready to respond as needed during the rescue should Hunter and Skye be successful in locating and liberating their loved ones. If everything went as planned, they would all rendezvous down at the harbor before first light where Lars would be standing by in *Windsong* to facilitate their timely getaway.

Locating the site of the "secret" auction had not been very difficult. Suffice it to say that at the Gathering, anything was available for the right price, and it didn't take much to loosen the tongue of a pub patron already in his cups to uncover the information that Hunter and Skye sought. At the bottom of the stairway the door was locked, but Hunter made quick work of the mechanism with his blade and they entered a flagstone hallway. Following it to the end, they made a series of left and right turns until finally coming to the empty auction hall where they entered a broom closet beneath the stairs to await the evening's activities.

* * *

TWO HOURS LATER, crouched in the cramped confines of the dark storage space, Hunter and Skye peered through cracks between the boards, expectantly awaiting the arrival of Anna, Lily and River. The high-ceilinged auction chamber was rapidly filling up with the usual jovial slave-auction crowd, who pleasantly greeted one another as they mingled, enjoying complimentary wine and spirits. The odor of tobacco smoke mixed with the distinctive musky aroma of burning cannabis drifted in the air.

From their vantage point beneath the stairs, the watchers could see only a portion of the raised auction stage at the far end of the room. Scanning the area visible through the cracks, they noted the intimidating arrival of more than a dozen heavily armed security guards posted strategically throughout the room and ringing the raised stage.

On the opposite side of the room, a uniformed officer was on hand to inspect the facility to ensure the safety of the Keeper, should the Gathering's founder decide to make one of his unscheduled appearances at tonight's event. A former marine-turned-mercenary, Von Hammer had worked his way up to eventually become commander of Royal Chen's personal guard. Five years ago he was promoted to Chief of Gathering Security. A physically intimidating figure, Von Hammer was six-foot-six, weighed two-fifty, and was smothered in muscles. He wore his spiked hair in a six-inch Mohawk dyed bright red with the sides shaved, and dressed in chain mail and brown leather with a metal breastplate and tall riding boots. The curved scimitar on his belt was one of his preferred weapons for close-quarters work, though of late he'd had very little cause to withdraw it from its gilded scabbard.

In appraising the man, Hunter judged correctly that he was someone high up in Royal Chen's chain of command. Noting the other's scimitar, Hunter wished for a longer blade of his own; his fighting knife, though handy in a clinch, was not a great match up against an opponent with a full-length sword. Due to the cramped conditions in which he knew he would find himself, Hunter had relinquished his own primary weapon—his trusty crossbow—leaving it aboard *Windsong* with Lars. He did, however, take comfort in the last-minute offering received from the sailing vessel's captain—a full framed .45 calibre Glock 21 which felt a bit awkward in the bulky holster at his side, but would no doubt come in handy should things happen to turn sour in the crowded confines of the auction.

Moving out of Hunter's field of view, Von Hammer continued on around the room inspecting every square inch of the facility, his disciplined mind attuned for any sign of the unusual, the abnormal, or the out-of-place. Disquieting information had been circulating lately—trouble was brewing between a couple of the major landholders—the source of the bad blood between them: a woman, of course. Their feud was no secret, having festered for several years now, but was reportedly approaching the boiling point.

Rumor had it that one was plotting the other's demise, though no hard evidence had yet come to light to prove it one way or the other. Proof would have allowed Von Hammer to step in and prevent something stupid from happening that had the potential of disrupting the flow of commodities, and thus the profits of his employer, the Keeper. Since both landholders sponsored teams competing in tonight's tournaments, the outcome could provide the tipping point, depending on how things turned out.

Compared to Von Hammer's other worries, their petty feud was child's play. Much more serious trouble was brewing down south where the self-styled anarchist calling himself Madsen the Just continued his depredations, targeting only Royal Chen's caravans, and seemingly at will. His well-planned and executed campaign of terror was creating actual scarcities in the commodities markets, infuriating Royal Chen, who had become a raving lunatic on the subject of "Madman Madsen." Like a phantom, the anarchist was damaging Chen's interests and miraculously getting away with it week-after-week.

Modeling himself after the renowned English outlaw, Robin Hood, the brash bandit had been very successful at liberating valuables from the richest man in the land and dispensing them to the poor. Madsen and his band of sanctimonious renegades enjoyed the favor of the commoners, who protected them, making it nearly impossible for Von Hammer to gain hard intelligence regarding the whereabouts of their base camp or any other vital operational information that might help the security chief bring them to justice.

And if that situation wasn't troubling enough, those ball-busting witch lesbians of the Sisterhood Alliance had really turned up the heat of late, collapsing entire networks of brothels and even taking out an occasional forced-labor camp with their devastating raids. They, too, seemed to enjoy the admiration of the people, especially among women and children, though many men supported them as well. It frustrated Von Hammer that no real progress to speak of had been made in his investigation of their outlawed organization.

Needless to say, the ongoing Madsen and Sisterhood crises were creating a major security situation that threatened to derail his career should they be allowed to continue much longer. Von Hammer was counting on his upcoming interrogation of the two captured witches brought in from the north on the trawler to provide his first real break in the Sisterhood case. He would use the information they provided to coordinate a massive attack on their hidden stronghold secreted away somewhere down south in the Redwood Empire.

He had already negotiated a deal with Coleman Black to provide his three-hundred man *Road Defense Force* cavalry in support of his campaign and was looking forward to the day he could burn the elusive Wolfhaven sanctuary to the ground. Black and Von Hammer were already well acquainted, having ridden together in Conrad's Raiders during the Southwest Border Disputes some years back, prior to moving west and taking up separate careers on the coast.

The thousand-credit bounty Von Hammer had advised Chen to institute against the Sisterhood was already paying off, and he planned to suggest the same type of incentive regarding Madsen and his merry men. Von Hammer found it somewhat ironic that many of those who had ridden with him and Black in the Raiders were now rumored to be riding with Madsen. He pondered what it would be like to look an old comrade in the eye while burying his blade deep in the unlucky bastard's heart. Actually, Von Hammer could care less who died, as long as he was being handsomely compensated for it.

Continuing his inspection of the auction room, he passed a closet door and casually tried the knob, but found it locked and moved on. Inside the cramped room, Hunter and Skye crouched frozen in place. With only a thin wooden wall separating them from the auction chamber, they watched Von Hammer approach their position and stop not six inches from their hideaway. The two remained absolutely still, barely daring to breathe, knowing that one small sound— even a suppressed cough or sneeze—could spell disaster, potentially dooming their rescue plan to failure.

Standing with his back to the dividing wall, Von Hammer scanned the crowd, his neck not six inches from Hunter's face. With broad shoulders, powerful arms, and the thick, muscular legs of a world-class athlete, the security chief was relaxed, yet poised, ready to pounce on any potentially troublesome situation. Trained in the killing arts since boyhood and quick to strike without hesitation, Von Hammer took his responsibilities very seriously. He had learned through experience over the years, that anything could happen anywhere at any time, and the possibility of an *incident* occurring during the heated bidding of a slave auction like this one was high, especially if there were some particularly desirable offerings on the block as was rumored to be the case tonight.

* * *

HIGH ABOVE THESE activities, unnoticed in the dead airspace between the first and second floors, Elise Planchet lay prone on the dusty rafters, watching the events unfold beneath her through the slightly angled fins of an aluminum ceiling vent. She and Jessi had crept in earlier with the help of the women they had met on the train who had provided them with local contacts and information. With their help, they had moved quietly into position hours before the room began filling up beneath them.

Balancing on the wooden joists, Elise wriggled into place just above and slightly behind the stage. A commotion arose at the near end of the hall—just behind her line of sight—and a hushed silence filled the room. She could hear the sound of shuffling footsteps as the audience began to murmur, softly at first, but gaining steadily in volume, until the whole place was abuzz with excitement.

In the cramped closet beneath the stairs, Hunter and Skye watched as the unlucky ones filed in through the far doors, miserable souls who had been caught out alone, or otherwise ambushed and ripped from their loved ones by the most vile of all creatures—*slavers*. The pitiful beings now entering the hall to be sold to the highest bidder hailed from all corners of the region, from as far off as Old Colorado and the high deserts, to north and south along the Pacific coast. The Afterworld was certainly no picnic, even for strong, fleet men-of-war, but for unaccompanied women, the very young, or the old and feeble, the new reality beyond the confines of one's home community could prove to be brutal—a landscape of potential terror and bondage from which no one was entirely exempt.

Nine out of ten communities were enclosed by high walls boasting robust gates that remained locked and heavily guarded after dusk. Their purpose was the same as in ages past: when lawlessness ruled the land and ordinary folks were forced to fend for themselves the barriers were there to protect life and property, and to keep out the rabble or worse.

Even traveling on the legendary Coast Road that connected dozens of towns and villages along its winding way, was becoming riskier than before. Ditches beside the cracked and jumbled thoroughfare hosted shallow, unmarked graves, bleak reminders of the growing danger.

Although the world-at-large was predominately populated by hard-working, well-intentioned individuals of integrity, the number of unsavory characters more than willing to earn a living by trading in human flesh was on the rise. It seemed more so in recent weeks, with young women disappearing at a frightening rate. Venturing out without an armed escort, even in once safe locales, was no longer advised.

Had Hunter known the extent of the slaving problem, he would never have come west. He couldn't really blame Skye, who, on the voyage south had broached the subject of the dramatic increase in kidnappings, confiding in him that with no previous attacks anywhere near the vicinity of his village, he had no reason to be concerned. Nevertheless, Hunter felt betrayed, not by anyone in particular, but by the pathetic remnants of his race who had obviously learned nothing from the lessons of the End War.

Hunter promised himself that upon completion of his rescue mission here, he and Elise would discuss returning home to Old Wyoming where their only real enemies were fur-bearing carnivores and the sometimes sudden, dramatic changes in weather. There was absolutely no doubt remaining in Hunter's mind that his species, though possessing the potential to exist in harmony and balance, was irreversibly doomed, cursed by the refusal of its members to rise above their base instincts. While the lemmings headed for the cliff,

Hunter preferred to return to the salvation and purity of the wilds, but first he would see this task through to completion.

* * *

PEERING THROUGH THE louvers, Elise's heart skipped a beat when she caught a glimpse of Anna and the Ravencloud twins among the captives below. Dressed in fine silks with their hair pinned up in attractive coiffures and faces painted like dramatic actresses from some ancient theatrical troupe, she barely recognized them. Wishing somehow that this was all just a bad dream—Elise would make any necessary sacrifice to wake up with everyone safe back home with their loved ones.

Witnessing the fear and hopelessness in the guarded faces of the conquered stirred a rage within Elise that had been simmering since the ambush. She had tried not to give in to it, knowing that the negative energy wasn't healthy for the baby—her developing child was nearing fifteen weeks old now and getting stronger every day. Barely besting her unruly emotions, Elise focused on the task at hand, determined to figure out a way to end this nightmare of broken dreams.

The buzz in the room increased sharply as the bidding began, the auctioneer barking out numbers as the audience set the pace with Anna as their prize. The amount in credits climbed rapidly until only three buyers remained in the bidding. A swarthy man with a balding head and gray-white beard raised his hand again, determined to add the blonde to his personal harem. He co-owned a dozen brothels spread liberally up and down the Coast Road—in which Royal Chen secretly held a majority stake—and was always in need of fresh girls, but this one was different; she didn't cower like the rest which he found intriguing.

After the brothel owner won the bid, Elise watched Anna being led away as Skye's sisters were brought to the stage—nineteen-year-old identical twins with flawless complexions and long, shiny, jet-black hair. As the oohs and aahs erupted from the crowd, Elise sensed the excitement building down below.

"To be sold together..." announced the auctioneer over the escalating murmurs in the room. "Every man's fantasy—a perfectly matched pair to satisfy their master's every whim."

As the bidding frenzy began, Elise felt sick to her stomach and was on the verge of becoming ill when the bidding suddenly stopped. Something had erupted at the far side of the room just beyond her line of sight. Amid panicked cries of alarm and the barking of a dog, someone was shouting orders. The tension below felt nearly palpable as the crowd stood frozen in place.

Frustrated by her limited view, Elise glanced over at Jessi who was glued to her vent and trying to assess the situation as well, but to no avail. Catching a glimpse of someone moving across the stage, Elise watched the auctioneer suddenly fly off into the crowd, ejected by someone beyond her line of sight. Almost immediately, a deafening gunshot rang out, startling her, and the crowd bolted, scattering for cover in a spontaneous display of frantic pandemonium.

* * *

DOWN BELOW IN the cramped closet beneath the stairs, Hunter and Skye had watched and waited with growing concern and frustration as Anna was brought forward to be auctioned off. When the bidding began, they glanced at each other, both knowing that with so many armed guards in the room, this was not the time to emerge from their hiding place. At least now they were certain that their women were actually on the premises, and they could wait until the auction was finished and the room had cleared out before tracking them down. Both were confident in their ability to affect a rescue during the wee hours before dawn when their chances of success would be much higher.

When River and Lily Ravencloud took the stage, something bizarre occurred that no one could have possibly foreseen. A workman entered the back of the room from upstairs and headed straight for the closet. When he tried the doorknob, he found that it wouldn't budge, so he pulled harder until the knob popped off in his hands. He thought it strange for the door to stick shut, as it had no locking mechanism on it that he knew of. Approaching one of the nearby guards, he asked if he would mind prying the stuck door open with his blade. The workman had been sent down here to collect a toolbox for his foreman who was working on some plumbing for one of the major stallholders.

Just as the frenzied bidding reached a crescendo, the guard inserted his large dagger between the door and the frame and pried with all his might, splintering the wood of the jamb in the process. By this time, Von Hammer had become interested in what was going on and walked over to interrogate the worker. Learning of his desire to gain access to the closet, he smiled and took out his own favorite tool—

one he had picked up during his stint with the Raiders, and from which he had derived his moniker which meant, 'of the hammer.' He approached the stuck door with his carpenter's hatchet in his hand—a combination hammerhead and notched hatchet blade.

After informing the worker that it would be the man's responsibility to fix any damage he might inflict in opening the door, Von Hammer stood with legs shoulder-width apart and raised his hand above his head to take a swing. Without warning, the door burst open and both Skye and Hunter came charging out, blade and pistol drawn, crashing fully into the guards and knocking them to the ground. They continued moving forward, racing through the crowd to the side of the stage where the shocked Ravencloud twins stood in stunned disbelief.

Leaping to the platform, Hunter grabbed the auctioneer with one hand and hurled him from the stage into the frozen crowd below. Skye gathered his sisters and the four began moving backward toward the rear of the stage as the guards quickly formed up in front to prevent their escape. With Von Hammer barking orders, his men surged forward in a flying V attack, swords drawn and blades glistening in the bright lamplight. Through the front entranceway, a dog handler suddenly appeared, his huge mastiff-wolfhound mix straining against its thick leather leash. Von Hammer ordered him to release the beast and the ferocious animal leapt forward, huge jaws snapping the air and racing straight for the retreating heroes.

The hollow-point bullet from Hunter's .45 entered through the man-eater's left eye, peeling back his skull and slamming him instantly to the floor where he lay sprawled out with his long legs crumpled awkwardly beneath him. At the sound and sight of the gunfire, the crowd scattered in panic, running helter-skelter through the room, pushing and trampling one another in their haste to escape the madness of the situation.

The unexpected gunshot caused Von Hammer's forces to hesitate—armed as they were with mere blades—and they looked toward him for guidance, but he was nowhere to be seen. With the sound of a scuffle at the back door, Von Hammer suddenly reappeared clutching Anna by her hair, his bright curved scimitar pressed up against her throat. He had watched the attractive trio as they entered the room together earlier and had perceived their obvious care and concern for one another when the bidding for Anna had first started. Taking a chance that his intuition was correct, he'd made a split-second decision and grabbed Anna as a hostage, threatening the two armed renegades with her death unless they immediately surrendered.

"Drop your weapons, or she dies! Now—or I finish her!"

Von Hammer's malice and determination to carry out his threat bore into the rescuers' eyes, offering them little choice but to give up their weapons. Skye dropped his blade and Hunter placed his pistol on the deck of the stage as the guards swarmed, wrestling them to the floor and binding them with ropes.

Unaware of the exact circumstances of the drama unfolding below, Elise anguished over her limited visibility when a squad of soldiers came into view directly beneath her position, with two tightly bound prisoners jostled between them. Though she could only see the tops of their heads, something about them seemed familiar. As one of the prisoners suddenly jerked his head free and looked up, she found herself staring straight into the eyes of Skye Ravencloud!

Nearly losing her balance from surprise, Elise almost fell forward through the ceiling, but caught herself at the last moment—her mind reeling from the realization that the two captives being hustled from the room were Hunter and Skye. Just when it had seemed to Elise that the situation couldn't get any worse—the men who had traveled all this way to save Anna and the twins—the two men she and Anna loved most in this world—were now in the hands of Royal Chen's security forces and on their way to certain torture and death.

CHAPTER NINETEEN

BURIED ALIVE

HUNTER LAY FACEDOWN on the cold stone floor, his hands and feet securely bound, the rough cloth blindfold wrapped tightly around his head effectively blocking his vision. Off to his right he could hear Skye's steady breathing as he lay nearby, as helpless as Hunter; both men still alive only because Royal Chen had a more titillating plan for their demise—something special for the restless crowd. Both would agree that theirs was not the most desirable predicament in which to find themselves.

They awaited their fates in a small, deserted anteroom adjacent to a large chamber filled with dignitaries and ringed by a contingent of Royal Chen's personal bodyguard. From a nearby open window came the sound of baying dogs and the roar of the crowd's approval from the arena below, apparently pleased with whatever barbaric spectacle they were witnessing at the moment. Hunter strained noiselessly against his leather bonds, his wrists chafed raw from the effort, in a vain attempt to create some space by which to extricate his tethered hands.

In the chamber beyond, surrounded by a court of fawning sycophants, Royal Chen stood before two half-dressed women also hogtied and facedown on the flagstones—recent captures by bounty hunters from the north who were delivered to the Gathering just in time for the Moontide festivities. He stood above them gloating, pleased at the prospect of the example he would make of them as the crowning glory of the evening's entertainment. Stroking his thin Fu Manchu mustache, he carefully looked them over, noting the matching indigo tattoos on their backs: a winged triangle within a circle, with an all-seeing eye in the center above an inverted cross.

Witches, Chen intoned to himself. *Dangerous, trouble-making witches from the hated Sisterhood coven. How they had harried him these past few years, attacking his interests at will—and growing bolder all the time. Nothing he had tried so far had even come close to deterring them from their destructive course; nothing until now. His newly announced thousand-credit bounty had already begun to bear fruit. These two were but the first of many such criminals that he looked forward to meeting in the very near future. But, what a pity,* he reflected, genuinely disappointed to have to destroy them—*such beauty and strength wasted on their doomed little war against him, all due to their own flawed, self-deluding philosophy.*

Since the early days immediately following the nuclear winter, no-one had dared to stand up to Royal Chen. Over the years, his power and influence had grown exponentially, stretching across the land and directly affecting the lives of nearly everyone in the region. As far east as Old Utah and Colorado, north to British Columbia and south to California, everyone knew of him and trembled... *and why shouldn't they?* Royal Chen's wealth and power were legendary, along with his reputation for ruthlessly demanding respect—the rumors whispered of the extraordinary lengths to which he would go to punish anyone who dared challenge his authority.

The occasional body rotting in a crow cage suspended from a tree or bridge, or the anguished cries of a crucified violator begging for mercy from a makeshift cross along the Coast Road drove home the message without requiring long speeches or explanations: DO NOT CHALLENGE ROYAL CHEN! And most everyone heeded the unspoken warning. The Keeper's ruling philosophy was derived from his study of three of the most infamous and successful conquerers of the Old World: Alexander the Great, Attila the Hun, and Genghis Khan. All were brilliant visionaries and military strategists as well as ruthless adversaries, who enthusiastically ground their enemies into dust without a moment's hesitation or remorse.

While Chen idolized the accomplishments of these ancient rulers, his preferred method of population control was financial manipulation rather than military conquest. With the majority of the regional populace trading for goods and services at the Gathering, he was already receiving a percentage of every transaction, and by further converting valuables such as gold, silver, and precious gems into *chens*, he gained an additional advantage in all business dealings.

The profit he realized from his sponsored gambling activities alone—not to mention the brothels, the caravans, the loaning of cash at exorbitant interest rates—was mind boggling. *The fact that he controlled the treasury and could mint more money at will made the entire financial system seem to him like an Old World board game.* Since childhood, Chen had dreamed of building an empire and running the world, and with each passing transaction, his dream became more real and his position more unshakable. However, there was a limit to his non-violent benevolence and anyone who directly attacked his interests soon found out they would pay the ultimate price for their folly. Otherwise, Chen believed that the masses would lose respect for him, and from his study of history he knew that along that path lay ruin.

The women lying prostrate before him were an abomination. In his world, females existed solely to serve men, to provide them comfort, pleasure and to bear them sons to follow in their father's footsteps. These witches who had dared reject their subservient station in life and who insisted upon directly participating in crimes against his empire and interests, would have to *burn*. Their stakes were already in place on a specially-built platform above the arena with plenty of dry kindling and firewood stacked in neatly tied bundles nearby.

Having finished with his inspection of the condemned, Chen nodded to Von Hammer, his ruthless security chief who, only this evening, had discovered a pair of armed infiltrators that had gained unauthorized access to the slave auction. The two men had been captured during a failed attempt to rescue some women who were scheduled to be sold. Von Hammer barked an order and four guards half-carried, half-dragged the two witches to his subterranean interrogation chamber.

In the anteroom next door, Hunter listened as Chen's entourage began to disperse, the sound of their receding footfalls growing fainter. Suddenly, the near doors opened and he heard two booted pairs of footsteps enter. The guards had returned with specific instructions from the Keeper: Take the male prisoners to the arena and throw them to the dogs as the next segment on the evening's entertainment roster.

The muscular guard assigned to Hunter was excited just thinking about it. Of all Moontide festivities, the punishment of the guilty segment was a special highlight, and tonight, a double witch burning was scheduled! The dog-pit segment, though, was undoubtably his favorite. Nothing aroused him as much as the thrill of watching unarmed wretches tossed into a circular pit containing a half dozen giant, starving canines, and to witness, with fascination, the humans' desperate fight for their lives. Although the outcome was inevitably the same, the guard enjoyed being witness to how inventive some could become in their life-death struggle against several 150-pound man-eaters. As he reached down to pick up the bound prisoner from the floor, he felt the sting of a flying insect on his neck.

As Hunter was roughly hauled to his feet, he thought he perceived an unusual puffing sound—like air forcefully expelled from a tube—shortly before his captor suddenly grunted and abruptly stiffened. Two seconds later the burly guard's grip dissolved as he collapsed to the floor in a heap, releasing Hunter as he fell. Almost simultaneously, the second guard gasped, surprised, and pitched heavily forward, his limp body sprawled partway across Skye's lower legs.

As the two bound and blindfolded men listened expectantly in silence, there came a faint shuffling from the back of the room and someone knelt down between them, deftly removing their blindfolds. Face down on his belly, Hunter was unable to make out who it was, but he detected the distinctive aroma of coffee and tobacco on the warm breath of the person leaning in close. Something about the man's presence seemed vaguely familiar and Hunter's mind raced to make the connection. Protruding from the side of the nearby downed guard's neck, Hunter noted a curious object similar to one he had seen a few years earlier...

For a fraction of a second—just at the perimeter of his peripheral vision—Hunter glimpsed the side of a brown man's fearsomely painted face, his long dreadlocks adorned by a colorful feather headdress, a strand of sharp jaguar claws circling his muscular neck. Tilting his adorned head, the savage man's gaze burned deeply into his eyes and suddenly Hunter remembered—the horse canyon killer! As his bonds were cut through, Hunter lay still, amazed and thankful for their mysterious rescuer's fortuitous timing. Then, as suddenly as he appeared, Dr. Constantine Sirocco was gone, having vanished through the doorway and back into the shadows of the darkened hallway.

Slowly rising to their feet, Hunter and Skye scanned the room, their silent benefactor nowhere to be seen. The antechamber was again empty, except for the two immobilized guards who appeared to be dead, but for the nearly imperceptible rising and falling of their chests. From a nearby bundle they hastily retrieved their weapons, and determined to affect a timely rescue of their own, proceeded carefully down the wide hallway, pursuing the echoing footfalls of Royal Chen's retreating retinue.

* * *

WITH THE CROWD cheering their favorite champions in the sports arena, the outer defenses were, for the most part, deserted. Each evening at dusk, the massive gates were locked and guarded as usual, but during the three-day festivities, the perimeter wall was sparsely tended by only a handful of disgruntled sentries who were displeased to be missing out on all of the excitement.

"This is crap!" Derek exclaimed aloud for the third time. The twenty-two-year-old rookie garrison guard spat out the words in frustration, but as he was alone, there was no one to acknowledge his protest. "Why is it that *I'm* always the one to get stuck with this duty while the others have all the fun?"

He was upset about pulling perimeter-wall night duty during the Moontide events *again*—for the third month in a row. His immediate superior, a tough sergeant named Olson, didn't appreciate Derek's hot shot, gung-ho attitude, most likely because Olson believed that it made him look bad. So the older man had singled Derek out, posting him as far away from the arena as possible during the festivities as punishment by sensory deprivation.

To Derek the posting was ludicrous—in the entire history of the Gathering there had never been a direct attack by anyone; especially in the twelve years since the tall perimeter wall was completed. With not one documented attempt to break into the Gathering, the chances of someone entering the grounds illegally tonight were next to nil. Pacing the cedar-planked walkway running along the inside of the wall, he surveyed the night, noting the torches at fifty-yard inter- vals along the perimeter, their flames dancing wildly in the stiff onshore winds of evening. In the distance, he heard the crashing of the surf against the rocky shoreline. Outlined by the throw of light from oil lamps lining the nearby docks he could make out the dark silhouettes of several ships an- chored out in the harbor, or tied up at the wharf. But with the full moon just rising above the coastal range to the east, the seaside portion of the boundary wall beneath him was smothered in darkness.

*   *   *

APPROACHING THEIR TARGET from the sea, Star led her Sisterhood Alliance against the enemy under cover of night. Cloaked and hooded in black, the six-hundred strong female force blended with the shadows as they maneuvered their agile boats the last fifty yards to the rocks at the base of the cliff. There, they assembled in teams and proceeded to scale the vertical escarpment. Glued to the wall like insects, they climbed effortlessly, seemingly unaffected by the pull of gravity, or the fear of falling to certain death far below. At the top of the cliff, they reassembled and fanned out, slip- ping invisibly past the roving dog patrols to gather again at the base of the wall, alerting neither the vicious canines, nor their deadly handlers.

The Gathering was located on a broad plateau overlook- ing a half-moon shaped bay where a modest river emptied into the sea forming a naturally protected harbor where docks and warehouses hugged the rocky beach. Here, the land rose steeply two-hundred feet to where Chen's mansion hugged the edge of the continent, before continuing on up to the top of the ridge. In the gradual incline between wharf and mansion, the higher the land rose, the more the sprawling settlement structures increased in number and density.

On the ocean side, the near-vertical cliffs above heavy surf crashing on the rocks below were considered an insurmountable barrier—formidable enough to dissuade even the most determined enemies from risking such a "suicidal" seaside approach. In taking advantage of this popular misconception, Star had chosen the seaside assault up the cliffs because the perimeter wall surrounding the complex was normally more heavily patrolled elsewhere, and the excellent physical conditioning of her lightweight fighters enabled them to execute the tricky climb with relative ease.

With all fighters accounted for and their wolven companions successfully hoisted up the cliff to the top, grappling hooks were tossed over the wall, their ropes pulled back until the leather-padded barbs caught the inside underlip of the wall's top cap. With the agility of an acrobat troupe, the fighters scaled the wall, step-by-step, hand-over-hand, until reaching the top.

Pausing on the top cap, scouts peered into the terraced lawns and gardens of the Keeper's magnificent estate—the secret guarded enclave of their most hated enemy. Scattered throughout the property, torches and lanterns flickered among footpaths and guard posts, casting eerie, animated shadows as the flames danced wildly in the wind. Rising from the center of a terraced plateau, Chen's three-story limestone chateau towered above the grounds, surrounded by a moat fed by a waterfall that cascaded down the mountain from above.

From her vantage point atop the wall, Star gazed out over the sprawling complex of buildings, walls, alleyways, and footpaths that formed the Gathering settlement. Pushing back the hood from her face, she drank in the moment with her companion Amaranth, at her side as always. Together they admired their army of silent warriors who lowered their wolven fighting partners and rappelled to the shadows below, preparing their minds and bodies for the coming battle. Among them was a newly met ally named Elise, who had arrived the previous day with young Jessi, Alena's daughter. Jessi had vouched for the newcomer, explaining how three of Elise's family had been kidnapped up north to be sold on the Gathering's auction block.

It was Jessi's message received two days ago alerting Star of the capture of her mother and Alibi that had sparked her decision to converge on the Gathering, something that Star had always considered might be necessary in the future, but she hadn't planned on ordering an assault until necessity had suddenly forced her hand. Star and Amaranth rappelled down to join the largest concentration of Sisterhood fighters in the history of the Alliance, assembled here in their enemy's stronghold to end Royal Chen's reign of terror once and for all.

Somewhere in the labyrinth beneath the complex, Star knew that two of her sisters were being held by evil men, probably suffering torture to force them to reveal the location of Wolfhaven and the plans and whereabouts of the Sisterhood Army. The captives faced execution simply for being members of her outlawed Alliance and Star felt the fa-

miliar anger rising within her breast. Her righteous wrath demanded justice and equality for anyone denied their human
rights in this dark and twisted world manipulated by tyrants.

Far from naive, Star understood that to the uninformed
masses, Royal Chen was considered to be a fine, upstand-
ing human being who, in raising his unique creation from
the ruins of the past, had provided a stabilizing influence
in their lives—an illuminating beacon, lighting the pathway
to a New Age. While they might be aware that Chen's justice was somewhat ruthless, most people believed that tough
times called for harsh solutions, and without a real government, no one was expected to coddle postwar sociopaths in
some namby-pamby reformatory prison system. Predators,
parasites, and other such conscienceless riff-raff who committed crimes without remorse could expect no mercy in return.

Chen was considered by those in the landed class to be
a true Renaissance Man, worthy of the respect and admiration of his fellows. To his many business partners throughout the region, he was fair and honest in his dealings with
them, but he was an acknowledged stickler, enforcing the
terms of their joint ventures to the letter. Those who kept
their agreements fared fine. Those who attempted to cheat
him, were short-lived. Flesh traders and others acquainted
with his darker side, respected him out of fear. While his
admirers considered him a visionary, others knew him as a
murdering dictator or worse—a cutthroat barbarian wrapped
in the flag of the Gathering—"The Last Civilized Marketplace On Earth."

The Keeper's sadistic appetites and habits were well
known to the Alliance—Star knew more about him than

she preferred to. The stories of his cruelty began surfacing through the grapevine several years back. Dark tales of a wealthy mystery man who enjoyed watching human beings suffer in extraordinary ways detailed the unspeakable atrocities he devised for his victims. Star shuddered, remembering several examples of his heinous crimes, and did her best to force the horrific images from her mind.

The use of his special breed of vicious canines was probably one of the most depraved aspects of his personality, though Chen had not originated the use of dogs to terrorize an enemy. Hernando de Soto, the Spanish conquistador commissioned during the 1500s to explore the New World of Cuba, Florida, and the southeastern United States, had bred and traveled with what some twentieth-century researchers described as mastiff-wolfhound mix "war dogs," that he used to intimidate native tribes into cooperation. Tossing naked, unarmed natives into a pit to be ripped apart and eaten alive by starving dogs was one of de Soto's favorite threats—a trick he had learned years earlier during his deployment in Panama under Balboa. Royal Chen had embraced the practice, making similar use of his specially-bred canines whenever he wished to impress the populace with his willingness to do whatever was necessary to protect his interests.

* * *

"THEY HAVE ESCAPED, Security Chief Von Hammer," the cowering officer in charge of prisoner security bowed his head, silently praying for a miracle of mercy, yet certain that no such grace would be forthcoming. Moments later, his spinning head flew halfway across the room, spewing streams of bright-red arterial blood, launched into orbit by the force of Von Hammer's wickedly curved blade. Wiping it clean on the dead man's tunic, he re-sheathed his weapon and barked an order to his suddenly promoted and newly appointed officer in charge of prisoner security to organize a search party to recapture the prisoners—with direct orders to speak to no one about this matter on pain of death, including the Keeper.

Von Hammer seethed as he headed down the hall to the stairs that led to the slave holding-chambers beneath the complex. He had a pretty good idea where the two escapees were headed and he planned to cut them down before they had a chance to cause him any more embarrassment. He clearly understood the ramifications of failing to nip this potentially career-ending catastrophe in the bud, and he was determined to do so, *well before* the Keeper ever knew what happened.

He would handle this annoyance personally and then get down to business with a strike against the Sisterhood's sanctuary. His crude but effective interrogation techniques had worked wonders on the captured Sisterhood witches, and he was looking forward to making a surprise visit to their redwood stronghold that he was certain they would never forget.

CHAPTER TWENTY

CRITICAL MASS

A S THE CROWD milled about the wide plaza that framed the raised arena ringed by guards, the master of ceremonies appeared on the center platform and gestured for quiet. The sporting events had just concluded and many in the crowd were standing around chatting or setting out to get something to eat or drink in anticipation of the next scheduled event. Crowding toward the stage, they looked expectantly at the speaker as he unrolled a parchment scroll and began to read:

"Fellow citizens and festival attendees! As you know, the surrounding region has been plagued by organized bands of criminals who prey upon the weak and vulnerable, taking what they want by force and leaving violated victims in their wake. Such lawlessness cannot be tolerated, and any civilized society must necessarily impose severe penalties for such behavior."

In response to his standard introduction to whatever particular punishments and executions would follow, several individuals yelled out their approval, while the rest of the crowd generally murmured words of agreement. People looked forward each moon to watch criminals be brought to justice, detesting those who made their already challenging everyday lives even more miserable.

"In order to combat this insidious plague, the Keeper has recently placed a significant bounty on the heads of such terrorists. Tonight two captured witches from the murderous Sisterhood coven shall be put to the torch for their crimes against humanity, including murder, robbery, and the disruption of business. Let all who witness the swift justice of the Keeper stand in awe!"

When he finished speaking, many in the crowd appeared stunned, completely taken by surprise by his words. While an isolated misogynist or two cheered the announcement, there were many more supporters of the Sisterhood among the crowd than not. The attendees, both male and female, began to loudly voice their disagreement with the execution order. Roaming guards scattered throughout the plaza sensed the crowd's unusual sudden change of mood and quickly made their way, in twos and threes, to the tunnel-like arched entranceways leading from the plaza.

*   *   *

IN HIS PRIVATE balcony above the arena, Royal Chen sat in his viewing box surrounded by a detachment of his personal bodyguard, and waited for the witches to be brought out. He was surprised by the negative reaction from the crowd, and rapidly became irritated by the catcalls rising from the plaza below. In all the history of his Gathering, where countless criminal punishments had been carried out during the Moontide Festivals Chen had never experienced anything like this. The public display of disrespect and disapproval of his judgment was offensive and unnerving. His bodyguards, too, sensed the changing mood, and as the milling crowd voiced their protest, his guards formed up around the Keeper, two deep, as a protective human shield.

Had Royal Chen been more connected to reality, especially to the sensitivities of the common people, he would not have decided to publicly execute the Sisterhood fighters. The common folks admired and respected the Alliance for their integrity and willingness to fight the oppressive "good old boy" network of brothels and work camps that robbed so many people of their freedom—women and children in particular. They had no idea that Royal Chen held a majority stake in such seedy enterprises, and if they ever found out that such was the case, would no longer hold him in high regard.

"What is going on down there?" Chen asked his Captain of the Guard, confused by the crowd's unruly reaction.

"They are upset about your execution order, Your Eminence," the concerned officer politely responded.

"But they always enjoy my punishments! It's one of the main attractions!" Chen inability to fathom their disapproval of the upcoming witch burning was symptomatic of how out of touch he had become.

The Captain of the Guard turned and caught the eye of his lieutenant, "Send word to the armory that we need more men up here immediately." The lieutenant ran to the tower to signal the barracks to immediately send a backup detachment. To a runner the captain barked, "Find Chief Von Hammer and get him up here now!"

Under his breath to Royal Chen the captain whispered, "Crowds can be very unpredictable, Sir, and can get out of hand very quickly, I saw it in the early days when food ran out and everyday people went crazy, killing each other over a few grains of rice."

Chen didn't need reminding. He vividly remembered that day on the Golden Gate Bridge when he had fled San Francisco—the madness of that mass hysteria returning to him in full measure. A rock suddenly sailed past Chen's head, thrown from below, prompting the captain to add in a calm, but firm voice, "Sir, let us escort you to the alcove, you'll be much more comfortable there."

He referred to the tower attached to the side of the arena with its covered catwalk to and from the viewing booth. It was designed to enable Royal Chen to come and go unobserved and protected from the weather, avoiding the typically rowdy crowds down below. Tonight a distinctly different energy was in the air, and the people were becoming more upset and unruly by the second.

When Jessi's mother, Alena, and young Alibi were led out onto the platform in shackles, hundreds in the crowd let out a roar of disapproval and surged forward in unison, seeking to stop the execution. Unnoticed in the darkness above them, Chen's archers began quietly filing in on the walkway behind the parapet surrounding the arena, and a ring of heavily armed guards poured from the backstage doors to surround and protect the front of the stage, physically blocking the mob's way. When the executioner stripped the condemned women to their waists exposing the bruises and lash marks inflicted by Von Hammer, the anger of the people rose to a fever pitch. Thousands in the crowd began shouting and pushing against the guards who shoved back with their shields and stood their ground, awaiting further orders.

Alibi trembled as the nervous executioner and his frightened assistant lashed her to an iron pole mounted on a raised platform ten feet above the stage. Her bound hands were fastened to a large iron ring welded to the top of the stake above her head, and her feet were secured to a matching ring at its base. Bare to her waist, young Alibi searched for a familiar face among the angry crowd raging just beyond the ring of guards that framed the arena's stage. She glanced over at Alena who had been so severely beaten by Von Hammer that she was slumped against her pole and barely conscious. As the executioner's assistant stacked bundles of kindling against Alibi's legs, the first heavy object was thrown by someone in the crowd and a sentry at the front of the stage went down hard from a rock to the side of his face.

* * *

AS THE TURMOIL in the crowded plaza escalated out of control, reinforcements arrived to quell the growing unrest. Unnoticed in the confusion, with the full moon just cresting the rise, six-hundred Sisterhood warriors, their battle-worthy wolven with them, poured over the perimeter wall three blocks away. They silenced the few remaining guards there and made their way along the wall's narrow walkways and down the stairs to ground level in the shadows. Streaming like a black river of ants with weapons drawn and nerves steeled for battle, they swept through the empty streets and alleyways of the Gathering in the torchlight, surprised at meeting zero resistance in their full-on sprint toward the plaza.

Suspicious of the absence of security personnel, Star was certain that their attack should have been challenged before now, at the very least by Chen's fearsome dogs and their handlers. She called a brief halt as her fighters fanned out to gather at each of the eight tunnel entranceways leading to the arena. Listening to the roar of the crowd which she mistook for the usual spectator enthusiasm, Star weighed her options, growing increasingly concerned about the specter of an ambush.

Somehow, the situation just didn't *feel* right. *Where were the sentries, the guards, the dogs? Could the lack of resistance be a trap? A ploy to draw them all in?* There was no way she could have predicted the spontaneous riot at the arena and the calling up of all reserve security personnel by Chen, leaving the perimeter wall and front gates virtually unguarded. As the moon peeked above the eastern horizon, Star noted her archers positioned on rooftops and parapets. Her lookouts signaled the "all clear" ahead, her wolven and their handlers were poised and ready—everything, it seemed, was in place just as she had planned it, but *where* were the enemy forces?

Taking a deep breath, Star made her decision. Throwing caution to the wind, she stepped into the tunnel and immediately broke into a full run, followed closely by Amaranth, Jessi, Elise, and her entire silent army of vengeance. Emerging from the darkened passageways, Star's forces poured into the plaza, and took out the few remaining sentries they found there before fanning out against the walls, momentarily thrown off guard by the unexpected scene taking place before them. The outraged crowd, though unarmed, outnumbered the guards two-hundred to one, and had attacked

Chen's forces with their bare hands and whatever they could find nearby to wield or throw, quickly overwhelming the sentries ringing the fence on the outside of the arena stage. Newly armed with the weapons of the downed guards, the crowd had fought its way through the two narrow gates in the fenced enclosure on either side of the stage and were engaged in hand-to-hand combat with the reinforcements guarding the platform itself.

On the raised platform, Alibi strained against her bonds as the executioner and his assistant frantically stacked bundles of firewood around her in a last ditch effort to carry out the Keeper's execution order. From their positions along the top of the wall, Chen's crossbowmen fired into the bunched up crowds at the two gates, and soon managed to clog the narrow openings there with the dead and injured. Bleeding and desperate to escape further injury, those who had been pierced by arrows cried out for help, and the dying writhed in agony, soon joining the dead on the cold, hard flagstones.

When Star's archers arrived inside the plaza, they immediately targeted Chen's bowmen with deadly accuracy. As flights of black-fletched arrows found their marks, the unnatural thudding sound of bodies crashing onto the flagstones from the heights above echoed throughout the square. Witnessing the carnage of the black archers, Chen's forces blanched in fear—panicked by the battle's sudden shift in momentum—and fled for their lives along the top of the parapet. From the plaza below, grappling hooks sailed over the top lip as scores of black-garbed female fighters scaled the walls on knotted ropes, and charged after the fleeing men, pairs of glistening katanas in their black-gloved hands.

Down below, teams of wolven and their fighting partners pushed through the gates on either side of the stage, and burst out onto the platform to savage the guards there. As they drove back the enemy forces, more of their sister-warriors were able to slip through and attack the remaining sentries inside the fence.

* * *

FROM THE PROTECTED alcove high in his stone tower, Royal Chen had watched in disbelief as the bloody insurrection below continued to spin out of control. When the first sentry went down, the mob became emboldened, and many more angry people in the crowd began throwing whatever they could get their hands on. Unfortunately for the guards, the planting beds in the plaza were ringed with fist-sized stones that quickly became deadly missiles aimed at Chen's men. When the crowd first attacked the guards ringing the arena, his personal bodyguard had whisked him to safety across the covered catwalk to his fortified tower well beyond the reach of the crowd yet still able to visually command his troops. Chen had reluctantly agreed to relocate to his bastion, but only until his forces managed to bring the situation back under control—which he was certain would be but a matter of minutes, perhaps half an hour at the most. He issued orders authorizing his troops to use any amount of force necessary to quell the riot, but to his surprise, the people refused to back down, and instead, became even more angry and violent.

Down below in the plaza, the people were now a raging horde, hell bent on rescuing the two Sisterhood warriors.

259

Shocked by the intensity of the crowd's reaction, Chen was certain that as soon as the protesters began taking on serious casualties they would retreat and scatter, and he would be able to mop them up later at his leisure. When he issued the order to his archers to begin firing into the agitated crowd, there was some hesitation among them. Derek, the young sentry from the perimeter wall who had been called up with the rest of the reinforcements, was appalled that he was expected to fire into the crowd of civilians which included many women and children. *I never signed on for this crap,* he told himself, deciding that there was no way in hell that he was obeying that bullshit order.

"Tell them to fire, by god, or I'll have their balls in a jar and yours alongside them!" Chen screamed at his Captain. As the officer drew his sword in a direct threat to anyone under his command who refused to perform their duty, Derek slowly eased back out of his line sight, fading into the background as best he could among the bunched up men along the parapet.

As the menacing officer approached his archers with sword raised, the crossbowmen began to let fly and the injured dropped to the flagstones in agony, many with bolts passing straight through them, or protruding from backs, necks, chests, and limbs. Some died almost instantly, but others writhed about in pain, screaming for help as they attempted to drag themselves to safety, leaving dark, slippery blood trails in their wake. Witnesses to the carnage cried out in horror and scrambled about in a panic, torn between the urge to flee to safety and to remain behind to rescue their friends and loved ones.

Chen was pleased to see the mob's attack begin to falter, but was stunned when, out of nowhere, a streaming black mass of fighters suddenly appeared, targeting his bowmen atop the walls with their own deadly accurate arrows. An involuntary flash of fear rippled through his opium-clogged senses as Chen saw the black-clothed warriors pour out of the dark tunnels, seemingly by the hundreds. *Who is this army?* he asked himself, *How did they gain access to my Gathering?*

In the flickering torchlight on the plaza, Chen's eyes were drawn to a fluttering white pennant emblazoned with a red-winged triangle within a circle, an all-seeing eye in the center and an inverted cross beneath. *It couldn't be— the Sisterhood Coven—here?* His befuddled mind failed to effectively process the rapidly unfolding events, as below him, vicious wolf-dogs went on the attack, overwhelming his guards at the arena gates and driving them back onto the platform itself. With his Captain of the Guard awaiting further orders, Chen partially snapped out of his mental paralysis, commanding the release of all reserve war dogs and their handlers, who immediately began flooding in to join the battle.

* * *

IN SPITE OF the Keeper's canine reinforcements, within minutes the Sisterhood had effectively wrested control of the plaza from Chen's forces. With their wolven out front as a vanguard, the women advanced through the entrance gates into the arena itself. With the ranks of Chen's bowmen decimated and the remainder in retreat, Sisterhood archers concentrated their fire directly onto the arena platform where the condemned women were bound. The three-man-deep ring of guards there began dropping to the floor, mortally wounded or too badly injured to continue the fight.

Amidst the din and confusion, Alibi looked on as Chen's trembling executioner scrambled about the platform on all fours, dousing the stacked firewood with lamp oil. He worked feverishly to complete his task, certain of his fate should he fail. All around him, dead and dying guards lay sprawled, impaled by the deadly black arrows that whizzed past his face, and ricocheted across the stage. Glancing over his shoulder, he was shocked to see his assistant lying wide-eyed dead, flat on his back with an arrow protruding from the side of his neck and another buried deep in his chest. Dropping his near-empty fuel can, the executioner reached for a torch as a black-fletched arrow pierced the base of his skull, severing his brain stem and shutting down his central nervous system like a switch. As his dead body collapsed, the torch bounced back and rolled away from the bundles of wood at Alibi's feet, settling against the discarded fuel can. With a *swoosh,* the oil ignited and bluish flames spread out across the wooden floor of the platform in a widening circle—hungry tongues of fire seeking anything combustible to devour.

CHAPTER TWENTY-ONE

JUDGEMENT

AS LARS APPROACHED the shallow inlet leading to the harbor below the Gathering, the sea was calm with a modest onshore breeze freshening his ship's partially furled mainsail. The full moon hovered above the peaks in the balmy night sky, not poised to slip into the Pacific until some nine hours after sunrise. The sea was running at the peak of the incoming high tide, carrying *Windsong* toward the shore at a good ten knots.

Blacked out with no running lights, the nimble craft sliced through the gentle swells as quietly as a razor, invisible even beneath the light of the full moon, to all but the most observant of creatures. Heading east, Lars could distinguish the silhouettes of ships anchored in the harbor, their watch lights and torches still burning in the hour before dawn. The barest hint of rose gently outlined the eastern skyline of the Cascades, betraying the coming daylight.

Heading for the pre-appointed rendezvous, he maneuvered his ship toward the northernmost dock located farthest away from the cluster of warehouses and storage facilities along the wharf. Looking up toward the settlement surrounding the hill, he wondered again how Hunter, Skye and his kinsmen were faring. He didn't envy them, hidden some-

263

where up there within the sprawling complex, surrounded by enemies, desperate and determined to somehow locate and liberate their beloved women before they were out of reach and beyond hope. His thoughts turned to young Jessi, wondering whether she'd made it safely back home to her people after her harrowing ordeal at the hands of the slavers. He would have been shocked to realize that Jessi and Hunter's Elise, were but a mile away across the bay, scaling the high stone wall alongside hundreds of Sisterhood warriors.

When he was a quarter mile offshore, Lars tossed out an aft anchor line, to enable the incoming tide to keep his ship's bow facing toward land. This prevented her from drifting in too close while remaining well hidden behind a rock outcropping that hosted a group of several dozen hauled-out harbor seals. Lars would remain here waiting, until he detected Hunter and Skye's retreat along the wharf, at which time he would continue forward to the far dock and glide alongside to take on the seven passengers and provide them a swift getaway. At least that was the plan. How much of it would actually play out the way they had figured it, no one could say, but Lars was prepared to act if and when he and his ship were needed.

* * *

ENTERING THE TORCHLIT plaza, Elise paused with her back against the stone wall to get her bearings and plan her advance. Before her was a scene of total chaos as the rioting crowd—suddenly caught between the Sisterhood fighters and Chen's security forces—scrambled to escape the mayhem with their friends and loved ones intact. Peering into the shadows beside the wall, her eyes scanned for an entrance to a stairway leading down into the heart of the subterranean catacombs. She had been told that it was there she would find Anna and Skye's sisters, and hoped to somehow rescue Hunter and Skye as well—if they still lived. When she had last seen them several hours ago, they were in the custody of Chen's guards and headed to an unthinkable fate—but she couldn't be distracted by that now. She must first focus on freeing Anna, River, and Lily, and to do that, she needed to access the lower levels beneath the complex.

From the shadows, Jessi suddenly appeared across the open ground, beckoning Elise down a set of wide stone steps almost hidden in the far wall. At the bottom they found a heavy wooden door partially ajar and pushed their way through it, proceeding cautiously with blade and crossbow drawn and senses strained. Meeting no resistance, they moved swiftly along the narrow, ill-lit hallway that wound around and down another set of steps identical to the first. The lower they descended, the more faint the sounds of the battle above them became.

Passing beyond yet another thick, wooden door, they perceived muffled voices and a commotion somewhere up ahead and instinctively picked up their pace, readying themselves for a fight. Bursting through a final doorway, they surprised a group of slave buyers and their bodyguards who were gathered in the center of a lamp-lit hall. Along the far wall, dozens of newly auctioned women and girls huddled in misery, crowded into grim holding cells fitted with rusting iron bars. Each one fearfully awaited her cruel fate—a life of bondage far from the comfort and safety of their own homes, and well beyond any hope of rescue by their loved ones.

Instantly sizing up the situation, Elise aimed her cross-bow into the crowd and fired, taking out one of the body-guards—as well as the unsavory character standing directly behind him—with a single bolt. As she quickly reloaded, Jessi attacked the appalled and speechless crowd, twin kata-nas held high and flashing diagonally through the air as she suddenly crouched down at the end of her swing. Bending nearly to the floor, she sliced into the two nearest pairs of legs just above their ankles. Elise took down a final body-guard with her second shot and the rest of the terrified trad-ers ran screaming for the exit at the back of the room.

In the sudden silence, Jessi stood over two men seated on the floor staring at their severed feet and shaking uncon-trollably, not yet able to comprehend that within the next couple of minutes they would both bleed to death. Grabbing the nearest by the nape of his neck, Jessi demanded to know where the rest of the captives were being housed, but the fool just looked bewildered, his ashen face frozen in shock. As he began to blubber something unintelligible, she deftly liber-ated his head from his shoulders with her blades. She im-mediately turned toward the other with her dripping swords raised above him.

"One level down, there, through that door," the terror-stricken man stammered, pointing to a side entrance partial-ly concealed by a tapestry. As the bright red blood squirted from his stumps, he pleaded with her, "Save me! Help me! I'm rich, I have *money*—look, many chens in my bags!"

Jessi lopped off his head as neatly as the first, sending it skipping across the floor like a melon. Wiping her swords on his still-seated torso, she dashed through the hidden door-way and took the steps leading down, three at a time.

Grabbing a large iron keyring from its peg on the wall, Elise rushed from cell to cell, releasing the captives. "Get up to the surface! The Sisterhood warriors are there to help you!" She pointed the way and they hurried from the bloody room, thanking her profusely—the tears of relief streaming down their cheeks. Following Jessi into the darkened stair-well, Elise listened for her, but heard no sound. She was awed by her young guide's fighting prowess, feeling extremely fortunate to have Jessi at her side as a worthy comrade-in-arms. At the bottom of the stairs with only one possible di-rection to travel, Elise sped off down a shadowed corridor at a brisk trot, adrenaline peaked and crossbow reloaded and at the ready.

* * *

FROM THE DEPTHS of the catacombs, Anna and the twins were being led from a dingy holding cell by their new master—the sour-faced brothel owner. Tied to one another with braided hemp bindings, they were jerked along the torch-lit corridor and up a set of rough stone stairs into the night air, when the first strange tremor rumbled beneath their feet. Glancing about in panic, their new master dropped the lead rope and ran for his life, abandoning the women to fend for themselves.

Startled by a deafening roar, Anna glanced back to see the ground collapse into a sinkhole, swallowing a section of the building they had just emerged from. All around them, structures began to sway and the ground bucked and heaved like ocean swells in a gale. Holding onto one another for support, they grabbed their lead rope and hobbled out into the open to escape falling objects being shaken loose from the surrounding buildings and walls.

While Anna had no idea what was happening, Lily and River understood earthquake phenomena, having experienced occasional tremors through the years. In the history of their people, the folklore of their culture spoke of a time when Mother Earth would shake off the imbalanced human culture, making way for a new world—a just society wherein all living beings would dwell together in harmony with the laws of nature and one another. As little girls, their grandmother had recounted the story of how the turtle who carried the Earth on its back would someday roll over to make everything new.

* * *

IN A DISTANT section of the underground labyrinth, Hunter and Skye made their way stealthily along a shadowed corridor lit with torches. At each new turn or doorway they expected to meet Chen's guards, but were surprised to find only a few on duty, whom they quickly dispatched before continuing their search. Uncertain of the way, they proceeded carefully, searching for slave housing, or some kind of holding pen where slaves might be held until removed by their new owners. At the end of a long hallway they entered through a set of iron-reinforced doors into a wide chamber filled with bunks fitted with leg irons attached to the bedposts.

At the far end of the room, Skye knelt on one knee with his ear pressed to the doors. He thought he could make out a commotion beyond, with men's muffled voices raised as if in argument. He motioned to Hunter and on the count of three, they burst through into the room, their glistening blades soon dripping with the fresh blood of their enemies and hungry for more. Without his crossbow or his .45—which Von Hammer had claimed for his own—Hunter had been forced to borrow a sword from the paralyzed guard who had no more use for the weapon.

On the far side of the room, near cages where a dozen huddled captives cowered, a handful of traffickers stood arguing about the ownership of a pair of young females. As they noticed the rescuers enter the room, the traders called out to their bodyguards, but too late. Hunter threw his heavy knife, dispatching one, and engaged another with his sword while Skye descended upon the rest, savagely slashing throats in an impressive display of controlled frenzy.

Racing to release the captives, Skye and Hunter moved rapidly through the adjoining rooms and corridors, calling out for River, Anna and Lily, when the first odd tremor rippled through the floor beneath their feet. Moments later, a second shock wave shook the ground and a crack appeared in the wall beside them, splitting the stonework and causing a wall-mounted torch and bits of the ceiling to come down.

"Run!" Skye yelled as he dashed to the nearest stairwell with Hunter hard on his heels. Both men instinctively understood that they must get to the surface immediately or risk being buried alive. As Skye vanished up the stairs, something heavy smashed into Hunter's right ankle causing him to lose his footing and crash to the cold stone floor.

* * *

DEEP WITHIN THE EARTH the internal pressure between two opposing tectonic plates had been slowly building
up for more than 500 years, and when it finally reached its
breaking point, a sudden subduction occurred as the Juan de
Fuca plate slid eastward beneath the North American plate.
Had there been a seismic activity recording device measur-
ing the event, it would have registered over 9.2 on the Richter
scale. Hundreds of miles off the coast, the ocean floor along
the seven hundred mile Cascadia Subduction Zone suddenly
uplifted, displacing billions of metric tons of water and generating a powerful wave that hurtled through the depths at an
initial speed of nearly two-hundred miles per hour.

Along the coast, the shock wave caused by the subduction rippled through the planet's crust, causing the ground
beneath the Gathering to undulate, transforming topsoil and
rock into a semi-liquid mass. As the planet reverberated from
the massive slippage, a deafening rumble filled the air, rising up from the ground beneath. In the hills surrounding the
settlement, huge slabs of rock broke off, cascading down the
mountainside and demolishing anything in their path. Mature trees were uprooted and crevasse-like fissures randomly
appeared—great yawning dirt mouths greedily swallowing
people and buildings like some geologic *Ouroboros* out to
devour the earth.

* * *

WHEN THE FIRST violent tremor shook the coast, the
raised witch-burning platform in the arena began to sway
wildly back and forth, and both Chen's men and the Sisterhood fighters froze as sections of the arena started to crum-

ble. The private viewing boxes where privileged attendees and owners of sporting teams had been celebrating before the riot, shook violently, knocking their occupants to the floor. Shrieks and cries for help rose up as heavy beams fell, pinning some and crushing the life out of others trapped beneath their weight. As the tremors increased, the structures began to shake apart at the seams, with massive balconies disengaging from their supports and collapsing down onto the crowd. With each brief lull, people lurched toward the exits that were fast becoming blocked by debris and the bodies of the dead.

When the riot first began, Stephan McClellan and his beautiful Rachel had been seated in their private box, surrounded by their fighters who were being congratulated for their sweep of the tournament. Champagne and beer flowed as the highlights of the evening were recounted and the boisterous team and their attendant girlfriends and wives celebrated, oblivious to the initial murmurings of the crowd down below. As the situation escalated, McClellan's lieutenant whispered something into the land baron's ear and he went to the railing to see what the excitement was all about.

The last thing that McClellan remembered hearing was an announcement about some witches who were about to be burned, but, as he was already well on his way to being pleasantly inebriated, he hadn't been too concerned about the goings on down among the rowdy crowd. The groundlings often engaged in fistfights during the tournaments anyway. *Let them have their fun,* he thought. He ordered that the privacy curtains be drawn, and walked back over to Rachel who was looking especially ravishing this evening.

When the first shudder of the quake shook their private viewing booth, McClellan and Rachel looked around confused as panic swept through their entourage and guests. During the rush to the covered stairway leading to ground level someone at the top tripped, falling into the others who had jammed the crowded stairway below. When the structural supports suddenly collapsed, the entire balcony, housing the twelve private viewing boxes filled with occupants, crashed down into the crowd below, instantly extinguishing more than two-hundred souls.

* * *

IN ROYAL CHEN'S tower high above the plaza the scene was surreal. At the quake's first shudder, bodyguards surrounded the Keeper to shield him from harm, but as the intensity of the earthquake increased, it was clear to everyone that they must immediately exit the area. Physically hoisting Chen to their shoulders, a half-dozen of his elite guard hustled him through a reinforced tunnel leading directly from the tower to a fortified safe room in the private chambers of his mansion.

* * *

FROM HIS RELATIVELY safe vantage point in the harbor, Lars waited aboard his vessel, oblivious of the battle still raging in the arena, as his view was blocked by tall perimeter wall. When the earthquake struck, he stood transfixed on *Windsong's* foredeck as the coastline shook, collapsing entire sections of the cliffs on either side of the harbor, that broke off into the bay like glaciers calving into the Arctic Ocean. The roaring growl from deep within the earth increased as random portions of the Gathering complex collapsed, swallowed by yawning trenches that suddenly appeared without warning. The rumbling continued for several minutes as wave after wave of energy reached the surface, wreaking havoc upon the land and its people. The reinforced scaffolding surrounding Royal Chen's nearly completed stone tower renovation came crashing down, and the tower itself swayed dangerously back and forth like a sapling in a violent storm. Countless oil lamps illuminating the walkways, corridors, and buildings of the sprawling complex crashed to the floor and burst into flames, and the fires spread quickly to anything combustible in their paths.

* * *

MOMENTS BEFORE THE quake struck, Star and Amaranth, along with a dozen fierce Sisterhood fighters had climbed over the dead bodies of Chen's guards onto the flame-engulfed platform that had been set ablaze by the dead executioner's dropped torch. They had barely finished cutting Alena and Alibi loose from their iron stakes when the settlement buildings suddenly lurched and hundreds of oil lamps tipped, spilling their flammable liquid down the sides of wooden structures and catching them afire. With the onset of the earthquake, the pitched battle at the arena had instantly ceased and pandemonium reigned as the panicked crowd scrambled to perceived points of safety. Star stood still, attempting to maintain her balance, and stared at the familiar scene before her eyes—*it was as if she had been here before.*

273

Suddenly, she remembered her waking dream, the vision she received that night in the glade with the drumming, the dancing, and the sacramental tea.

The flaming city, the screams of terror, the barking of dogs, the snarling of wolves—it had all been shown to her in advance—*the clash of swords as the battle ensued, the panicked crowd crying out in fear and confusion*—she'd seen it all before. Looking to the east, she noted the hint of pink above the towering Cascades. Sunrise had arrived—just a few more moments before the dawn.

* * *

RIPPING THROUGH THE Earth's vulnerable crust, the powerful quake brought all human activity on the affected portion of the surface to a standstill. The shaking became so violent that humans, dogs and other animals all lost their footing and tumbled helplessly to the ground as the land lurched, the roar of its groaning nearly unbearable. Some people screamed uncontrollably while others lay silent, frozen in shock, dazed by the drunken swaying of the ground.

All over the settlement, ceilings collapsed and walls caved in as the geologic undulations took on mammoth proportions. Down below in the tunnels, Jessi and Elise braced themselves against the supports of the shuddering walls, fully aware, without needing to verbally acknowledge the fact, that at any moment this place might become their tomb. Knowing their only chance of survival was to find their way to the surface, the women forced themselves to their feet and ran drunkenly for the stairway at the end of the hall.

As dust filled the air making it nearly impossible to see through the thick haze, they felt their way along the floor, determined to somehow make it to the top. Grabbing a fallen torch, Elise got to her feet during a lull, and she and Jessi lurched forward along the half-collapsed corridor, arriving at a set of stone steps similar to the ones they had used to descend into the labyrinth.

Ascending the stairs, they could hear the screaming and confusion above them grow louder and they doubled their efforts. As a new wave of aftershocks arrived, they felt the stairs begin to give way beneath them. With a final effort, Jessi and Elise pushed through a pair of heavy doors and burst out into the midst of a chaos unlike anything either had ever witnessed before. With a full moon rising above the scene, the morning sun was cresting the ridge to the east, and in shadows cast by flickering torches and broken lamps, the plaza was littered with bodies sprawled upon the flagstones. People crawled, or cowered in small groups of two or three, too frightened or disoriented to regain their footing and flee.

The arena itself was coming apart at the seams. Huge timbers listed awkwardly while fires fed by smashed oil lamps, raced along the ground, tracing a path along anywhere that oil had spilled. As they moved away from the stairs, Jessi looked up to see the scaffolding surrounding Royal Chen's new stone tower suddenly buckle. Elise pulled Jessi out of the way as heavy planks and bamboo framework crashed to the plaza floor, bringing down piles of rock that had been tediously hauled up by the masons for use in completing the tower's exterior surface. This was immediately followed by a rending shriek, unlike anything either of the women had ever heard, announcing the arrival of a jagged crevasse, that

275

ripped a six-foot wide swath across the middle of the plaza, swallowing everything in its path and heading straight toward them.

* * *

TWO HUNDRED MILES offshore, the submerged wave raced toward the shallows as fish and marine mammals sensed the danger and headed for deeper waters. Perceiving the change in water pressure dynamics through a subtle increase in barometric pressure, thousands of seabirds simultaneously took flight, abandoning their nests and circling out to sea, somehow conscious of the impending danger. A pod of orcas a half mile off the coast felt the change and broke off feeding to race into deeper water.

On the mainland, within several miles of the coastline, animals lucky enough to have escaped the initial effects of the quake fled to higher ground, intuitively sensing the upcoming disaster, whether through a shift in the Earth's magnetic field, or a change in atmospheric pressure, they instinctively understood that something catastrophic was about to occur, and instantly reacted to those stimuli, fleeing for their lives. Above the beaches, throughout the hills and forests spanning the Coast Road, herds of elk and mule deer scrambled up hillsides, joining bears, coyotes, and all manner of smaller woodland creatures making their escape to higher ground.

Less than a mile offshore, the immense volume of displaced water met the shallows and the sea began to rise up into a Great Wave over forty feet high and hundreds of miles long. Bearing down on the shoreline like a charge of heavy horse from an epic battle of the Ottoman Empire, the tsunami harbored enough energetic potential to obliterate every living thing in its path.

*   *   *

WHEN THE SALTWATER began to flow out of the bay, suctioned by the tsunami speeding toward the coastline, Lars instinctively understood what was happening and turned to look out to sea, but was unable to discern much in the dim gray of dawn's first light. With scant time to react, he drew his knife and slashed his anchor line, allowing *Windsong* to be drawn toward the mouth of the inlet by the strong current created by the receding waters.

As someone familiar with the behavior of ocean currents, tides, and the principles of oceanic hydrology, Lars knew that when an earthquake-generated tsunami encountered the shallower waters of the continental shelf, the physical force of the displaced ocean would cause a drawing back of the water near the shore. He wasn't sure exactly how much time he had left, but he was certain that within a matter of minutes, a killer wave spawned by the earthquake would engulf the bay, and explode against the shoreline, and he didn't want to be caught inside the harbor when it hit.

Manning the wheel, he steered her on a beeline through the mouth of the inlet, awed by the sheer volume and velocity of the water being drawn from the bay; even the river was draining faster than its natural flow. Harbor seals sensed the danger and headed for deeper water, along with any remaining fish in the bay, all ripping through the swells as fast as they could swim. Glancing back one last time, Lars wondered what the chances were now for Hunter and Skye to escape.

As *Windsong* cleared the mouth of the inlet, the epic wave reached the continental shelf, just as the sun broke the plane of the ridgeline to the east, and Lars could see white caps cresting in the distance—growing taller with each passing moment. Reaching the shallows, the wave rose high above the surface and Lars realized that *Windsong* could not possibly clear the incoming crest. Dashing to the mainmast, he scrambled up to the topmost crosstie and perched there facing the sea. Clinging to the rigging, he wished for some way out of his predicament—some miracle that would allow him to evade the enormous wall of water bearing down on him at nearly one-hundred miles per hour.

CHAPTER TWENTY-TWO

AFTERMATH

PROUD, SELF-ABSORBED HUMANS—*when would they ever learn? The Old Ones had witnessed their fruitless struggles for more than two-hundred millennia, rarely intervening on their behalf, preferring to avoid the contamination of their violent, three-dimensional universe. Mostly they simply observed their predictable shenanigans with a detached curiosity, pondering their unenlightened, self-destructive nature.*

This was not their planet to tame and control. The spinning sphere, orbiting third from its life-giving star to whose crust they perilously clung, was a complex dynamism in constant flux, ever changing, never the same, one moment to the next.

It wasn't their fault, really—what with geologic time being so vast compared to their own tiny existences, and galactic reckoning even more so. Such infinite considerations made it difficult and awkward for beings with eighty-year lifespans to willingly recognize or dare to admit to the relatively inconsequential nature of their human existences in terms of making any significant contribution whatsoever to the fundamental processes of their home planet they so affectionately called Earth...

* * *

THE DAWN BROKE cool and clear with a gentle breeze blowing in from the sea and an unusual silence encompassing the land. The displaced waters of the tsunami receded quickly where the raised landmass of the rugged coastline had blocked its advance. However, in places under forty feet above sea level, the wall of water had swamped the shore, flooding the mouths of river valleys as it pushed its way inland and far upstream, stripping the terrain bare of foliage for several miles.

From Vancouver Island to San Francisco Bay, the Pacific Northwest coastline was battered and bruised, with convoluted piles of twisted wreckage strewn along beaches, rocky shores, and bobbing haphazardly in the shallows. Drifting with the tides in the cold, jetsam-filled waters were great floating islands comprised of uprooted trees, demolished buildings, and vessels large and small, some nearly intact, sloshing about in the offshore swells as far out as the eye could see. Many offshore islands and landmarks had either disappeared or were so altered in appearance as to now be unrecognizable to anyone familiar with the pre-wave landscape.

Below the Gathering, the harbor itself had suffered extensive damage, the surge having swept away the docks and wharf, and any vessels unlucky enough to have been caught in its wake. Onshore, the road leading from the wharf to the gates had vanished, eroded by incalculable tons of churning sea water.

Higher up the hill, the settlement itself had escaped the flood, but select sections of the complex had suffered grievously, appearing as if someone had suddenly pulled a rug out from beneath them. Structures of all shapes and sizes had partially or fully fallen in or down, or now leaned dangerously to one side, threatening to collapse at any moment. Strong aftershocks continued throughout the morning, with further cave-ins a common occurrence. Several sections of the great wall had crumbled from the terrible shaking of the earth, randomly burying unfortunate victims beneath its rubble.

Immediately following the quake, in the misty light of dawn, shocked survivors hugged the ground or lay curled up and huddled together out in the open, fearing what might happen next, and afraid to venture too far in any direction lest they fall into one of the narrow jagged trenches crisscrossing the plaza. As the trembling receded, the survivors slowly began moving about, some walking aimlessly in a daze, while others frantically called out in search of missing loved ones.

In the growing light of morning, a scene of unprecedented devastation revealed itself to the living. Perched proudly on the cliff, Chens's palatial mansion was burning, one section of its roof engulfed in angry orange flames, sending billows of black smoke far into the pale summer sky. A section of exterior wall had sheered off, tumbling into the sea, and with it, a cascade of luxurious home furnishings had spilled out upon the rocks.

Like a vision from Hell, thousands were sprawled across the jumbled landscape. With each new aftershock, involuntary cries arose from the hillside as the shaken masses

281

scrambled from one place to another, dragging themselves to perceived points of safety, only to be threatened with death as a new section of wall or building suddenly collapsed without warning or pattern.

Within the transformational context of the natural disaster, the previously warring factions were suddenly thrown into survival mode by the surrounding chaos, their alliances temporarily meaningless, uniforms no longer recognizable as friend and foe alike were camouflaged in a thick layer of dust. Enemies, who moments before had been fully engaged in exterminating one another, now worked together to free those who were trapped and pleading for someone to save them.

As the morning fog was burned off by the warming sun, smoke from smoldering fires lent an acrid stench to the air prompting survivors to cover their faces with scarves or shirts to filter out the stinging particles. By noon, the seabirds began returning from wherever it was they had escaped to, revisiting the coastline and dropping into nesting colonies to find chaos and confusion there as well. Nothing, it seems, had been left untouched, even among the various animal species.

* * *

TWO STORIES UNDERGROUND, Hunter and Skye lay covered in a thin coating of dirt in the pitch black darkness, hopelessly trapped in the remains of the stone stairwell that had collapsed to form a small narrow space two feet high and barely long enough to lie down in. Fallen roof beams and heavy tunnel support posts had come to rest in a jumbled pile above them, preventing the two from being instantly crushed to death, but now, untold tons of rock, soil, timbers and debris blocked their way to the surface.

After what seemed an impossibly long period of time, during which they spoke words of encouragement to one another and voiced their determination to try to dig their way out, another major aftershock tore through the earth's crust, simultaneously opening up the ground above *and* beneath them, and hurling the pair in opposite directions.

When the dust finally settled, the blessed light of the morning sun streamed in from above, giving them hope, yet, at the same time, illuminating their precarious predicament. Skye found himself lying perhaps twenty feet from the surface, stretched out horizontally on his belly and covered in dirt and debris. Beyond a few bruised muscles and scrapes, he was miraculously unharmed.

Thirty feet below him, Hunter wasn't nearly as fortunate. During the aftershock, something large had bashed into his ribs—the same ones damaged by Bull Mitchell during the retaking of New Eden some five years earlier—and he felt something give way as intense ribbons of pain radiated from the point of impact. His ankle, too, had been crushed in the earlier cave-in, forcing him to balance upright on one leg. Looking about at his immediate environment, Hunter saw that he was perched on an exposed section of rock jutting from the side of an apparently bottomless chasm. From deep within, the planet groaned again as if in labor and sent innumerable tiny aftershocks shivering through the earth's destabilized crust.

* * *

CONDUCTING A MENTAL inventory of his physical condition, Skye heard the distinctive cry of a raven's loud "caw" from somewhere nearby and wriggled free of his impediments to see the large black bird perched on the end of a thick broken branch hanging out over the edge of the precipice. It was strutting up and down the limb making a huge racket and Skye acknowledged its presence, appreciating the obvious encouragement. He immediately began calling out for someone on the surface to send down a rope.

The raven flew off as faces appeared and before long, a knotted line was lowered down. Fashioning a makeshift safety harness, Skye was hauled up by several people on the surface, and he arrived at the top in high spirits, despite the shocking scene of devastation all around him. For the moment, he was just happy to be out of the ground and alive.

As Skye moved back from the edge and stepped out of the harness he heard a woman's familiar voice calling his name. Turning around, he looked full into the face of his sweet Anna, who was instantly in his arms and crying for joy and relief, and a dozen other wonderful reasons, joined moments later by his sisters, Lily and River. All were covered in dirt and soot, but appeared to be okay, at least physically, considering their incredibly trying ordeal. His heart overflowed with joy as he hugged and kissed them all before suddenly remembering his friend.

Dashing back to the edge, he spied Hunter down below in the shadows still clinging to the wall of the chasm. Calling to him to hold on, Skye began lowering the safety harness, but realized that the rope was about ten feet too short. He called out for more line and after what seemed an eternity, someone brought another length of rope which he joined to the first. As he turned back to the edge to drop the lengthened line down to Hunter, another aftershock knocked Skye to his hands and knees.

As Hunter awaited the rope, another jolt shook the earth, and rock and rubble poured into the trench from above, bringing with it a young girl—not more than seven or eight years old—who crashed into him on her way down into the bottomless hole. Reacting out of pure instinct, he grabbed the child's clothing with his free hand, gripping the rocks with the other. Pulling her back from the open trench, he saw the fear etched into her features as she clung to his legs with both arms, screaming unintelligible words in a fit of terror.

"I've got you now, don't worry, you're safe with me." He spoke to her in a calm, soothing voice. Flashing her a smile, he pulled her up onto his hip and glanced back toward the surface to see Skye reappear at the edge of the precipice. On his face was an expression of shocked disbelief at seeing that Hunter was now somehow holding a small child in his arms.

"I'll tie her off and you can hoist her up," Hunter called out, and Skye dropped the line. Wrapping the strong hemp rope around the girl's legs and waist, he fashioned a smaller harness for her slight frame and looked into her eyes with his face close to hers.

"You are such a brave little girl! Hold on tight to the rope now and don't let go. They'll get you at the top."

He smiled into her wide, frightened eyes and she bit her bottom lip, managing a slight nod of her head in response. Calling out and giving Skye a thumbs up, Hunter balanced on the rock with the ball of his good foot, guiding her with both hands as she slowly ascended from the pit. Watching the frightened little girl spin slowly on the end of the receding rope, he suddenly had a crystal clear image of Elise, safe back in British Columbia, and smiled, wondering whether the child developing peacefully in her womb was a boy or girl.

Hauling in the thick, braided line, Skye was joined by fellow tribesmen, Walker Dan and Paints-His-Face-Red, who, though bruised and battered, grabbed the rope to give Skye a hand. He received an even greater shock when Elise suddenly appeared. According to Hunter, she was waiting safely back at their village in Old Canada. Reaching down, Elise caught hold of the child, lifting the little girl into her arms. Glancing into the chasm, she spotted someone down below on a narrow rock ledge. As she carried the child to safety, a growing realization began to blossom in the back of her mind as another strong spasm shook the ground beneath her feet, nearly causing her to drop the terrified little girl. Passing her off to Anna and the twins, Elise rushed back to the edge, the familiar shape clinging to the wall vividly outlined in her mind.

* * *

WITH THE CHILD safely at the top, the ground shifted again and Hunter felt the rock on which he balanced tremble and begin to slide, threatening to drop away beneath his foot. At the same time, the wall he held to began to crumble and he looked up at the thin sliver of pale blue sky one final time. Above him on the surface, Skye was jolted by the tremor and thrust out his arms for balance, going down on one knee. When he recovered, he glanced over at Elise, still having a hard time believing she was really here. Pushing the obvious questions aside, he made sure that the little girl was safe before recoiling the rope and dropping it down to his waiting friend.

Leaning over the side, he was about to call Elise over to assist in Hunter's rescue when he realized that something was wrong. Squinting deeper into the trench, he looked beyond the dust billowing up from the pit, trying to locate Hunter who had been perched on the narrow rock slab moments before, clinging precariously to the wall. During the last aftershock, the entire slab had broken off, cascading into the black chasm below.

Lying down on his stomach at the crumbling edge to have a better look, Skye scanned up and down the trench, hoping for any trace of his friend—thinking that he may have been able to grab ahold of something further down. As his eyes swept the jagged subterranean landscape, he sensed Elise's presence beside him when another section of wall collapsed, carrying tons of rock and dirt into the depths. As the avalanche rumbled far below, the sobering realization dawned on Skye that his courageous friend, brother-in-law, and worthy comrade-in-arms—the strong, silent Hunter who had so valiantly fought and sacrificed that others might remain free—*was gone...*

* * *

WHEN VENERABLE WU's three-ship armada approached the Gathering's harbor two days later, he could hardly believe his eyes. All along the coastline, any vegetation or manmade structures below sixty feet above sea level had simply vanished. Buildings, docks and warehouses had been smashed to bits by the massive wave and carried off in the tide. Piles of debris clogged the shoreline with the remains of downed trees, splintered boats, and pulverized structures floating among the general wreckage in the tidal flats and shallows.

Standing off from the shore, he ordered a pigeon released with a message appraising his Red Dragon subordinates of the dire local situation, ordering that a flotilla immediately set sail loaded with security and construction personnel, food, water, medical supplies, and building materials to assist in local rescue, cleanup and rebuilding efforts. He had no idea at this point that the Bay area had suffered significant tsunami damage of its own. He swiftly organized a shore party comprised of crew members from his two escort ships along with a platoon of his personal bodyguard led by a senior officer. They went ashore in the longboats to establish contact with Royal Chen and set up a command post if needed.

Forty minutes later, Wu received good news and bad news when his onshore semaphore operator signaled that Royal Chen was currently unaccounted for, and that the Sisterhood Alliance was in complete control of the local situation, having already established a command post, a triage and first-aid center, search and rescue operations, as well as a victim identification process. After a flurry of messages back and forth, the shore party officer finally gave an all-clear, confirming that the area was secure, and Venerable Wu went ashore—prudently surrounded by a squad of wary bodyguards—to personally assess the situation and determine his next course of action.

Arriving at the open field headquarters where rescue operations tents had been erected adjacent to the race track, Wu was met by a contingent from the Sisterhood Alliance, led by their founder, an attractive, intimidating woman with a commanding presence named Star, whom Wu immediately sized up as intelligent, competent, and extremely dangerous—both physically and strategically. Their meeting was polite and formal, with Star more than candid about all that had taken place prior to, during, and after the quake and tsunami, including an explanation of her army's presence here and the reason for their assault on Chen's forces.

She outlined her willingness to declare a truce as long as Chen's thousand-credit bounty was officially cancelled by whomever assumed responsibility for his estate in his absence. The slave auctions secretly sanctioned by the Gathering would also have to be cancelled and forbidden in the future, and the new Keeper (should Royal Chen not return to power for whatever reason) must declare slavery officially outlawed throughout the region.

From the knowledge that Star had amassed over the years through her network of eyes and ears, she was convinced that Venerable Wu was the natural successor in line to assume the day-to-day physical and financial operations of the Gathering. He was known to be a major stakeholder in Chen's empire with huge resources in the south, and with no sign or evidence that the missing Royal Chen was likely to reappear anytime soon, Wu would most likely fill his predecessor's shoes. In addition, her spy network, with operatives in nearly every household in the region where women worked as domestic help, had provided her with recent intelligence of a plot by Wu to topple Royal Chen and claim the

Gathering for himself, most likely by the end of the year. It never ceased to amaze her how much servants could find out about the schemings and intrigues of their upper class employers. Like flies on the wall, they were commonly privy to a bevy of sensitive and potentially damning information.

Wu was frankly impressed by the Sisterhood's organizational skills as demonstrated in their competent handling of the disaster-relief efforts, and was cognizant of the fact that Star's well-trained and outfitted army currently outnumbered his own boots on the ground five to one. As a student and proud direct descendant of Sun Tzu, (whose name was written *Sun Wu* in the simplified Chinese language) Wu wisely agreed to her demands, with the stipulation that if Royal Chen should be found alive, any policy changes affecting the Gathering would, of course, have to be deferred to him. Besides, Wu knew he could always reverse his decision once he was in a stronger negotiating position, but at present, he was more than happy to comply with Star's demands since the effective efforts of her Sisterhood Alliance volunteers were much needed and appreciated.

Wu was surprised that in the immediate aftermath of the disaster there had been no looting of food, water, or trade goods and other valuables, this being another confirmation of the respect that the common people held for the Sisterhood Alliance forces. Even Royal Chen's financial records had remained intact, secure within his locked, undamaged accounting office and currently under the trusted supervision of chief accountant Su, who had miraculously emerged from a collapsed building in the pleasure district without a single scratch. Chen's treasury, too, was secure, locked and guarded by members of his own security forces who, though initially disarmed by Star's fighters, had been allowed to retain their emancipated status and were free to do their jobs as long as they refrained from demonstrating aggression toward others.

Chen's cliffside mansion had sustained significant damage, mostly from a collapsed exterior wall on the seaside, as well as from a raging fire that had destroyed half the roof. An admitted racist who took great pride in the fact that over fifty percent of his organization was comprised of pure Chinese stock, most of Chen's household staff were at least of Asian descent. Wu spent several hours interrogating them about Royal Chen's final moments and his speculated whereabouts.

He was shown the reinforced panic room to which Chen had retreated during the onset of the quake and Wu could see that it had suffered only superficial damage—some cracked plaster, a couple of broken lamps, and a collapsed wall unit, but nothing major. The fact that Royal Chen had not been seen since being barricaded inside the room was a troubling mystery. With only one way in or out, which had been locked from the inside and guarded by two external sentries who claimed never to have left their posts—even during the fire—where could he have gone?

After a second headcount of the living, injured, and dead reconfirmed that Chen was still officially unaccounted for, Wu authorized three special search parties, each team comprised of six hand-picked men from his personal guard, each man an expert at tracking and capturing large prey and killing men. They were commissioned with the solitary objective of locating the Keeper, dead or alive, with Wu offering a generous reward to the first team to find him. Making it clear that recovering Chen's *remains* was the hoped-for result of their efforts, Wu pledged an almost obscene additional bonus to the man willing to perform any necessary *coup de grace* to guarantee the Red Dragon Triad chief his desired outcome.

In Chen's absence, Wu wisely called a meeting of the Keeper's security forces, guards and their officers, reassuring them that their paychecks would not be interrupted and their affairs would be properly looked after in the interim until the whereabouts of The Keeper could be discovered. Without their employer, they had no choice but to comply with Wu's wishes, and several of them, including a high-ranking officer, were already secretly on his payroll anyway.

Old Chang— another well-placed Wu spy—had made it through the earthquake and fire with only a broken arm which he received in an heroic effort to save his precious pigeons by releasing them from their cages. The birds housed here from outlying message stations immediately flew straight back to their home lofts, some carrying messages explaining the mass exodus and requesting a fresh supply of doves be returned to the Gathering as soon as possible. Birds hatched locally flew only far enough away to escape the flames and smoke, and had returned to the proximity of their nests as soon as the coast was clear. They now roosted atop the damaged structure until it could be repaired.

Happy to find his favorite, most valuable niece, May Ling, safe and sound, Wu provided her with lavish accommodations in the spare master suite aboard the *Sea Witch*, and shuttled her there in his longboats along with her servants and belongings salvaged from Chen's damaged chateau. As she was his ancient, but still-living, mother's favorite granddaughter, Wu was greatly relieved that she had made it through unscathed.

There was only one other name remaining on the missing person's list causing Wu concern. Von Hammer had not been seen since before the riot, and it was rumored that he'd gone into the catacombs beneath the complex less than an hour before the earthquake struck. Wu knew from the damage reports that most of the tunnels and chambers there had collapsed and he held out very little hope for Von Hammer's survival. Secretly, he was pleased not to have to eliminate the man himself, something any prudent successor to Chen's throne would be obligated to do. Not that he had anything against the man personally. He just knew that he would never be able to trust him and he wasn't comfortable allowing him to remain alive as a potential threat. Von Hammer was powerful and had many connections, friendly and otherwise, throughout the land. The fact that he was a former mercenary and captain of Chen's personal guard was bad enough. That he was an outsider with vast intimate knowledge of the inner workings of the Gathering's security systems and standard operating procedures placed a large bullseye on his chest, and to avoid upsetting Von Hammer's personal friends and allies, Wu would prefer not to have to personally pull that trigger.

* * *

WITH THE ARRIVAL of Venerable Wu on the scene, search and rescue efforts were redoubled and by the sixth day, most of those trapped and still alive had been located and extricated from the rubble. The wolven, too, were employed in more benevolent ways, sniffing out survivors and locating the bodies of the less fortunate. The dead were taken to an open field where they were laid out and identified as well as could be expected. The wounded were brought to the field hospital staffed by many volunteers including a large cadre of Sisterhood fighters who worked wonders applying their expert first aid skills—setting bones and stitching wounds—as well as applying various herbal and homeopathic remedies.

A written accounting of all survivors was compiled and a list of the missing dwindled as these were cross-referenced with the dead and seriously injured who were able to be identified. Once every effort had been made to identify those who had lost their lives, their corpses were buried in the local cemetery or burned downwind in funeral pyres before they began to decompose. Later, Wu dedicated a memorial shrine to the fallen on a nearby wind-swept bluff overlooking the sea, where master masons crafted a lovely stone altar and half-circle arch that perfectly captured the setting sun each July 15th on the anniversary of the disaster. Friends and relatives of the lost were invited to pray and meditate there, placing flowers or other private offerings as they saw fit.

Once Star realized what a richly gifted healer Elise was, she was placed in charge of the hospital, directing the care of the most seriously injured patients. There in her element, Elise worked diligently, providing comfort and encouragement to all she interacted with. Ironically, many of her charges were members of Royal Chen's guard who had been wounded in the battle prior to the quake. Their most common injuries were puncture wounds inflicted by arrows, and traumatic animal bites received during wolven attacks.

With the arrival of each new patient, Elise subconsciously expected to see Hunter, but as the days passed, her hopes faded with them, her heart numb and filled with an emptiness she had never before known. Anna and the Ravencloud sisters served in the hospital as well, in spite of undergoing their own harsh ordeal prior to arriving at the Gathering, and the trio circulated around to the kitchen, or care center for orphaned children as needed, doing whatever they could to alleviate the suffering of others. There were several children who had lost their parents, from infants to early teens, including Jewel, the little eight-year-old girl saved by Hunter and pulled to the surface by Skye and the others.

Anna did her best to look after Elise, knowing how inwardly devastated she must be after losing her best friend and the love of her life. Hunter's continuing absence and presumed death was a void too vast to fathom, and nothing she could say or do would be able to reverse her sister's soul-wrenching loss. She didn't try, but simply sought to look out for her in little ways, such as making sure that she ate properly and got enough rest. In both their wombs, their children grew, and Anna hoped that with time, Elise would at least partially offset her pain with the joy and challenges that motherhood would bring.

As word of the disaster spread, many concerned and generous souls streamed in from the surrounding countryside to help, and Wu wisely offered generous compensation to anyone willing to contribute to the cleanup and rebuilding efforts. He realized that the sooner the Gathering was fully operational, the quicker it would begin turning a profit again, and he committed whatever resources were at his disposal to that end. Everyone healthy enough to contribute worked in some capacity in the effort, even young people and older children. All able-bodied survivors interested in helping out for pay were organized into various brigades to ensure the recovery effort was balanced and lacked nothing. Locals who were able to resume their normal responsibilities and duties did so, whether they were cooks or vendors, maintenance personnel or guards, accountants, traders, or livestock managers, most everyone found purpose and stability in simply getting back to work.

Outside the damaged perimeter wall, the large horse stables and corrals housing thousands of animals belonging to the visiting attendees had been graciously spared. Volunteers took over managing the herds while their owners worked, making sure they were properly fed and watered and generally looked after. Anna spent much of her spare time in the barns, assisting with livestock management.

After an intense first week, most of the buildings and walls that collapsed had been thoroughly searched and it was determined that the likelihood of additional survivors was slim. All resources were then redirected to the enormous clean up and rebuilding efforts. Skye, Paints-His-Face-Red and Walker Dan had led the initial rescue efforts alongside teams of Alliance fighters and Gathering security personnel, everyone working shoulder-to-shoulder to save as many victims as possible. When rescue efforts moved into the recovery phase—removing bodies as opposed to removing live people—the trio turned their attention to the salvage and clean up operations in the harbor. With the exception of the pylons sunk deep into the seabed, all evidence of the docks and wharf had vanished, stripped away by the massive wave; the only evidence of their existence being the splintered posts sticking up at various heights above the waves. Floating in the surf or stranded high on the rocky beaches, tons of wreckage spoiled the once pristine shoreline, attracting hundreds of scavengers who stayed busy picking over the piles of twisted fishing nets, buoys, assorted lumber, pieces of boats and buildings, furniture—anything they could salvage and sell.

At the time of the tsunami, more than two dozen boats and ships of various shapes and sizes were tied up at the docks, or anchored offshore in the bay. The majority of boat owners had survived the riot and the quake, and spent their time scouring the beaches for salvageable bits of their personal property. Nearly anyone with a serviceable watercraft of any kind was offshore, checking over the flotsam and jetsam for goodies, for the traditional law of the sea, going back many centuries, was one of "finders keepers, losers weepers."

* * *

WILL AND SAM, twenty-something partners in a local fishing concern, drifted in their eighteen-foot skiff alongside a bus-sized floating island of harbor wreckage sucked out to sea by the tsunami. With gaff hooks on long wooden poles they slowly pulled themselves alongside the pile, their busy eyes scanning the jumbled mass for anything of value. Suddenly Will caught a glimpse of something large and black bobbing lazily in the shifting island's midst, partially covered by seaweed and a hopelessly tangled section of fishing net. It looked like a big steel chest or container as tall as a man and twice as wide, though it was hard to tell exactly what it was, being ninety percent submerged and shrouded in shadow. The top was emblazoned with Royal Chen's official red and yellow crest, the same one sewn onto his banners and embedded in tile above the Gathering's massive gates—rumored to be the Chinese character for a *gathering* or *building where people assembled.*

Calling Sam over, Will pointed the thing out to him and they got busy clearing away the clutter and debris, cutting the curious, buoyant container free with their knives. Once separated out from the floating island, it did a lazy roll onto its side and the two partners gasped as the front door of a large black safe became visible for a few moments before again slipping beneath the gentle swells. Looking at one another in exaggerated disbelief, they hastily covered their find with a tarp, securely lashing it to the stern of their boat with a doubled over section of fishing net. Manning the oars, they made a beeline for a small barren island some three miles away.

"You know they'll kill us if they find it." Sam said in a matter-of-fact tone of voice, his face exhibiting no emotion as he rowed.

"Who will?" his partner replied, knowing that it didn't really matter *who*. Anyone seeing the safe would definitely kill them for it, period. No questions asked.

"Wonder what's in it?" Sam asked, just to hear it, knowing already that they'd have to wait until they got it open to know for sure.

"What do you mean, what's in it?" Will replied sounding a bit annoyed. "You know what's in it same as me. Freedom's in it. Never have to work another day in our muckraking lives is in it. I'm the rich guy so don't mess with me is in it, you thick-headed crab picker! If this is the safe they kept in the office on the wharf to pay for shipments, there's bound to be... hell, who knows how many credits in there... maybe five, ten thousand?"

Sam smiled and giggled with glee, "Five thousand credits apiece—I'm gonna be the richest clam digger on the west coast!"

"Don't go countin your chickens just yet, Sammy, we still gotta open this damn thing."

Sam didn't care about that, he just thought about all the stuff he could buy with his credits and didn't stop grinning all the way to the island.

Once there, they struggled to bring the cumbersome safe ashore, but instead, got it stuck in the sandy bottom near the breakers, standing almost perfectly upright. Knowing they were in for a long night, Will stayed behind to guard while his smiling partner returned to the mainland to grab some food, lanterns, a sledge hammer, cold chisel, large crowbar, pick, and whatever else he thought might be useful in getting the thing opened.

"Not a word, Sammy, not a word to anyone—you hear me?"

Will made a gesture like a dagger being drawn across his throat and made him promise. Watching Sam become smaller and smaller until finally disappearing altogether, Will looked out for other boats, hoping that nobody he knew passed by in the interim. When Sam returned hours later, it was nearly sunset and the tide had gone out, exposing the entire safe to the whole world and anyone who might happen to pass by.

In the yellow glow of the lamplight they looked over their amazing find, noting the huge dent caving in one side where it must have been hurled against the rocks by the tsunami. Working as quickly as they could in the cool evening breeze with billions of uninterested stars bearing witness to their efforts, they banged away at the door and hinges for hours without much luck, the sound of their pounding echoing across the water for more than a mile. Will concentrated on hammering the chisel into the front seam of the door until he had a small lifted place big enough to stick the crowbar into, but even using their combined strength, try as they might, the stubborn door simply wouldn't budge.

As the rose-colored dawn spread across the sky from the east, and with a growing realization that others would be soon taking to their boats in search of floating treasure, an exhausted Will grabbed the twenty pound sledge out of pure frustration, and began wailing away at the demon safe like a madman, angered by the proximity of such promise and potential, yet having no real way to redeem it. With a final reckless swing, he bashed the side with the huge dent in it and the front door fell off into the shallow waters of the incoming tide.

"Holy crap! You did it! How in hell did that happen?" Sam stared at the fallen door as Will, who could care less how it happened, let go of the sledge and picked up a lantern to have a closer look. The interior dimensions of the safe measured six feet high, three feet wide, and three feet deep and was divided into three equal compartments, one on top of the other, each containing three identical slide out drawers similar to those in a filing cabinet with spring latches holding them in place. Pulling out the first drawer, Will held up his lamp and gasped. The compartment was lined with rows upon rows of tightly stacked *chens,* a hundred to a row, twenty rows across, and twelve rows deep.

The partners just stared with mouths open not saying a word. All nine drawers were identical and filled to the brim with chens. There were three drawers for each denomination: ones, tens, and hundreds. Noticing a small compartment on the inside of the fallen door, Will stooped down to open it. It, too, contained chens—eight of them, but these were different. Instead of being white with red markings, they were black with white lettering. Will held his palm open as they stared at the ceramic disc.

"I didn't even know they came in thousands." Sammy whispered.

Will just shook his head, his mental calculator trying to figure out how many credits were actually in the safe, but he gave up after a couple of tries. Had he known that this was Royal Chen's personal household safe, the one that had fallen out of his secret hiding place into the ocean during the earthquake, he would have more easily understood the situation. It was Chen's policy to always keep the safe filled with eight million credits as an insurance policy, his personal stash hidden away for the day he might ever need to leave hastily in the dead of night, taking with him a bit of start up cash to ease his transition. Of course, his treasury contained a thousand times more, and he could always produce as many as he needed in his official kiln.

When Venerable Wu eventually moved into the Keeper's restored mansion upon officially becoming the *new* Keeper of the Gathering, he searched high and low for Chen's secret room, certain that it had to be there somewhere. Chen's chief treasurer, a thin, bespectacled fellow named Lo, confirmed Wu's suspicions under rigorous interrogation, admitting to making regular deliveries to the Keeper's chateau. Unfortunately, he was unable to pinpoint the exact location of any safe, as he merely delivered the credits to Chen's residence where the Keeper always took possession of them before sending Lo on his way.

*   *   *

ELISE STAYED BUSY, her days filled with the ever-challenging, deeply rewarding work of caring for the injured at the hospital. In the two weeks since the quake, they'd moved indoors out of the tents and she had seen much improvement in the vast majority of her patients, however there were those heartbreaking instances when there was really nothing that could be done to make it all better. In those cases, the goal became one of making the patient as comfortable as possible for as long as possible, using whatever remedies and potions she could provide.

One of her patients showing considerable improvement was Amaranth, Star's companion and confidant, whose collarbone and three ribs had been broken and her shoulder dislocated when a heavy beam collapsed during the quake, pinning her beneath its crushing weight. She was one of several Sisterhood warriors whom Elise was honored to care for, and she found herself being deeply moved by their stories about the Sisterhood's remarkable campaign to free all women and children from bondage.

Star would come by quite often to visit, and she and Amaranth would sit together in pleasant conversation for hours, especially in the evenings when Star's duties had wound down for the day. The love they shared was obvious in the way they related to one another, and Elise thought it was sweet how Star would take her aside to find out how Amaranth was *really* doing. Occasionally, the Sisterhood chief would bring young Jewel with her, the eight-year-old orphan girl rescued by Hunter and Skye from the abyss. Jewel was a lithe, wiry child having thick orange curls that framed her sweet, freckled face. Flitting about like a hummingbird, she demonstrated and almost insatiable curiosity and was capable of carrying on conversations on a level that was far beyond her years. Among her many notable attributes, Jewel possessed the most remarkable ice-blue eyes that Elise had ever seen, her irises ringed in flames of bright yellow gold.

Whenever Jewel would visit, she would run up to Elise and give her big hug, looking up into her face with a bright smile to thank Elise for saving her life. Each time it happened, Elise wanted to blurt out that *she* wasn't the one who saved her, but rather it was *Hunter* who caught her before she disappeared forever into the bottomless pit, but she never did, finding it still too painful to say his name out loud. As the days passed, Elise began to notice that whenever Jewel embraced her, the baby in her belly started kicking and being excited as if her child recognized Jewel's voice and presence, and wished to somehow acknowledge that fact.

As the days turned to weeks, a bond began to develop between Jewel, and Elise and her baby—a deep physical and spiritual connection wrought in the crucible of love lost, and the unnerving vulnerability of an unsolicited new beginning.

This genesis was not of their own choosing, but had been forced upon them by circumstances beyond their control. All were entering a new phase in their lives, one in which the love and security of the past had been greatly diminished.

Jewel had lost her entire family and was all alone in the world, compelled to rely on strangers to protect and guide her through the immediate gauntlet of this life. Likewise, Elise was suddenly on her own and responsible, not only for herself, but for her unborn child as well. Her baby had lost a parent and was now destined to miss out on whatever love, protection, and guidance that Hunter would certainly have been able to provide during the child's vital formative years.

Although Elise understood that there were caring family members willing to provide a safety net for her, she was disinclined to avail herself of that option and accept their hospitality. Her spirit resisted the temptation to slip into that addictive dependency, which quite often provided the appearance of stability and security while actually reducing one's self-determination to live fully. In such circumstances the comfort and convenience of the arrangement could inadvertently anesthetize one's desire to stretch the boundaries of potentiality to attain a deeper life.

Looking to the future, Elise was at a crossroads, a turning point in her life's journey from which there could be no going back. With the coming of her child, commonsense told her to return with Anna to Skye's village to enjoy the benefits of family and friendship, and where her son or daughter could grow up cocooned in the love and attention available within the framework of an extended family.

Yet, in her heart, she yearned for something more, something she hadn't yet experienced, but that she knew was out there somewhere: a projection of her most heartfelt dreams and wishes perhaps, or maybe just a wholesome land, green and welcoming, real and rare, and just beyond the next ridge. Whatever it was, Elise could not go back to her old life— not to New Eden, not to her homestead in the Wind River Range of the Rockies, nor to a sedentary life in Skye's village to become a complacent single mother, surrounded by the predictable and the comfortingly mundane. Where Elise would ultimately end up was a place she had not yet experienced. She was excited about the possibilities ahead, and was looking forward to discovering this new incarnation as it unfolded, day-by-day, and moment-by-moment.

The following morning when Star came to visit Amaranth, little Jewel ran up for her big hug as usual, but instead of thanking Elise for saving her life, she announced with a wide smile and a twinkle in her bright little eyes, "Elise, we are going to Wolfhaven in three days and you should come with us!"

The baby in her belly seemed to leap with joy and Elise was suddenly overcome by Jewel's words and the obvious love pouring from her sweet, innocent soul. She found herself unable to respond—her heart shouting *yes*, but her mind still in flux. Star walked over smiling and played with Jewel's beautiful hair, saying something about how well Amaranth was doing thanks to Elise's expert care. Elise just smiled, the words only partially registering. With welling tears in her eyes she excused herself and hurried away—not wanting Star or Jewel to witness her outpouring of emotion.

* * *

WITH THE DISASTER nearly a month behind them, many who received relatively minor, recoverable injuries were well on the mend and travelers who had come in specifically for the festival—but had stayed on earning money in the cleanup up and rebuilding efforts—were packing and heading for home. Skye and his people had booked passage on a ship sailing north to Seattle. Anna was closing in on being five-months pregnant and wanted to get home before traveling became too uncomfortable. Everyone had been working very hard and the credits they received in exchange for their efforts were more than enough to buy supplies and provisions, and pay for their passage north.

Word from Canada was that the tsunami had done significant damage on the coast, but for the most part their village was spared, being located miles upstream from the sea and high on the bank above the river. When the surge came through, some canoes and kayaks had been lost, but miraculously, no one was injured, and while the quake certainly shook things up, the worst of it had lasted less than ten minutes.

With so many hardworking souls arriving from all over the region, attracted by Wu's offer of unusually high wages, clean up and rebuilding efforts were progressing nicely. The interim Keeper had even temporarily rescinded the one percent rule, which was hailed by the traders as an act of notable generosity. Chen's mansion had a new timber-framed roof and exterior wall in place, but the finishing touches on the interior would take months to complete. Trading was beginning to return to normal, though the upcoming Moontide Festival had been postponed for at least another month and maybe two, as rebuilding and repairs continued on those portions of the settlement that had been destroyed.

Scavengers had been scouring the coast and further inland for weeks like army ants, collecting anything of value and bringing their finds to the Gathering's stall owners who, in turn, resold them at an even higher price. Following the ravaged riverbed inland for some three or four miles upstream, a group of diggers made a surprising discovery. High atop a muddy embankment, thirty feet up in an ancient gnarled oak, a beautifully crafted wooden sailboat rested upright on her keel, tipped slightly to starboard, embraced in the tree's thick, outstretched branches.

Her tall mainmast had been sheered off ten feet above the deck, leaving a broken, splintered stump with boom and jib still attached. Dangling from the tangled lines, her shredded mainsail hung nearly to the ground, fluttering in the slight afternoon breeze and flapping lazily against the tree's broad trunk. Miraculously—but for her shattered mast—*Windsong's* hull, keel and deck were fundamentally sound, her proud dragon prow unaffected by her encounter with the massive wave.

* * *

FOUR WEEKS AFTER the most powerful earthquake and tsunami in more than five-hundred years devastated the Pacific Northwest coast of North America, a group of salvagers returning from the sea spotted a half-naked man signaling from the wreckage-strewn beach of a tiny offshore island. Drawing as close to the rocks as they dared, they watched him dive into the chilly surf, swimming hard for the boat. Several minutes later they pulled a slightly battered Lars aboard, undernourished and thirsty, but alive.

As luck would have it, when the tsunami collided with the shallow seabed, the rising water had lifted his ship's bow up, flinging him over the end of the prow, where he barely cleared the 40-foot force of nature. Catapulted from the mainmast, he was carried out to sea in the wave's backlash and eventually managed to climb aboard a matted bundle of flotsam. For several days and nights he drifted with the currents until finally washing up on the small rocky island some nine miles offshore and sixty miles down the coast from where he started.

Pounds thinner, with dozens of superficial scratches scabbed over and multi-colored bruises on the mend, Lars made a rapid recovery from the dehydration and exposure he had been forced to endure. In the ensuing weeks, he fully regained his strength and with his amazing luck holding, made it back to the Gathering just in time to lay claim to his dragon ship that had incredibly survived the Great Wave. Refitting her in his off-time while helping to rebuild the Gathering's wharf, Lars planned to put *Windsong* back into service and head home to his *Crow's Nest* before the coming storms of autumn diminished the joy of the voyage.

One morning while working on the wharf, Lars unexpectedly met up with Skye and his kinsmen who filled him in on the details of everything that had happened after Lars had dropped them off at the beach the day before the quake. He was interested to get their take on the riot and the battle between the Sisterhood Alliance and Chen's security forces, some of which he'd heard about from co-workers. Lars vividly remembered watching the earthquake from the bay and was able to share with Skye, Red, and Dan his experience of the both the quake and the subsequent tsunami, vividly describing the pulling away of the water from the coastline just prior to its arrival. Of course, Skye and the others had obviously not had the opportunity to witness the approach of the wave from their vantage point within the damaged settlement, having been rather preoccupied with their own challenges at the time.

Lars was quite saddened to hear the news about Hunter, sincerely liking the quiet man who'd had a rough time out on the water aboard ship, but who hadn't complained once. Lars had hoped to get to know him better perhaps, as they all lived in the same relative vicinity within fifty miles of Vancouver Island. He was relieved to hear of the successful recovery of Anna, Lily, and River, and was glad that everyone seemed to be doing so well.

The following day, Lars was surprised by a brief visit from Jessi and her mother, Alena, who were told by Skye that Lars had been found alive and was working down at the wharf repairing his ship. Lars was happy to see Jessi smiling, and noticed the resemblance to her mother, who was obviously recovering from some pretty serious injuries. Had he known the half of it, he would have been thoroughly appalled and disgusted.

Von Hammer had been especially brutal to the older Sisterhood *witch* during his rigorous interrogation of her, and young Alibi's resolve had dissolved quickly after being forced to watch the sadist perform unspeakable acts with Jessi's mother. The slave boat's crew had been choir boys compared to the vicious mistreatment Von Hammer had visited upon Alena's body and soul. Threatening to strangle the semi-conscious woman with his whip before performing those same bestial acts on her, Alibi had broken down, answering his every question in explicit detail.

Afterwards, she felt like a traitor, having revealed Wolfhaven's location to the merciless brute, but she had done so out of pure terror, honestly fearing for their lives. In retrospect, she was convinced that the only reason that she and Alena weren't put to death immediately after she disclosed everything, was the fact that Chen had scheduled the witch burning spectacle for the crowd to see, and Von Hammer didn't want to insult and upset the Keeper by ruining his plans. Alena's physical recovery was slow but sure, the bite and lash marks taking longer to heal than her bruises, however the emotional and psychological toll on her spirit from the hellish ordeal she had endured would take a lifetime of love and nurturing in a safe environment to gradually recede into the background.

Alena thanked Lars for his gracious rescue and benevolent treatment of her daughter. Taking his hand, she placed a white ceramic disc the size if a silver dollar in it. On one side was the warrior's mark in red, and on the other, a crescent moon and star. "If you ever run into trouble, show this to any Alliance fighter or ally and you will receive whatever aid they can muster." She smiled and turned to go as Jessi said her goodbyes, giving Lars a quick hug and peck on the cheek, and assuring him how much she appreciated what he had done for her. Watching them slowly walk away along the wharf, Lars regretted that things hadn't turned out better for them both, wishing that this troubled world was not so broken, and that bad things never happened to good people. Later, he made a leather pouch for the disc and wore it around his neck for luck, hoping he'd never need to ask that favor.

* * *

WITH AUTUMN FAST approaching, Star, Amaranth, and the remaining members of the Sisterhood Alliance collected themselves and struck southeast up into the Klamath Mountains and away from the busy, crowded confines of Venerable Wu's rapidly recovering Gathering. En route to bisect the north-south railroad line, they planned to catch the *Bent Rails Transfer* train south down into the heart of the Redwood Empire, returning home to their beloved Wolfhaven after an extended absence of well over a month. Most of their remaining fighters had headed back more than a week ago, but Star wanted to stay behind until her last sister warrior was able to make the journey home with them.

With a heavy heart, Star glanced back to several reed baskets strapped to a pair of stout, black Montana mules. Within the baskets were urns housing the carbonized remains of 59 of her Sisterhood warriors who had lost their lives in the battle and subsequent earthquake. Their recovered bodies had been ceremoniously cremated atop a massive cedar funeral pyre on the beach, and the ashes then poured into clay jars for their final journey home. All told, 66 fighters and five wolven had been lost, though seven of the women were still missing-in-action and presumed to be dead as their bodies had never been found. Star and the others had decided that upon their return to Wolfhaven, they would build a timber-and-stone memorial to their brave comrades who had made the ultimate sacrifice while riding to the aid of their captured sisters.

Amaranth was mending nicely and was able to ride without too much discomfort. She wouldn't be doing any galloping soon, that's for sure, but at least she was able to sit atop her horse and maintain a gentle walk. Normally, it would take no more than two days to cross the mountains and drop down into the valley through which the iron rails ran, but Star maintained an especially easy pace today, having several wounded fighters among their ranks. Besides, the slower speed would only add an extra day to their short journey, and with the upcoming train ride saving them more than two weeks, she was in no great rush.

Glancing back, she could see her new friend, Elise on her pretty buckskin Mustang, riding beside young Jewel on her little dapple-gray Welsh pony, the two in animated conversation about something in which both appeared to be extremely interested. Jewel had collected several plants at their last halt and Elise was naming them and describing their useful properties—not going into too much detail just now—but giving her a general overview that was readily grasped by the inquisitive child's sharp, young mind. Jewel seemed to find it fun to memorize each plant's name and unique physicality, noting its color, its texture in her hands, and the fragrance of its leaves, roots, and fruits, if any. By the end of the day she had succeeded in committing to memory nine different specimens.

Watching Jewel's curiosity and excitement grow as the bright girl gained the ability to name and describe the properties of a few common plants, Elise fondly recalled being similarly mentored back in New Eden by *Little Bird* more than two decades earlier. With a serene smile gracing her countenance, Elise inhaled the heady scent of the conifer forest, all of her senses alive on this perfect bluebird day, sunny and mild, with her horse friend strong beneath her and warm against her legs. She was happy and relieved to finally be back in the saddle, having missed riding terribly during the entire past month working in the sick ward.

Her thoughts went out to Anna, recalling the crushed and confused look on her younger sister's face when Elise broke the news that she had decided to join the Sisterhood at Wolfhaven in the Redwood Empire. She was committed to embracing their communal lifestyle—living, working, and fighting alongside them in the struggle to free their oppressed sisters from bondage. Over the past week, Elise had become aware of the undeniable bond she shared with Star, Amaranth, Jessi, little Jewel and the others—a deep spiritual connection made obvious during their collectively-experienced ordeal. In sharing her decision with her sister, Anna had cried, expressing her deepest sorrow and regret over Elise's loss—feeling partially responsible for Hunter's death, as he had descended into the catacombs to effect her rescue.

Skye had withheld judgement of Elise's decision, honoring her autonomy. Gazing into his sister-in-law's emerald-green eyes at their parting, he delved her soul and smiled, and Elise sensed his understanding of her life and of the chosen path before her. Her baby stirred as she embraced the courageous shaman and she silently acknowledged Skye's gift of fertility, forever grateful for his miraculous intervention in her life. Though their parting had been tearful, on some higher level the letting go of the past was a deeply liberating moment for Elise.

From the azure sky above, a golden eagle cried out, returning Elise from her reverie, and she looked up toward the ridgeline to see there an image of Hunter on his favorite horse, strong and steady, tried and true, quietly studying the lay of the land. With the wind in his hair, he breathed it all in—whole, calm, and completely in his element. Drawing closer, she watched his image slowly dissolve into ryegrass, sagebrush, and quartz-laced granite.

Feeling his presence, Elise loved him now as she had always loved him—as she always would. He was a part of her forever—in the way he built a fire, or checked on the horses, or breathed life into her soul on those cold winter nights beneath their furs. Her baby was his gift, as was little Jewel, plucked from the abyss by his hand, along with his respect and stewardship for the natural world and all things in it.

She recalled that night around the fire during their first great adventure together, the first time he opened up and shared with her his flying dreams, and she could hear his words as he spoke to her from across the flames, his handsome face awash in wavy, orange light: *I wished that perhaps in another life I would be reborn as a bird of prey or maybe a large heron or crane..."* and she smiled through her tears as the warmth of the sun became the warmth of his embrace, and the caress of the wind was his fingers through her hair, and the energy of the storms would be his passion for her always, for he was as much a part of her now as every element in the universe surrounding her—and she could never be alone, for he was ever with her, in the stars, in the moon, and in the snow-capped peaks of the towering mountains.

The eagle cried out again, this time higher and nearly out of sight, and Elise felt the baby in her belly move and she smiled, whispering softly to the wind, *"Fly Hunter, fly."*

EPILOGUE

IGH ATOP A remote mesa, a hundred miles due east of the Gathering, a fierce-looking bronze-skinned man wearing ochre face paint, an ornate feather headdress, and jaguar claw necklace, slowly shuffle stepped around a crackling fire, chanting singsong words in an ancient Amazonian dialect. Coming to an abrupt halt, he retrieved a coal-tipped cedar stick from the blaze, turned, and began marking sacred runes and symbols on the naked, quivering body of the hooded captive lashed to a cross-pole and trussed up like a pig on a nearby spit. Working with precision beneath a waning full moon, the singer smiled to himself, his preparations for the human sacrifice nearly complete.

Stepping back from the condemned, he rolled himself a cigarette using a packet of glue-edged rice papers he'd picked up from a vendor near old San Francisco sometime back, and a pinch of Deep South tobacco from the supple leather pouch at his side. Glancing up from time-to-time, he kept close watch on the pair of massive canines he'd named *Shiva* and *Karma*, fitted with studded collars and heavy leather harnesses, chained side-by-side to the ground. Their keen eyes were riveted on his every movement as they obediently awaited his next command.

Bending down on one knee to retrieve a burning twig from the fire, Sirocco lit the cigarette, taking a long pull of the thick, fragrant smoke deep into his welcoming lungs. Relishing the rich flavor, he closed his eyes and smiled, exhaling blue-gray funnels through his nostrils as nicotine-enriched blood surged through his veins and arteries, delivering a rush to his brain and a heightened sense of wellbeing to his soul.

Tonight he was particularly pleased with himself, already sensing *the anointing* rising up within his breast like an anthem—a double portion by the feel of it. The smiles of the gods were surely upon him, blessing his work—his sacred quest for justice in this world of many sorrows. He was certain that the spirits had ordained tonight's sacrifice—this once-powerful man with decades of victims in his wake who now awaited the knife and flame of retribution and cleansing.

Drawing near with a purposeful look on his face, Sirocco removed his captive's hood and leaned in close to blow a thick stream of tobacco smoke directly into the man's terror-filled eyes, whose eyelids had been pinned open with cactus thorns. Though unable to physically respond due to the potent blowdart-delivered *curare* immobilizing his muscle receptors, the infamous Royal Chen, *former* Keeper of the Gathering, could see, hear, smell, taste, and feel everything that was happening to him.

Sirocco had waited for him in the panic room, the one place the Voices told him that Chen would go when the earth storm came. It was there, in the place where this creature felt most secure that he caught him by surprise like a spider catches a fly. Watching through the peephole, he waited until the cowardly guards ran away from the door, fleeing the growing flames, before carrying Chen out in a rolled up rug thrown over his shoulder—and away they went into the dawn, invisible to the fearful masses huddling in abject terror before the terrible groaning of the Earth Mother.

Retrieving his favorite skinning knife from its scabbard, the Ivy League avenger proceeded to skin the inside of his victim's legs to the crotch, leaving the curling, pale-yellow shreds dangling down onto the bundle of firewood stacked neatly beneath his naked form. Salivating from the sight and smell of human blood, the hungry mastiff-wolfhound war dogs sat up on their haunches and began to whine and strain against their chains as they licked drooling lips, eager for a taste of the human flesh—their only staple since being weaned from their mother in the Gathering's kennels. Taking a flaming brand from the bonfire, Sirocco thrust it into the kindling beneath Chen's rune-covered body and looked on with interest as the dry twigs and bark quickly caught fire, the flames racing up the curling shreds of skin to scorch and blister his unprotected belly and privates.

Spinning him around to face his dogs, Chen's horror reached its crescendo as Sirocco began removing generous filets of flesh from his buttocks and thighs (taking care, of course, not to sever any major arteries), while playfully tossing the meaty strips to the ravenous beasts. Sirocco took his time in this as an artist would, savoring the moment with no need to hurry. He understood how much Royal Chen enjoyed watching people being fed alive to his dogs and felt it his duty to provide him with this unique opportunity to witness *himself* being eaten alive by animals personally raised on human flesh at his own command, in order for him to fully appreciate the significance of the experience.

Trapped inside his paralyzed body, yet fully conscious and painfully aware of his predicament, Chen's brain throbbed in excruciating agony as Sirocco's knife sliced deeply into his flesh while the growing flames beneath him roasted his unprotected belly and genitals. Unable to even writhe about, he tried holding his breath, hoping in vain for unconsciousness and death to release him from his agonizing torment.

With legs quivering in excitement, eyes bright with interest and tails wagging with delight, the famished man eaters took turns snapping up the tasty morsels from mid air, swallowing them down with barely a chew before licking their dribbling jowls and eagerly whining for more. As the aromatic fragrance of the burnt offering filled the air, the anointing suddenly rose up within Sirocco's breast and burst forth from his lips, prompting him to lift his voice to the heavens in an extended primal scream. He was immediately joined by the canines who howled out their pleasure, noses pointed at the moon in a dissonant primordial bonding between man and beast lasting several minutes.

Afterwards, Sirocco removed Chen's living face and scalp in one piece to later shrink and fashion into a trophy to add to his growing shrunken head collection. He hung it on the pommel of his saddle beside the other fresh skin, the one sporting a shaved scalp with a spiked, bright red Mohawk down the middle. With his sacred mission here complete, Dr. Constantine Sirocco released the starving canines, who made short work of Chen's still-living carcass, tearing off large chunks of muscle and bone with their massive jaws and greedily wolfing them down.

END OF BOOK TWO

The adventure continues in *The Sisterhood-After The Fall, Book Three*, an excerpt of which begins on the following page.

THE SISTERHOOD

P R O L O G U E

THE WOLVEN

K *eep running!* The terrified girl silently commanded her faltering legs as she fled across the open field in the darkness. With her adrenaline beginning to peak, she sped as fast as she could in the moonlight, barely eluding the relentless men not far behind tracking her on horseback. Their excited voices grew louder, leaving no doubt in her panicked mind that they were gaining on her. Too afraid to look back, she dared not consider the chilling outcome should she lose her desperate race and fall into their hands.

Suddenly, a large barn loomed out of the shadows ahead and she ran straight for it as the hoofbeats grew louder, filling her ears with impending doom. Dashing around the corner of the two-story structure, she made it halfway down the side when a dark horse and its rider bearing a torch appeared around the opposite end. Spinning back, the second stalker emerged from the corner behind her, urging his horse forward to trap her between the two.

In the dim light of the pale moon, the frantic girl let out a futile cry for help, protesting to the universe-at-large the unjust brutality of her fate, but the rough men just laughed at their prey's predicament, her fear heightening their excitement as they pressed in to take her by force. Making a final attempt at escape, she tried to slip between them, but both charged forward, horses snorting and stomping their hooves, their large heads switching this way and that to effectively cut off her last ditch effort at freedom.

"Looks like we caught ourselves a tender little night blooming flower, brother James—a real looker, too!" He held his torch aloft to see her better.

Conley smiled and shot a glance at his older sibling who sat gloating over the evening's good fortune. There weren't many available females of breeding age in the surrounding territory, so opportunities for sexual adventures were extremely few and far between. He'd only been with two women in his entire life; the first, old enough to be his mother and the last, barely old enough to have fun with. Both had been short-lived encounters. Usually his older brother, James, took first dibs on them, but this time he'd promised Conley that he could have his way with her first. The younger brother had been going crazy just thinking about what it was going to be like to be the one in charge for a change.

"Yep, Con, she's a ripe one alright," James spat, wiping the dribble from his scraggly beard with his shirtsleeve and coveting her youth and beauty—long, dark braids soft against the hint of developing young breasts beneath her sweater.

"Looks like she's gonna have some real grown-up fun tonight—aren't ya, cutie?" A strange light shone from his eyes and he could feel his manly parts twitch in eager anticipation.

As the sobbing girl collapsed into a fetal position against the rough wooden siding of the barn, Conley slipped from his saddle and took a single step toward her, braided length of rope in one hand, upheld torch in the other. Blinded by his lust, he failed to notice the barn door slide noiselessly open beside her. Without warning, something large rushed out with a deep, guttural snarl, flashing past the cringing girl and colliding head-on with the surprised Conley. Clamping down hard on the human's throat with fang-lined jaws, the beast ripped out his larynx with a single violent toss of its shaggy head.

Looking on in stunned disbelief, James witnessed the three-second attack, unable to react in defense of his younger brother who already lay sprawled out on the ground, bleeding out. Behind him, the hayloft door swung out silently on newly oiled hinges and a dark silhouette leapt through the air, landing feet first on the back of James' horse. With a dagger instantly to his throat, the attacker sliced clean through both windpipe and jugular before back-flipping off the startled animal, slapping it hard on the rump with the flat side of the dripping blade in one fluid motion.

Wide-eyed in horror, James gasped for breath, clutching his badly hemorrhaging neck, simultaneously dropping the torch which bounced beneath his mount to collide with the horse's legs. The spooked animal jumped sideways to avoid the flames and tore off into the night, toppling James from the saddle in the process. As he fell, his right boot became caught in the stirrup and the would-be rapist disappeared into the night, dragged face down behind his galloping horse across the darkened field.

"Are you okay?" the phantom silhouette asked, kneeling beside the breathless girl, a gloved hand resting gently on her shoulder. Daring to look up, she was surprised to discover that her rescuer was a woman.

"Yes, I think so," she exhaled slowly, trying to calm her rapid breathing, "just exhausted from running so hard," she managed a fleeting smile, "so scared."

"You're lucky I was here—you're safe now."

The dark-garbed warrior rose and went over to her black wolf-dog companion named Soot, gently tugging his ears and pressing her face into his. From a leather bag at her side she produced a jerky treat and Soot sat on his haunches munching contentedly, glancing over at the savaged corpse from time-to-time to emit a low growl that rumbled way down in the back of his throat.

Returning to the traumatized girl, the mysterious woman introduced herself, offering two crossed hands in formal greeting, "I am the one they call *Arbor*, from the Empire of the Redwoods on the Pacific coast where the indigo sea caresses the rocky shore, and you are?"

"I'm Kristen from Minnetonka, Minnesota, beyond the Great Desert and the snow-capped mountains, across the Great River on the far side of the world."

The twelve-year-old clasped hands with Arbor and began to relax, feeling safe for the first time in weeks. Her parents had fallen ill on the Overland Road and died from the bad fever, leaving her alone in the world with no one to help guide her through the labyrinth of this life. She briefly shared her story with Arbor and the Sisterhood warrior adopted her on the spot, offering to take her back to Wolfhaven where she would be safe from the depredations of the male-dominated

Afterworld. Having no better plan in place, Kristen readily accepted Arbor's offer, extremely grateful for her amazing rescue and certain that their meeting was a providential answer to her desperate predicament.

Retrieving her horse and other belongings from inside the barn, Arbor offered a famished Kristen some dried fruit and nut mix along with a generous chunk of the venison jerky. Welcoming her first real meal in several days, Kristen soon felt her strength returning and the dreaded fear of the unknown lift from her shoulders like mist dissolving in the morning sun.

Leaving the dead man's body where it fell, Arbor left her calling card—a circular ceramic tile with the Warrior's Mark on it in red. She placed it carefully on his still-warm forehead as a warning to anyone who would presume to violate the human and civil rights of any woman or child. As the Sisterhood were not thieves, the man's person and belongings—except for his horse which was now orphaned and in need of a caring guardian—remained undisturbed, and as the rose-streaked sky quietly announced the coming dawn, the two newly acquainted travelers made a swift departure from the barn, heading west.

Kristen rode the dead man's five-year-old with ease—a well-mannered chestnut mare she promptly named Cinnamon. The horse was initially uncomfortable and suspicious of her new rider, but settled down after realizing that the girl did not use a switch, nor was she rough with the reins like her former master had been. As they moved through the gentle countryside, Kristen noted with some degree of surprise and curiosity that Soot remained mostly out of sight on the fringe as they traveled, keeping to cover and scouting the trail. The large, dusky *Canid* with intelligent, perceptive eyes maintained an effortless fluid lope, appearing briefly out front, or to one side or another. His movements were apparently in response to silent hand signals from Arbor who allowed her horse its head, maintaining an easy, rhythmic pace at a canter—neither too fast, nor too slow.

Arbor rode effortlessly in perfect form, her demeanor one of guarded confidence, passing through the land as someone with a purpose and a destination in mind. She led them along a winding dirt track flowing easily over grassy hills and through scattered groves of eucalyptus and madrone. The air was pleasant and warm, and alive with hummingbirds, bees, and colorful butterflies, all sipping nectar in fields choked with multicolored wildflowers gracing the surrounding landscape. During feeding, these winged benefactors simultaneously cross-pollinated the flowers in an intimate choreography ingeniously designed to ensure the continuity of the native floral species.

*   *   *

IN THE GATHERING dusk, Arbor and Kristen made camp beneath the stars among some jumbled boulders, with a rock ledge blocking the stiff onshore breeze blowing in from the ocean now just a few miles to the west. As they sat around the crackling fire eating a hastily prepared meal of roast rabbit and fresh wild onions and garlic, Kristen wondered about Arbor's large, quiet companion she called *Soot*.

The lean, muscular animal had positioned himself on the ground behind Arbor with his back nearly against hers. Almost invisible in the dark, he rested there, just outside the throw of light, relaxed, but poised—his sharp senses probing the surrounding darkness. From time-to-time he would quietly melt into the blackness and then, just as silently, re-appear a few minutes later, as if he'd never left. When Arbor moved around the modest camp, his long ears tracked her like radar dishes, eyes aiming away from the fire to protect his extraordinary night vision.

"What about your friend?" Kristen asked, certain that the animal was more than a pet, or guard dog, "what exactly *is* he?"

The large canine was unlike any dog she had ever seen. He was physically very powerful, almost frighteningly so, and his personality aloof, yet he was very much in communication with Arbor and affectionate toward her, but on some deeper, mysterious level than the usual master-dog plane. It was almost as if they could communicate through thought, without the need for clumsy, inadequate words.

"Soot? Yes, amazing, isn't he?" She smiled and reached back to stroke his long, luxurious tail. "We've been together since he was born—four years ago now. His father—an alpha wolf whom we call Thor—came down out of the wilderness to mate with one of the Sisterhood's breeders, a black german shepherd female named Akela. Soot was the only black pup in their litter, and the only male."

"How did you train him to fight like that?" Kristen shuddered involuntarily, wanting to understand how Soot knew to go after the bad man and not herself.

Arbor laughed. "It's not really so much a matter of *training* him, as it is a matter of pure cognizant intuition for *Wolven*—the name our founder, Star, gave to the Sisterhood's unique breed of wolf-dogs."

She added a log to the fire and continued. "Wolven behavior stems from genetically handed down pack principles, along with some specific learned behaviors assimilated through living exclusively with human females." She reached back and gave Soot a big hug.

"I guess it's a new twist on a much older relationship, not unlike the earliest interactions between wolves and humans, with archeological evidence demonstrating the start of the human-canine bond as far back as 30,000 years."

Taking it all in, Kristen thought it amazing to have wolven as companions and hoped that someday *she* might be granted the honor of sharing her life with such an awesome friend. Later on, with her tummy full and her heart warmed by the fire and the grace of her newfound benefactors, the young girl from Minnetonka, Minnesota drifted off into a deep and restful sleep. For the first time in weeks, she slept through the night without waking up once in fear, knowing deep in her subconscious that the formidable Soot and his capable warrior companion were on guard, protecting the camp from danger.

Excerpted from:

The Sisterhood-After The Fall, Book Three

Anticipated release early 2013.

www.ingramcontent.com/pod-product-compliance
Lightning Source LLC
Chambersburg PA
CBHW070644180626
46817CB00006B/2237